LORD AUGUSTUS

Sons of the Marquess

Book 3

A Regency Romance

by Mary Kingswood

Sons of the Marquess Book 3: Lord Augustus

Published by Sutors Publishing

Copyright © 2018 Mary Kingswood

ISBN: 978-1-912167-08-1 (paperback)

Cover design by: Shayne Rutherford of Darkmoon Graphics

Sons of the Marquess Book 3: Lord Augustus

About this book: *A traditional Regency romance, drawing room rather than bedroom.*

Lord Augustus Marford has only one interest in life - horses. It's an expensive hobby. When his brother, the Marquess of Carrbridge, finds himself in financial trouble after his agent disappears with much of his fortune, Gus is happy to help the family finances by finding work with horse auctioneers Tattersalls. His first job takes him to the wild Northumberland coast to assess some stud horses for the eccentric Duke of Dunmorton.

But Gus's hopes of a quiet trip are soon shattered as he is drawn into the Duke's family problems, and finds himself in the unlikely role of matchmaker for his elderly host. And then there's Amaryllis Walsh, the demure widow living quietly on the Duke's estate. Gus is powerfully drawn to her, but her history is mysterious - who is she really? Are there dark secrets in her past? And even if he can answer those questions, he daren't risk falling in love, when he can't afford to marry.

Book 3 of the 5-book Sons of the Marquess series, each a complete story with a HEA, but read all of them to find out all the secrets of the Marford family!

About Sons of the Marquess: the Ninth Marquess of Carrbridge is happily married to the former Miss Constance Allamont, he has an heir and a spare in the nursery, and all seems set fair for a life of perfect bliss. His five younger brothers are a bit of a handful, but young men like to spread their wings a bit. If only they weren't so expensive! And whatever happened to that huge income his father used to boast about? It seems to have vanished in a generation. And now there's the unknown son of his father's who claims to be the legitimate heir to the Marquessate. It's a bit much for a Marquess to deal with. Fortunately, his wife has some ideas about recovering their position...

Book 0: The Earl of Deveron (a novella, free to mailing list subscribers)
Book 1: Lord Reginald
Book 2: Lord Humphrey
Book 3: Lord Augustus
Book 4: Lord Montague
Book 5: Lord Gilbert

Table of Contents

1: The Cherry Tree Inn

Lord Augustus Marford knew all the foremost inns on every major road in England. The foremost inns, naturally, being those which would best attend to the needs of his precious horses. If they served edible food and a decent claret, and provided beds with clean linen, well, that was an added benefit, but not, in his view, essential. He was happy to eat and drink whatever was put in front of him, and could sleep on the floor if the situation demanded it, as he had proved on more than one occasion. But allow his beloved animals to be tended by half-drunk ostlers and careless grooms? No, it was inconceivable.

So it was that Gus and his travelling companion, Captain Michael Edgerton, found themselves at the Cherry Tree Inn at Kelthwaite, even though the White Hart opposite and the George and Dragon just down the road looked more salubrious and had more patrons.

"You sure about this, Marford?" Edgerton said, looking up at the peeling paint on the sign over the door.

"Have I led you astray yet?" Gus said genially. "You are free to stay elsewhere if you wish, but I shall not entrust Jupiter to anyone else."

And as soon as their little party had clattered under the arch to the yard, ostlers scurried out from all sides to attend to them, and led the horses into well-appointed stables. Gus stayed long enough to ensure that Jupiter was receiving lavish attention from his own two grooms, and that the other horses were being cared for to his standards, then he made his way at a leisurely pace into the inn.

The pained tones of Captain Edgerton echoed about the low-beamed taproom. "No parlour? No parlour? Whatever sort of an establishment is this, to be so deficient in accommodation, and when you have the brother of a marquess condescending to stay here, too. It is excessively disappointing."

Gus could not hear the innkeeper's replies beyond a gentle murmur at intervals, but this was not a place where bluster and rank would have much effect. If he had wanted flunkeys bowing low enough to sweep the floor with their noses, he would have gone elsewhere.

"Edgerton, it is not the innkeeper's fault if his rooms are all taken. There are only two parlours here, after all, and the taproom will serve us very well."

"Your lordship is most understanding," the innkeeper said, a little dumpling of a man, as innkeepers often were. "My humblest apologies, but one of my parlours is under new paint, and the other is already taken by a lady."

"But only the daughter of an earl," Edgerton protested. "I believe Lord Augustus takes priority."

Gus laughter. "No, no, no, that will never do! Turn a lady out to sit in the taproom? Where is your chivalry, Captain? Do you have chambers enough for us to sleep in, my friend? Two would do it, if the grooms sleep in the hay store, but if you have only one, then the valets must have it, and the captain and I will take the hay, too, for I owe it to my cravat to ensure that Willett enjoys perfect repose."

"We have rooms, my lord, but— Ah, my lady, one moment, if you please."

"One moment? We have waited a great many moments already, and— Gus? Gus Marford, as I live and breathe!"

"Erm..." Gus was never good with names. So many ladies drifted into his view at balls and dinners and theatres, and he was usually thinking about something else and not paying much attention. Now he gazed at the statuesque lady with pale blue eyes, a mouth overfilled with teeth and a mountain of frizzy fair hair topped with a froth of lace, and scrambled to recall who on earth she was.

She gave a throaty chuckle. "How mortifying! You do not remember me at all, do you? Emma Frensham. Heavens, Gus, we played spillikins as children often enough, and you pushed me into a pond once. You were seven and thought it vastly amusing. I was fourteen and feared never to recover my dignity."

He laughed. "Emma! Of course. Where are you bound?"

"To Maria's place, at Carlisle, to comfort her in her grief." She rolled her eyes. "Prostrate, she is, as you can imagine. Hated the man when he was alive, but is inconsolable in widowhood, apparently. Oh, let us not stand about in this foolish manner. Come and share our parlour with us. There is only the one, so there is no running off and hiding, as you are wont to do, Gus. Do come in. Yes, bring your handsome friend with the Four Horse Club waistcoat. We have a splendid blaze going."

"In August?"

"You know what Aunt Prudence is like."

"Ah, Lady Prudence. Now *her* I remember," Gus murmured. Emma only laughed.

There was indeed a splendid fire going, so splendid that the room seemed hot enough to bake bread. Gus felt his shirt collars wilting as soon as he stepped into the room. Beside the fire, an elderly lady sat ramrod straight in a wing chair. Her hair was as white as snow, although mostly covered by a voluminous black crepe cap. Her gown was black bombazine, and she wore black gloves and a great quantity of jet beading. She turned small, intent eyes on them, then raised a lorgnette to examine them more closely.

Emma waved the two men through, and whispered, "As soon as she has her claret, she will nod off and we can let the fire die down." Then in a raised voice, she turned to the old lady. "Aunt Prudence, look who is here! It is Gus Marford, Carrbridge's brother, do you remember him? He used to play at the hall when I was a girl."

"Of course I remember him, you silly girl. Just because I am a little hard of hearing does not mean I am in my dotage. Well, m'boy, not seen you for an age. Daresay you turned out ramshackle. All you young men are ramshackle these days. Still, better ramshackle than silly, like this niece of mine. Who is your friend? Military man, by his bearing, although the waistcoat is a trifle overpowering."

"Lady Prudence, Lady Emma, may I present Captain Edgerton, formerly of the East India Company Army, but presently engaged at Tattersall's, as am I."

"Your sense of direction is failing you, Marford," Lady Prudence said. "Tattersall's is in London." She cackled, hugely amused at her own wit. Gus raised a dutiful smile, and Edgerton tittered almost convincingly.

The innkeeper entered, ushering in a servant with a tray bearing two wine bottles and four glasses. Lady Prudence brightened perceptibly.

"Over here!" she called out. "Whatever took you so long? We have been waiting forever, and what could be simpler than claret? Every half-decent inn in the country has such a thing to hand. Yes,

yes, just put it down. I shall pour my own, since you would undoubtedly spill some. Cannot do the simplest thing, you people."

The servant rushed to oblige, setting one bottle and a glass on a small table beside her. Lady Prudence poured herself a large measure of wine, and drank it without pausing. Then a second, which she consumed in two draughts. The third took a little longer. Then, with a heavy sigh, she set down the glass, leaned back in her chair and closed her eyes.

"She will be asleep soon," Lady Emma whispered. "Poor dear, the carriage *will* bump her about so, and she does like her sleep in the afternoon."

And before long, gentle snores emanated from the wing chair, and then, as the lady's mouth fell open, rather louder rumbles.

"Do not mind her," Lady Emma said in her normal voice. "We may be easy now and enjoy a comfortable coze before dinner. Captain Edgerton, may I trouble you to pour the wine? So tell me all the news of Drummoor, Gus. Lady Carrbridge is increasing again, I hear, and what is this about Humphrey? I heard a whisper that he is to be wed soon."

"Done already," Gus said.

"Oh, a hasty business. You know what will be said of *that*, I am sure. But she is quite something, my spies tell me. Rides as hard as a man, and shoots tigers before breakfast."

Gus laughed. "Not before breakfast, perhaps, but she certainly shot our land agent one afternoon."

Emma sat bolt upright in her chair, mouth wide open. "No! Intentionally?"

"Oh, very. He was harassing a lady, so Miss Blythe — Lady Humphrey now, of course — shot his hat from his head, and then, when he tried to make good his escape, asked Humphrey if she might kill him. *'No, better not,'* says he, so she hit him in the shoulder instead. As fine a shot as he had ever seen, Humphrey said. They will deal very well together, for she is every bit as insane as he is. More so, perhaps."

"She sounds gloriously original. Oh, I do hope he will bring her to Melton this autumn. I should so like to meet her. And what of the agent? He survived, I take it?"

"Oh, certainly, which is more than he deserved. A great deal of havey-cavey goings on are suspected, and as soon as the surgeon had dealt with him, he disappeared. Even his wife has no idea where he is."

"With Lady Humphrey taking pot-shots at me, I might be inclined to disappear myself," she said, laughing. "But tell me, what brings you so far north? I do not often agree with Aunt Prudence but she is quite right on one point — it is novel to meet two Tattersall's men so far from London. You are on Tattersall's business, I take it?"

"Indeed. We are to catalogue and value the stable of the late Marquess of Darrowstone, and arrange for the transportation of anything of unusual interest."

"Oh, poor Darrowstone, God rest his soul! And his poor father! The duchess gave him three sons who all survived to adulthood, and all of them dead now. The poor duke!"

Gus shrugged, not much excited by the Duke of Dunmorton's sons. Edgerton was interested, however.

"That is most unfortunate. What happened to them?" he said.

"George, the youngest, smashed his head in falling from his horse. Edward, the middle one, died on the Peninsula, as so many of our brave young men have done. And now Henry, the eldest, has gone out in a boat and drowned himself. It is a dangerous business, getting into a boat. I have never dared to do it myself. And now the duke's heir is some paltry third cousin from Cheshire, who is an attorney or some such. Dreadful business. But Gus, if you are going to Castle Morton, you must be sure to tell the duke that I am still unwed, and would be very happy to provide him with a lusty heir or two."

"Emma! You cannot be serious! Why, Dunmorton must be sixty if he is a day."

"And what is that to the point?" she said, looking rather pink about the cheeks. "He was one and sixty last spring, and, I make no doubt, still a fine looking man. He used to stay with us sometimes when he was younger, for he and Papa were at school together. I always liked him, and I think we should rub along very well together. Far better than that evil witch of a wife of his, may she burn in Hell for tormenting him so. And let us be honest, Gus, who else would have me but a man with failing eyesight? I am one and thirty years old, with a face more like a horse than a woman. My own mother used to weep when she looked at me, and Papa did not want to spend a penny on my come-out, for what could be a greater waste of time, he said? And he was quite right about that. All of my sisters took at once and are countesses now, but I shall end up an old maid like Aunt Prudence and be required to chaperon my nieces about. One glare from my frightful gaze and all their unsuitable suitors will shrink away in horror. But I should *so* like to be a duchess and outrank my sisters. So will you tell him? Please?"

She was so earnest that Gus dared not laugh at her, but he thought it a foolish notion all the same. If a man of more than sixty years were to take a wife, and that man a duke, he would hardly look at a tired spinster like Emma Frensham. He would pick up a pretty little debutante and put a smile on his face for his declining years. But he said all that was proper, and soon after the servants arrived to prepare the table for their dinner, Lady Prudence woke with a snort, and all sensible conversation was at an end.

The dinner was indifferent, the service slow and the taproom noisy enough to penetrate even to the parlour. Lady Prudence kept up a continuous monologue of grumbles, which only Captain Edgerton attempted to respond to, by upbraiding the servants whenever they put in an appearance. However, by the time the third bottle of claret was getting low, and only the cheese and nuts remained on the table, she retreated to her chair to sleep away the hours until it was time to go to bed.

Edgerton then turned his attention on Lady Emma, engaging her in a light flirtation that had her giggling and blushing like a debutante. But when Gus went out to check on the horses, Edgerton followed him out.

"She is quite something, your Lady Emma," he said.

"Not mine, nor ever like to be," Gus said. "If you are going to ask about her dowry, I have not the least idea, but if she could lay claim to anything substantial, I make no doubt she would have been snapped up years ago. Huntsmere is not a man to flaunt his wealth, which usually means he has none. Mind you, Landry runs expensive, by the look of it."

"Huntsmere? Landry?"

"Your pardon, Edgerton, I forget you have not grown up with these people. The Earl of Huntsmere, father to the Lady Emma. Viscount Landry, only son and heir to the earl, and Emma's brother."

"Right. So not much money, and the heir is running through what there is of it, if I understand you correctly."

Gus laughed. "You are not serious, Edgerton? About Emma?"

"A titled wife? That would suit me very well, if she has a reasonable dowry."

"You must have a good income, surely? You hardly need to look for a rich wife."

"I do not *need* to, no. I have fifteen hundred a year, few expenses and an expectation from a great-uncle. But a little more would make me very comfortable. I should like a snug little hunting lodge and a string of hunters like yours, Marford."

"I can see the attraction in *that*, to be sure, but marriage is a high price to pay for the pleasure, I should have thought. I have my hunting without the need to become leg-shackled first."

"You are a queer fish, Marford. You think more of your horses than of any woman."

"Of course I do! Look at Jupiter here — such a splendid creature, and see the intelligence in those eyes! And no need to have any conversation, or dance with him, or bring him posies of flowers. Horses are far superior to humankind, Edgerton."

"Hmm. I wager you will find yourself leg-shackled eventually, nevertheless. Bound to happen."

"Not if I can help it," Gus said firmly.

2: Castle Morton

Gus and Edgerton, with their valets and grooms, were on the road early the next morning, long before Lady Prudence and Lady Emma had emerged from their bedchambers. Early rain gave way to clear skies and a soft breeze, with just a hint of salt in the air as they neared the coast. They made good progress, and one more night saw them within reach of their destination. They woke to steady rain, and by the middle of the afternoon, thoroughly sodden, they had reached the bustling town of High Morton, which abutted the castle grounds.

Castle Morton had once perched awkwardly on the cliffs above the pounding seas of the German Ocean. It had been twice burnt to the ground, once by the marauding Scots, and once by a lazy kitchen maid who neglected the hog on the spit. The duke of the time decided to take advantage of this fortuitous event by leaving behind forever the damp stone walls, spiral staircases and draughty arrowslit windows, and building himself a fine modern castle.

He could not quite bring himself to abandon the origins of the house, however. So it was that when Gus, Edgerton and their entourage came to the gates of Castle Morton, they saw at the end of the drive before them the epitome of a solid Norman stronghold, complete with four massive corner towers, turrets, battlements and oriels, and an inner keep. There was no moat or drawbridge, and the bailey housed pleasure gardens rather than the ducal army, but Gus thought it an amusing deception.

Edgerton's eyes were round. "All this for one man?" he said in awed tones. "It is larger than Drummoor, in my estimation."

"Possibly. Drummoor sprawls rather, whereas this is more compact. Shall we ride on?"

The gates, massive wrought iron affairs more than thirty feet high, stood wide open, although no one tended them. Beside it, a neat little lodge sat in its own hedged gardens, chimneys gently smoking.

The road from the gate ran arrow-straight to the castle, passing at first through tree-fringed parkland, and then formal gardens with neat clipped hedges and square beds. An arch three storeys high and almost as wide led through the nearest side of the castle to the interior, but the wrought-iron gates were closed. Steps to one side rose to massive double doors from which emerged a butler and six footmen. Leaving the footmen, blank-faced, in a line on the top step, the butler descended the steps without haste.

"May I help you, sir?" the butler said, in a wispy little voice that made him sound like a girl.

"The duke is expecting us. I am Lord Augustus Marford, and this is Captain Edgerton."

"I was not informed of any arrivals. Is your visit a matter of business or a social call, my lord?"

"Business. The duke invited us to come, and since we have journeyed from London to attend him, might I suggest that you refer to him for instructions?"

"Very well, my lord. Your lordship may wait inside while I inform his grace of your presence."

"And what of my friend? May he not wait inside also?"

"No, my lord. His grace's instructions are that those of noble blood may be admitted without question, whereas those of the commons must await an explicit invitation from his grace."

"My friend may be of the commons, little man, but he is still a gentleman," Gus said with disdain. "The duke is discourteous to refuse him hospitality. I shall wait out here also. Now get off to your master, and be quick about it."

The butler bowed impassively, for he must be used to such responses, and in the same unhurried manner mounted the stairs and disappeared into the house, his flunkeys following behind.

"How unspeakably rude!" Gus said.

Edgerton laughed. "Marford, you are quite splendid when you become lordly and haughty! But I do not mind being snubbed by a duke, you know. These great men have their quirks."

"Quirks are one thing, but discourtesy is unacceptable no matter how high the rank. My father always said that one should make even more effort to be civil to those of lower rank, because they cannot point out that one is being a pompous ass. They are obliged to smile and bow and accept whatever we choose to do. So it is up to us to set the standard. But clearly the duke follows different precepts. I should have liked the opportunity to dry out in front of the fire, too. Still, if we stay under the arch then at least we are sheltered from the rain."

This was not of much help, however, for the wind howled through the archway and rendered all of them thoroughly chilled. Even walking the horses back and forth brought no relief to men or animals. Gus began to fret for his horse, and was seriously considering riding away to the town and returning alone, later, when the great doors creaked open again. With careful steps, the butler descended once more, the footmen following in his wake.

"His grace bids me welcome you to Castle Morton, my lord. If you and the captain will follow me, your servants may follow the footmen round to the stable entrance, and then—"

"I like to see my horse attended to myself," Gus said. "Edgerton, you go on inside, and I will join you when I am sure that Jupiter has taken no harm from being left to stand about for half an hour."

"As you wish, Marford, as you wish." But he followed the butler inside with a smile on his face.

With two footmen showing them the way, Gus, the grooms and valets led the horses round the outside of the building. The castle was arranged with perfect symmetry, with four wings in a square and a tower on each corner. Each of the wings boasted a massive archway in the centre. From the western side, they plodded dutifully round the corner to the northern side, past its archway with its closed gates, and round the next corner to the eastern side, to find another archway identical to the first. Again the gates remained closed, but an open door gave access to the stables.

"If both they gates were open, we could've come straight across, instead o' goin' all round," one of Gus's grooms said.

"Aye, and nd there's a road, too, right across the middle," said the other. "Fancy sending us all round the outside like that. S'pose they only opens them for weddin's and fun'rals and such like."

Gus laughed, and thought he was probably right.

It was a long time before Gus was satisfied that Jupiter had come to no harm, and allowed the last remaining footman, who was lounging against a wall exchanging ribald jokes with the groom, to lead him through the house to his accommodation. He had half expected to be sent round the outside again, but the footman took him up two flights of stairs and then through endless broad corridors and past innumerable closed doors. Here and there a door stood open, revealing furniture swathed in holland covers.

Eventually the footman led him to one of the towers, where he found Edgerton at his ease in a cosy parlour with his boots off, his feet in a mustard bath and a glass of wine in his hand. A fire burning merrily gave the room a pleasant warmth, and the butler was pottering about with decanters and glasses.

"There you are, Marford!" Edgerton said. "What a martyr you are to that horse! Here, get some claret down you. Or there is brandy over there, you know. Is this not snug? There are two bedrooms on this floor for us, and Willett and Gardner are two floors above us. Convenient, eh? We are to dine in here too, but you will not mind that, I imagine."

The butler coughed. "Not quite, sir. His lordship is to dine with his grace in the keep."

"Oh — the noble blood business again?" Edgerton said, and laughed. "Now, don't be looking like a thundercloud, Marford. If his grace wishes to dine with you, then you must go and no nonsense about it. I shall do very well here, I assure you, and it's only natural his grace wants to be with his own kind, and not mingle with ordinary folk like me."

"His grace dines promptly at five, my lord," the butler said.

"Good heavens, I had better get changed then. Is there any chance of a bath?"

"The hot water should have arrived already, my lord, and your man awaits you in your room. I shall collect you at ten minutes to the hour precisely."

A hot bath and the ministrations of Willett partially reconciled Gus to the prospect of dining with the duke. He had supposed he must do so at some stage, although he had rather have been treated as the paid agent that he was, as if he were a lawyer or some such, a man doing business with the duke but not a guest. Still, it would have to be got through, somehow. He wondered idly how many of the duke's family would be there. The duchess was long dead, but was there a dowager? He could not remember. The grieving daughter-in-law would be there, no doubt, and an array of aunts and uncles and cousins and nephews and nieces. Probably the heir, too, the attorney from Cheshire, looking horribly out of place. He sighed. So many names he would have to remember! It was a pity he had not Edgerton with him, for he was much better at that sort of thing. So it was with resignation that he followed the slow-paced butler.

The duke lived inside the castle in a separate tower, fancifully called the keep. Although it had an entrance at ground level, there was a bridge at the level of the third story connecting the keep to the northern wing of the castle, and it was by this means that Gus was led to the duke's domain and was announced.

It had not occurred to Gus until he entered the drawing room that his host might be alone. Yet so it was. The duke sat forlornly by the fire, a rug around his legs. Were it not for the rug, he would have seemed a hearty sort of man for his age, solidly built and with the ruddy complexion that came from too much outdoor living, or too much port wine, or possibly both.

"Ah, Marford, come in. Forgive me not rising — gout's devilish bad at the moment."

"Duke," Gus said, making his bow. "Very kind of you to invite me to dinner. Had no expectation of it, since we are only here to execute some business for you."

"Hmm. Carrbridge's boy — have to make an effort, don't you know. Come and sit down. Well, you have the Marford nose, that much is certain. Are you like your father in other ways, eh?"

"Hard to say."

The duke gave a bark of laughter. "Diplomatic answer. He was a wild one, your father. Would bet on anything, anything at all. You a betting man, Marford?"

"On horses, yes, but not cards or dice. That is a fool's game," Gus said.

"Ha! True enough. I won a little, lost a lot when I was younger. Have no stomach for it now. It seems exciting at the time but it leaves a man empty, and looking for something else to fill the void. And then it becomes impossible to stop. Fool's game indeed."

The butler came in to announce dinner, and a burly footman took hold of the duke's chair and began to push. It was on wheels, Gus now saw, as he followed the duke into the dining room. The table was long enough to seat fifty or sixty in comfort, but it was laid for two. The duke's chair was wheeled to the head of the table, and Gus sat at his right hand. Like the drawing room, the dining room was darkly wood-panelled, with old-fashioned heavy furniture and a painted ceiling, this one depicting some blood-curdling battle. For a while, as the dishes were set out on the table and the duke carved, they talked of nothing very much beyond the food and a few commonplaces. But the duke looked at Gus from under his bushy brows.

"So how is that brother of yours doing?"

"Which one, sir? I have five brothers."

"Five." The duke stared at him, the animation wiped from his face. "Six sons should be enough. All alive still?"

"So far," Gus said. "Although Gil, the youngest, is like to kill himself before he is much older. He is wild, if you like. But the others are remarkably well settled."

"And the eldest? The marquess?"

"Carrbridge is very contentedly married, with two sons in the nursery and the expectation of another before the spring."

"Two sons… a good start, but not enough, not nearly enough. Three was not enough for me, Marford. Three sturdy boys, and all of them gone now. All gone."

"I am very sorry for it," Gus said. The duke fell into a reverie, and when the silence threatened to stretch indefinitely, Gus said, "I am surprised to find that your family has abandoned you at such a difficult time, Duke. I should have thought they would have rallied round you."

"Hmm? What is that? Oh, the family — ha! No desire to have *them* underfoot. What, you think those mealy-mouthed daughters of mine would be any solace to me?"

"Your heir, perhaps?"

The duke laughed so hard, Gus was afraid he might rupture something vital. "That useless piece of flotsam? An attorney from Cheshire, here in *my* house? I think not."

Tentatively, Gus said, "Do you not think that it would be good for him to learn from you, sir? Just so that he might have an idea what will be expected of him?"

"Nothing will be expected of him," the duke snapped. "Whenever he finds himself inheriting all this, I shall be long dead, so it is of no concern to me. He may do as he pleases."

And Gus was so flabbergasted at this disinterest in the succession that he missed the opportunity for a second portion of salmon before one of the eight footmen in attendance whisked the dish away and replaced it with spiced mushrooms.

Later, they played cribbage for an hour, after which Gus thought it reasonable to leave.

"Thank you for a most pleasant evening, Duke," he said, as he made his bow.

"Was it? Ha! Very civil of you to say so, but cribbage with an old man is not your idea of a lively evening, I wager."

"Not lively, sir, no, but I enjoyed it all the same," Gus said.

"How so, when you lost every game?"

"Because nothing was said that did not relate to the game. I find that very restful, not being a great conversationalist."

The duke gave another sharp laugh. "I hope you are wrong about that, young man. I depend on you to cheer me up while you are here. Maybe I shall draw you out a little more tomorrow, eh?"

Gus's heart sank. Tomorrow? Was he expected to dine with the duke every night? That would materially diminish his enjoyment of the visit. "If you want better company, you might invite Captain Edgerton to dine. He would keep you well entertained, and is an excellent card player, too."

The duke's face darkened. "Not in the keep! No one enters here unless they are of noble blood. That is my rule. In the castle — well, sometimes it is necessary, but the keep is my private domain and I choose my own guests."

"Of course, sir," Gus said, with another bow, and with very few further words was able to make good his escape.

Edgerton was still up, half-dozing over his port. He was agog to hear all about Gus's evening, and wanted the dishes, the plate, the footmen, the furnishings all described in the minutest detail.

"*Eight* footmen? For just the two of you? Great heavens! And two full courses? But where is the rest of his family? He has daughters, does he not?"

"I... think so," Gus said. "Not sure how many. They will be married and gone, though, if there are any."

"Five daughters, all married," Edgerton said. "So different from Drummoor. That was as full as it could hold."

Gus smiled fondly. "Ah, Connie loves to fill Drummoor with visitors! Whereas this huge place is big enough for an army and just the one man rattling round in it. But he seems to like being alone."

"No one likes being alone," Edgerton said. "Why else invite *you* to dine? If he truly wanted to be alone, he would not have done so."

"It is a courtesy to a guest," Gus said, but even before Edgerton raised his eyebrows in disbelief, he was aware that courtesy to guests was not uppermost in the duke's mind. "Well, if it is my witty conversation or brilliant card play he is seeking, he will be sadly disappointed. I suggested he invite you for that sort of thing, but he would not have it, I regret to say."

"I thank you for the compliment, Marford, but my ignoble blood is against me, I fear. It will be necessary for me to receive my intelligence second hand, for as long as you are willing to indulge my curiosity. But the picture you paint is not a happy one. Poor lonely old man. Did you mention Lady Emma at all?"

"Lady Emma?"

"As a wife, Marford. Have you forgotten already? She seemed very keen to be Duchess of Dunmorton."

"Oh, that. No, I did not think to mention it. He is so against his present heir that the thought of a new wife must occur to him without any help from me."

"But he might not think about that particular new wife," Edgerton said. "You must raise the matter with him tomorrow."

"Perhaps," Gus said with a shrug. "It is really not my place to discuss such a matter with him."

"But who else will? His butler? His valet? And Lady Emma is depending upon you, Marford."

Gus sighed. "If the opportunity arises, then perhaps, but I make no promises. I shall head for my bed, I think. We have a long day ahead of us tomorrow."

By the time Willett had undressed him and readied him for sleep, Gus's mind was already running ahead to the next day's visit to the late marquess's stables, and he had forgotten Lady Emma Frensham entirely.

3: A Ride In The Woods

Gus was up early the next morning, his head full of the day's plans. Today he would get his first look at the horses owned by the late Marquess of Darrowstone. He knew Edgerton was a late riser, so as soon as he was dressed he set off to walk the short distance to the marquess's stables, which was situated at the southern end of the castle grounds. He knew very little about the project, except that it was an attempt to breed race horses for greater speed. He wondered just how successful such an enterprise would be, here in the bleak north-east of the country, and how enthusiastic the marquess had been. He had rarely been seen at the southern race courses, and on the few occasions Gus had met him, he had found the man silent to the point of surliness.

The castle and its outer pleasure grounds were ringed by trees, but once he had passed through those, Gus discovered that the whole southern end of the park was given over to the horses, divided into neatly fenced paddocks holding dozens of mares and foals. At the centre, a square of two storey stone buildings housed stables, breeding yards and quarters for the grooms, with everything tidy and in general good order.

He had no wish to approach the stables just yet, so he stopped to lean on a rail and admire a particularly fine pair of mares, their foals gambolling energetically. He had not been there long when a small man in a well-fitted coat and polished top boots approached him.

"Help you, sir?"

"Thank you, but I am just admiring these fillies. Excellent bearing, and the foals look promising, too. Lord Augustus Marford."

"Ah, thought so. Johnny Waterbury, head groom here. Very kind of you to speak so well of our handiwork, my lord."

"This is a larger enterprise than I had supposed. How many mares do you have?"

"Forty three at present, my lord, and seven stallions, all individually chosen by the marquess, may God rest his soul." His voice wavered as he spoke. "Had a ten-year plan for breeding, to enhance the speed and stamina, and at an earlier age than the common way. This is his lordship's life's work, here in these fields, my lord. A tragedy — that's what it is. To cut a man off in his prime like that, before his work here is done. A tragedy."

"My clergyman brother would say that one should not question God's will in such matters," Gus said gently.

"Indeed, and I do not question it," Waterbury said. "I grieve for the loss of a good man, as anyone would do who knew him as I did. But the horses... everything we have worked towards... to be destroyed and cast aside as if all of it were nothing. And then there will be no memorial to him, my lord. Once the horses are gone, and the grooms have left, and everything is shut up... why, there will be no memory of him, and it will be as if he had never lived."

~~~~~

After a hasty breakfast with Edgerton, the two men paid a more formal visit to the stables, and were shown the stalls and feed stores, the workers' accommodation and the office, where the marquess had kept his stud records and plans for future breeding.

His notebooks spread over shelf after shelf of the bookcase, each filled with the marquess's neat hand, recording the history of every horse, its strengths and possible weaknesses, and potential matings between the fastest horses.

"Where did they all come from, these horses?" Gus asked Waterbury. "For they did not pass through Tattersall's, that much is certain. Darrowstone bought a few hunters there, but no racing stock."

"These are all northern-born horses," he said. "Used to the weather here, and not bothered by a bit of snow. That'll give them an advantage when they go south to race, or so his lordship reckoned."

"An interesting idea," Gus said. "Do you not agree, Edgerton?"

"It may be so, who can tell? Are you going to read those books all day, Marford, or might we make a start on listing the stock?"

"Of course. Might I look at these another time, Waterbury? There is much to interest me here, and I should like to understand Darrowstone's philosophy."

Edgerton laughed. "Philosophy? Truly? In horse breeding?"

"Why not? To put it in less grandiose terms, I should like to know how the marquess was thinking as he chose which horses to buy, and which mare to put to which stallion. I have not had much to do with stud work before, and it intrigues me. But I shall read these when I am at leisure. By all means let us make a start."

For three days, they industriously examined every single horse owned by the late marquess, inspecting teeth, lifting feet to examine hooves and running expert hands over flanks and rumps and manes. Then, in a notebook of his own, Gus wrote down the horse's details and Edgerton's valuation. Gus had not been at Tattersall's long enough to be trusted with this important aspect of the work, and since the horses were auctioned he could not quite see the point of it. They fetched whatever price a buyer was prepared to put up, and that was an end to it. But in this case there was a point, because the very best animals would be walked all the way to London to be sold to the wealthiest stud owners. The rest would most likely be sold locally, for lower prices. Yet as he looked around at the lush paddocks and gleaming coats of the well-cared-for occupants, he was aware of a pang of regret that such a carefully devised enterprise should be broken apart.

The morning of the fourth day was spent laboriously writing a long missive to Tattersall's, detailing their findings.

"Now we must wait and see what they say," Edgerton said, as they emerged from small inn room that acted as the local post office. "We have a few days at leisure now until further instructions arrive. Shall we begin our investigation of High Morton's public houses? Or something livelier, perhaps? Do you not wonder what these northern women are like?"

"I shall stretch Jupiter's legs, I think," Gus said. "It is too long since he was given a run."

"Pfft, let your groom exercise him."

"No one rides him but me. He is too evil-tempered to leave to the grooms."

"What a strange fellow you are, to prefer your horses to the company of womankind," Edgerton said. "Well, the loss is yours. We may compare our afternoons this evening, and we shall see then which of us has had the pleasanter time." And with a cheery wave, he disappeared down the main street.

Gus hastened back to the castle, his spirits rising with every step. At last! He was so accustomed to riding every day, that the loss was keenly felt, especially here where the country was open and wild and calling to him. From now on, a ride every day would be an absolute necessity. He ordered the horse saddled and went to change. When he returned to the castle stables, he heard the commotion even from outside.

Jupiter was still in his stall, snorting and kicking up his heels. Three grooms were holding his head, while Gus's own two grooms tightened his girth and made final adjustments to the bridle.

"He's terrible wild, milord," Fred Carson, one of his grooms, said.

"So I see. Where is the best place to let him burn off his megrims?"

"There's an exercise track around the edge o' the stud fields, milord. Or through the southern gate to the gallops on the cliffs."

"That is no good. I dare not take him anywhere near the stud horses. He will wreak havoc in this mood, jumping all the fences into the paddocks and terrifying the foals. Nor can I go west, through the town. What is through the eastern gate?"

"A steep path to the beach, milord."

"That will never do, either."

"Beyond t'northern gate is woods, milord," one of the other grooms said. "Very quiet, no one goes that way much, these days. Too many gates to jump or open, but ye'll not regard that, I reckon."

"No, a gate is no obstacle to Jupiter. Right, to the north it is then." He swung himself into the saddle, as the horse reared and then kicked again. "None of that nonsense! Easy, now. Very well, stand away and open the gate."

As soon as he was released, Jupiter shot out of his stall and towards the open door. Gus knew better than to try anything clever with him except to point him in the right direction, and that was enough of a challenge to keep him fully occupied for some minutes. At first the beast seemed determined to head for the sea, and it took all Gus's strength to dissuade him from the notion. But at length he got the animal pointing towards the north, and let him have his head. They raced out from the encircling trees into the open park, Jupiter still snorting and tossing his head, but eventually he settled to the gallop. Ahead, another belt of trees hid the northern gate, but the gravel drive pointed the way, and the symmetry of the castle was such that Gus knew exactly what he would find — a small lodge with a hedged garden, and the high gate standing wide open.

Except that it was closed.

Jupiter burst out of the trees not twenty yards from the great iron gates, skidded to a stop, reared and whinnied in rage. Spinning as he dropped down, he reared again, and when that did not answer, began to kick his heels.

"Gate!" Gus yelled, trying desperately to hold on as the horse reared again. "Gate, dammit!"

A small figure in an apron bobbed up from behind the hedge, where she had presumably been weeding. She dashed out of the lodge gardens, and raced to pull open the gate. Before one side was even half open, Jupiter bolted for the gap, still snorting and kicking. The figure screamed, so close that the sound echoed in Gus's head and then, somehow, the horse had squeezed through and was away, galloping as if the devil was on his tail.

For a while, Gus simply hung on, happy to let the beast expend his energy. Besides, there was only one route, a wide track under high trees, with no risk of a low-hanging branch. The thud of hooves on the soft earth and the horse's heavy breathing were the only sounds. They came upon a low wall, with a five-barred gate set into it, but Jupiter sailed over it without breaking stride. Not much further on was another gate, and then a third, but the horse never faltered. Gradually, both horse and rider settled into a steady rhythm, and Gus laughed out loud in exhilaration. Oh, the joy of a fast horse! There was no feeling on earth to beat it.

Gradually, as his concentration was needed less on his mount and his thoughts were free to wander, he remembered the small figure in the apron, and that piercing scream. Had she been hurt? Was she even now lying unconscious, or even dead, before the gates? But there was nothing to be done about it, for there was no point trying to turn Jupiter until he had released the first burst of energy.

The trees thinned and the ground began to rise. The track forked, but Gus let the horse choose its own way and before long they emerged from the woods onto open grassland, longer tufts swept by the salty breeze. For there to the east was the sea, a dull grey today, seabirds wheeling over the cliffs. And a little way ahead, the craggy ruins of the original Castle Morton, a couple of towers still standing in obstinate defiance of the corroding sea and wind.

Jupiter slowed and Gus reined him to a halt, gazing about him. Beyond the castle ruins, the land dropped away again and he longed to explore, to see if the cliffs hid a sheltered cove, or a fishing village, or perhaps, on the far horizon, the smoky haze of some great town. Instead he turned and trotted the horse back the way they had come, jumping the gates more circumspectly now. The great iron gates beside the northern lodge stood wide open, and to Gus's relief no crumpled figure lay beside them.

He loosely wrapped Jupiter's reins around the bars of one gate, for he was docile enough not to wander now, and knocked at the front door of the lodge. Within moments the door opened and a face peeped out at him, then, recognising him, the door opened fully to reveal the aproned figure he had seen before.

He had not had time to observe her previously, but now he saw a slender young woman, wearing a matron's cap although she was not much above twenty. She was pretty, too, with a heart-shaped face and wide blue eyes.

"I am come to proffer my apologies," Gus said. "Are you uninjured? My horse did not kick you?"

"Oh, no, sir! I was well able to jump aside, and your horse was not close enough to hurt me. I beg your pardon for screaming, but his abrupt movements startled me and it just burst out, you see." To his surprise, her accent was good. He had expected the lodgekeeper's wife to be a local woman, of low standing, but, now that he looked more closely, he realised that her clothes, though simple, were of good quality.

"That is entirely understandable, under the circumstances," Gus said, tempted to smile at the serious manner with which she apologised for screaming when faced with a bolting horse. "He is an evil beast when he has been kept indoors for a few days. I should have screamed myself, in your position."

She giggled at this, raising a corner of her apron to hide her mouth. "But he is a beautiful creature, sir! I wish more such might pass this way, for there is nothing like a fine horse at a gallop for raising the spirits. One cannot repine when there is such magnificence in the world. What is his name?"

This was so much in accordance with Gus's own feelings on the matter that he smiled at her in delight. She was clearly a woman of excellent perception. "Jupiter, and mine is Lord Augustus Marford."

"Oh!" The apron rose again, this time to hide her confusion. She bobbed a curtsy. "Beg pardon, my lord. I did not realise."

"How should you, indeed? May I have the honour to know whom I am addressing?"

She coloured at his politeness, and bobbed another curtsy. "Mrs Edward Walsh, my lord."

"It is a pleasure to meet you, Mrs Walsh, and I am happy that you have taken no hurt from our first encounter. I plan to ride each morning at eight from now on, so it might be best to leave the gates open at that time."

"Indeed I will, my lord."

Gus made his farewell, and rode Jupiter at a more moderate pace back to the stables, wondering how a well-bred woman came to be living in a Castle Morton lodge, and what cause she might have to repine when there were no horses for her to admire.

But when he mentioned her name to the duke that evening, he sneered and said only, "A charity case. One has to do something for these poor foolish creatures."

After that, he would say no more about her, and Gus could only assume that she was a distant relative who had fallen on hard times, perhaps married beneath her. But it puzzled him, all the same.

4: Two Dinners

Gus was restless. A fast ride on Jupiter usually burnt away any petty worries and left him feeling full of life. That evening, he ached all over from struggling to control the horse, the duke's company had been even more boring than usual, and Edgerton had finally returned close to midnight, very much the worse for drink and insufferably pleased with himself.

"It seems to me that your afternoon was a lot less… *relaxing* than mine," Edgerton said with a smug grin. "Wrestling with that fiend of a horse of yours, a dull ride in the woods, and then a terribly civil conversation with some servant or other… you are such a slow-top, Marford. Was she pretty, this gatekeeper's wife? Maybe I should go and call, eh?"

"Leave her alone, Edgerton," Gus said, sharply. "I cannot say who she is, but her accent proclaims her gentry, at least."

"Oh ho, so is that how it is?" Edgerton said, winking. "Very well, dear boy, she is all yours."

"You are drunk and offensive, and one can only hope that both states will be improved by a night's sleep," Gus said. Edgerton only laughed.

But the next morning Gus woke refreshed and leapt from his bed as enthusiastically as usual. He had given instructions the previous day, so Jupiter was saddled and ready for him when he reached the stables. The horse still reared once and kicked out twice, but Gus could tell it was more for form's sake, because the creature felt it was expected of him and he had a reputation to maintain as the meanest horse in any stable.

This time it took no more than a tweak of the reins to persuade the horse to head north, and although he put his head down for the gallop, it was not the mad headlong chase of the day before. Through the copse, Jupiter slowed of his own accord, the memory of the previous day still in his mind, no doubt. But there was the little lodge with its trim garden, and beyond it the gates stood wide open. Jupiter needed no urging, for he snorted and sped up, his own pleasure in the ride just as great as Gus's.

This time they took the other fork, away from the ruined castle, and found themselves in a wide meadow filled with the purple fronds of rose bay willow herb. Jupiter cantered on contentedly until they came to farmland and a view over a wide river valley, housing what looked like a thriving township of mills and manufactories. Not wanting to broach the farmer's crops, Gus turned aside on a rutted farm track that led him by a circuitous route back to the ruined castle, where he turned for home.

When he reached the lodge, the young wife was there, hanging washing on a line between two apple trees. She turned at the sound of their approach, and dropped into a curtsy.

"Good day to you, Mrs Walsh," Gus called, reining Jupiter to a halt. "A fine day for a washing."

"Good day, my lord. Indeed it is, and a fine day for riding. Did you go all the way through the woods? There is a splendid view of the old castle from the far end."

"Indeed I did. I went first a little inland, to a place with a view of a mill town."

"Oh, that would be Drifford!" she said, clapping her hands together excitedly. "That is where I lived, before... before I came here." Her animation slid away, and he wondered again about her history, and whether what had happened *before* was what caused her to repine.

"It looks a prosperous place," he said, but when she did not answer, he went on, "Then I rode past farms and came in time to the ruins on the cliff. A bleak place it seems to me. Who would want to live in such a situation?"

"Anyone who had an interest in keeping the savage Scots at bay, I should imagine," she said, with such a twinkle in her eyes that he laughed out loud.

"That would have been a powerful motivator," he said. "I am thankful we no longer have to worry about the wild men of the north coming down upon us, be they the Scots or the Vikings. Let us be glad that we live in civilised times."

"Are we civilised? I suspect we have some way to go yet. But do not let me detain you with my chatter, my lord. The breeze is quite cool so early in the day, and I should never forgive myself if Jupiter were to take a chill."

He gave a small bow as he made his farewell, and she bobbed another curtsy. He wheeled the horse and trotted slowly off, his mind pondering her words. Why would she feel the world was uncivilised, and what had happened to her... *before?*

~~~~~

That evening, the duke was not alone. Gus almost jumped in astonishment at the sight of a lady sitting in a chair opposite the duke, the chair that Gus had almost come to regard as his own. She was in her thirties, so thin and pale of complexion that in her white muslin gown she looked like a veritable ghost.

"Ah, there you are, Marford. Come and meet my daughter-in-law. Edith, this is Carrbridge's brother."

She nodded politely. "Lord Augustus."

Gus cast about in his mind. Daughter-in-law? Was this the marchioness, the widow of the duke's eldest? Yet she wore no black. Had either of the other sons married? He had no idea, but he had to make a guess as he made his bow.

"Lady Darrowstone."

No one corrected him, so he assumed he had guessed correctly. But if she was the Marchioness of Darrowstone, her husband had died barely three months ago, so why no widow's black? And she was not dressed for evening, either.

"I daresay you are wondering to see me here," she said to Gus. He was not, for why would she not visit her father-in-law sometimes? "I came to tell the duke that I have invited his heir to visit me. *Someone* needs to take the poor boy in hand and make sure he will not disgrace the Winfell name when he inherits."

"Meddlesome woman!" the duke said. "You had no right to interfere, and as for inviting him to stay—"

"I may invite whomsoever I please to my own house, I believe."

"Just so long as you do not bring him to *this* house, madam."

"Never fear, he knows he is unwelcome. In point of fact, the boy is abjectly terrified of you, and it was all I could do to persuade him to come north at all. I hope I may be able to stiffen his spine somewhat. He arrives tomorrow, Lord Augustus, and you are invited to dine with us, and Captain Edgerton, also. We sit down at around seven."

"Ha!" said the duke. "You will be lucky to get sight of the soup before nine, Marford. Never knew a more disorganised household."

The marchioness rose. "You are a disagreeable old man, and will die alone in your bed, unmourned. I shall see you tomorrow, Lord Augustus, and I shall expect a full account of your brother's wife."

"Which one?" he said, amused, although he guessed the answer.

"The one who shot the tiger."

"I believe it was seven tigers, one bull elephant and my brother's land agent."

She laughed in delight. "How positively delicious! I cannot wait. Until tomorrow, then."

As she swept out, with the click of the door the butler entered and announced dinner in his oddly thin voice.

"About time," the duke said. "It is almost ten past the hour, Bedford. Just because that woman is here is no reason to keep me from my table. What is it tonight, eh? Is there any decent fish? I hope it is turbot. And pigeon — I asked for pigeon yesterday, and did I get any? Not a sign of any pigeon."

The butler made no answer to any of these grumblings, which Gus imagined was wise of him. They progressed slowly out of the drawing room and into the adjoining dining room, the duke muttering all the way. Only when he had been positioned at the head of the table with the first course set out in front of him did he relax, and say with the hint of a smile, "Now, Marford, tell me all about the tiger lady."

So he did, and by the time the duke had drunk most of a bottle of claret and partaken liberally of every dish on the table, including two helpings of pigeon in redcurrant sauce, he was far more mellow.

"I despise that daughter-in-law of mine," he said musingly, as he passed the port to Gus, "but Edith is right about one thing. I shall certainly die alone in my bed, and probably unmourned. My sons are dead, my daughters are too busy to spare a thought for their father, and who will care when I am gone? Not Edith, that much is certain. She hates me almost as much as she hated Henry, and has never made any bones about it. Well, it is entirely mutual. Cannot stand the woman, although I will give her credit in full measure for doing her duty by Henry. Nine babes in all, although three never breathed, three died in their cradles, and the three who survived were all girls. No, both of them tried their damnedest, and maybe the tenth would have been the one. Except that Henry had to go out in that wretched boat. Clear day, no cause for concern, yet down it went, and all my hopes with it. And now this boy is here, no doubt sizing up his inheritance. Ha! An attorney from Cheshire! It is almost enough to make my father rise up from his grave in revolt."

"Still time for you to marry again and cut out the attorney," Gus said.

"Ha!" The duke shook with laughter. "Oh, a fine idea, Marford! And who on earth would have me, eh? I am one and sixty years of age, and so riddled with gout that I never leave these rooms."

"You still have most of your hair and all of your teeth," Gus said. "Besides, you are a duke. Any number of women would be delighted to be a duchess and provide you with an heir or two in gratitude. And why not?"

"Why not? Because... ack, would I want some woman fussing over me? I am set in my ways, Marford, and I have no intention of changing now."

"No need to change, sir. You set the rules. Which would you rather have, a pretty young thing keeping you warm, or the attorney moving in as soon as you are in the ground?"

"Hmm." There was a long silence. "And how would I find a wife, eh? Take myself off to London and shuffle about with the debutantes at Almacks? You want me to make a cake of myself? I should like to retain a shred or two of dignity."

Gus had not until that moment considered how he would broach the subject of Lady Emma. Even though she had authorised him to mention her directly to the duke, he hardly liked to do so. The duke had an uncertain temper at the best of times, and telling him in unvarnished terms that the lady wished to marry him might have exactly the opposite effect to that desired. But the idea of a wife was in the duke's head now, and something had to be done.

"I have not the least idea how it might be achieved," he said. "However, I know a lady who might be able to help you in the matter. Do you know Lady Emma Frensham?"

"Frensham? One of Huntsmere's girls?"

"Indeed. She is a... a skilled matchmaker, and also very well acquainted with all the best families. She would be able to advise you." This was improvisation, and Gus was uneasily aware that this was not his strong suit. He wished he had Humphrey with him to suggest some ingenious device to bring the two together without the duke suspecting that he was being led by the nose.

"A bit of a girl?"

"Oh, no, she is quite old. Above thirty, I should say."

"An old maid, then. What will she know about matchmaking when she could not find a husband herself?"

Gus took a sip of port to give him time to think. This was not proving to be easy, and already the duke was finding all the flaws in his scheme. At length he said, "Spinsters are the very best matchmakers. A married woman is always on the catch for her own daughters and nieces, and a young woman has not enough experience, but a spinster past the marriageable age has a clear insight into the business. Lady Emma has seen her own younger sisters married, and any number of cousins, and she is worldly enough to understand the practical aspects. Why not invite her here, and see what she suggests? At least that way you might discuss a few ideas with her in private, without the whole world knowing what you are about."

"That is a good point. It is a service that Edith should provide, if she were less selfish. She is discreet, this Lady Emma?"

"Oh, very," Gus said at once, and could only hope that was true.

"Hmm. Compose a letter, then, Marford, and if I deem it good, I shall send it to her."

~~~~~

The dinner at Lady Darrowstone's was late, as the duke had foreseen, but nevertheless was more enjoyable than Gus had anticipated. He was not the most sociable of people, but after his solitary dinners with the duke, there was some pleasure to be had in the company of those bent on revelry. He was aware that he and Edgerton were being brought onstage to provide a diversion for the locals, and if Gus himself was not likely to be an entertainment, Edgerton was more than capable of entertaining for two. Nothing delighted him more than a ready audience for his badinage, which he regarded as the epitome of wit. A little flirtation with the ladies, a political joke or two and some ribald remarks with the gentlemen over the port, and he thought himself a capital fellow, and the most popular man in the neighbourhood.

Lady Darrowstone lived within the town of High Morton, no more than ten minutes' walk from the castle, but Edgerton was concerned for his stockings if there should be any mud about, so Gus took them there in his curricle, which had now arrived from

Drummoor. It was hardly worth putting the horses to, for the marchioness's town house lay not twenty paces from the main square with its statue of an earlier Duke of Dunmorton, a forbidding bronze figure on his horse. The house was neither imposing nor elegant, but inside it was warm and packed with what Gus supposed were the leading figures of High Morton. Nor was the dinner anything terribly grand, for although it was the full two courses, the dishes were comparatively plain. Gus thought of the duke, dining alone on an array of rich sauces and elaborate desserts, and here was a lady who might have been a duchess, who yet preferred simple food and good company.

The heir was not especially memorable. He was young, no more than five and twenty, but already showing signs of portliness. His wife was even younger and even portlier. Neither displayed any sense of style or fashion or intelligent discourse. Gus was no great conversationalist himself, but Mr Winfell, when he could be induced to speak at all, was inclined to talk in platitudes and homilies. Every other sentence began, "As the estimable Mr Fordyce would say...", and there was only so much of that nature that a sensible man could stomach. His wife needed no inducement to speak, rather it was the greatest struggle to prevail upon her to stop talking. The size of the rooms, the furnishings, the number of servants and their liveries, even the number of logs on the fire, all met with her approbation, in a constant stream of verbiage that no one seemed to attend to in the slightest. After a while, everyone, even Lady Darrowstone, ignored both of them.

Edgerton, however, would never be ignored in any company. The discussion of tigers and elephants lasted all the way through the first course, and into the second. Having been in the East India Company Army, he had a bottomless well of exotic tales for all occasions, and kept the company enthralled. Gus had heard most of the anecdotes before, but he was very happy to keep to the shadows and allow Edgerton his hour in the sun. It was not until the company was relaxed by too much to eat, drink and listen to, that someone finally came round to asking an obvious question.

"So, Lord Augustus, what brings you so far north?" said one of the portly burghers filling the table.

"We are here on behalf of Tattersall's," he said. "The duke has asked us to evaluate the late marquess's stud with a view to selling the horses."

The chatter around the table died away. The marchioness set down her wine glass with a crash.

"The *horses*? The *duke* asked you to come?"

"That is so. You did not know?" Gus felt a prickle of alarm.

"I did not," she said crisply. "You should be aware, gentlemen, that my late husband's horses are not the duke's to sell. They belong to me, and are not likely to be for sale, now or in the future."

5: *Widows*

"Now we are in the soup, and no mistake," Edgerton said gloomily, as the curricle clattered over the cobbles of High Morton. "I wonder the duke did not mention that his daughter-in-law owns the stud."

"He may not be aware of it," Gus said.

"How could he not be aware of it? There must have been a will, so it would have been quite explicit."

"Not necessarily, and there may be factors of which we are unaware," Gus said. "The stud is on the grounds of Castle Morton, for one thing. The duke may have put money into the venture. Or even if he has not done so directly, if he paid his son an allowance, and the marquess spent that allowance on horses, the duke may feel he owns them by proxy. Or perhaps the lady funded the venture, and now feels it is rightfully hers. It will be a matter for the lawyers, I feel."

"Well, they have one in the family now, so that will be helpful," Edgerton said, chuckling.

Gus laughed. "I never saw so unpromising a ducal heir. Does he read nothing but sermons? For I swear he quoted nothing else, and he has not an original thought in his head."

"And the future duchess is even worse," Edgerton said. "An apothecary's daughter — can you imagine? She will be torn to shreds in London."

Gus shrugged. "They may not care. In fact, their hides are so thick, they may not even notice." He sighed. "We shall have to write to Tattersall's again, informing them of this difficulty. And doubtless we will be stuck here for weeks now until the matter is resolved."

"There could be worse situations," Edgerton said with a grin. "There are many attractions to a small town like High Morton, especially when the residents are so friendly. That red-haired friend of Lady Darrowstone's, for instance, Mrs Masterson — now that is a most agreeable lady. Her husband is going away tomorrow, so perhaps I may call on her, to enliven her long, lonely hours." And he laughed, delighted with himself.

~~~~~

Gus kicked his heels at the keep all the next morning, waiting for the duke to be up and about. He was eventually shown into the duke's dressing room where the duke reclined in bed in a voluminous nightcap drinking his morning chocolate.

"What is this, Marford? Could it not have waited until this evening? Noon is an uncivilised hour to be socialising."

"This is not a social call, Duke. I am obliged to inform you that Lady Darrowstone is claiming ownership of the stud in its entirety. You may wish to consult your legal advisers."

"Consult my—!" He went so red that Gus thought he might explode in an apoplectic fit. "I shall do no such thing! Consult my legal advisers indeed! You may tell Edith that if she suggests such a thing again I shall come round to that miserable little house of hers and flay her alive."

"I am not acting as intermediary in any quarrel between two family members," Gus said, without rancour. "I act only for Tattersall's, and clearly there can be no further dealings in the matter until you can prove ownership."

"Get out! Go on, clear out, you insufferable booby! I am surrounded by fools and incompetents and ignoramuses. Get out!"

Gus got out. He bore the duke no ill-will, and had met far more eccentric great men in London. Sometimes it seemed as though the higher a man's rank, the more outrageous he became. Perhaps Mr and Mrs Winfell were in fact typical of the mass of the lower gentry, and their conversation, which seemed so boring to him, was taken as the height of civilised discourse in Cheshire. And perhaps when they became the Duke and Duchess of Dunmorton, their very banality would be smilingly approved and half the peerage would begin to ape their manners. With that depressing thought, he returned to his room to change into his riding clothes.

He found Edgerton bound on the same objective. "Will you show me this woodland ride of yours, Marford?" Edgerton said. "And the pretty little wife at the lodge, of course, if I promise to keep my hands off her?"

"Truly, Edgerton, sometimes I suspect you think of nothing but women."

"What else is there for a man to think about?"

"Horses, of course."

Edgerton snorted. "You are not natural, Marford, I swear."

Gus laughed. "Perhaps not. Edgerton, I believe we know each other well enough now to be on Christian name terms. You may call me Gus."

"Thank you! I began to think you despised me so thoroughly that we should never get to that point. And you may call me Michael."

In a spirit of cautious amity, the two rode across the castle's parkland to the northern gate. Having been ridden daily, Jupiter was not in a great hurry, but even so his long legs soon outpaced Edgerton's more restrained mount. The gates were closed when Gus approached, but Mrs Walsh must have heard him coming, for she rushed to open them and he barely had to hold Jupiter in at all before the way was clear and the horse sprang forward and raced off into the cool depths of the woods.

At the fork, Gus waited for Edgerton, Jupiter dancing with impatience, and the two rode on together to the old castle.

"What a fine spot for an assignation," Edgerton said.

That made Gus laugh. "See? Always thinking of women. But you will not get your Mrs Masterson up here, nor any housemaids. It is too far from the town to walk, and there is no way to get a carriage here."

"No, but that would be no obstacle to a lady who rides," he said, grinning widely, and nothing would do but for him to scramble all over the ruins while Gus held his horse. "It would need a rug or two, but it could be done. Splendid! Now do not look so thunderous, Gus. You should not be so censorious about such matters, as a Marford. Your family has some history in that line."

"My father, you mean?"

"And your youngest brother, too, not to mention that rackety cousin of yours that you never acknowledge."

"Every family has a few bad apples. The present generation is not half so wild as my father was. Any number of affairs within the *ton*, and now we are finding the little presents he left with housemaids and the like."

"Only just finding them? Usually they get underfoot from the start and make a thorough nuisance of themselves."

"He seems to have paid them off — money or a house, that sort of thing," Gus said. "Then, on his deathbed, he appeared to regret not doing more for them, and made Carrbridge promise to take care of them. Which he does, when he finds them, but there are no records anywhere, so sometimes it is a matter of recognising the Marford nose. One turned up who was the image of Humphrey — quite uncanny. There could be scores of them for all we know."

"Well, if he paid them off, his duty is done, I should say. Shall we ride back, now? Will you introduce me to Mrs Walsh? Wait — let me pick her some flowers. Ladies like to be given flowers."

"Michael..."

"No, I shall be very good, I promise, but I should like a closer look at her, you know. Besides, if you like her, you are such a slow-top that you will need someone like me to bring you together, otherwise you will ride by her house twice a day without ever doing more than to bid her a good morning in passing."

"She is a married woman," Gus protested, but Edgerton just laughed.

"The best kind," was all he said.

At the lodge, Edgerton dismounted, clutching his bundle of wild flowers, and insisted Gus dismount too and knock at the front door. He was uncomfortable about it, for they had no real reason for calling, but Edgerton was perfectly capable of going alone, and Gus had no wish to impose his friend on Mrs Walsh without being there himself to shield her from the worst of his foolishness. Or so he told himself. So he tied Jupiter's reins loosely to the gate, and the two men walked into the little front garden, filled with herbs and bees humming, and up to the front door.

She answered it almost at once, which made Gus suspect she had been watching out for them. He made the introductions, Edgerton presented his flowers and she blushed prettily as she thanked him. Gus was conscious of a momentary pang of envy for the unknown Mr Walsh, with such a delight to come home to at night. For some ten minutes Edgerton chattered away to her on the front step, and although she blushed, she responded very readily. She told them, which Gus already knew, that she came from Drifford, the mill town some twenty miles away by road. No, she had not been born there, but when she was fourteen, her clergyman father had had to give up his living through ill health and had rented a small property there. She had met her husband when he had been quartered at the army camp near the town.

"Militia?" Edgerton said, with a soldier's interest in his fellow professionals.

"No, the Regulars. He… he was killed not long after he went out to the Peninsula. His first action. He was very brave, his colonel said." Her voice wavered, her fingers clutching the skirt of her gown and Gus thought he saw tears on her lashes, but she blinked them away. Poor woman! How unfortunate to be left a widow at such a young age.

"I am very sorry to hear it," Edgerton said, but he cast a speaking look at Gus, which seemed to say, *'A widow! Now you need not hold back'*. "Gus's brother is on his way to the Peninsula, is he not, Gus?"

She lifted her chin. "Ah, such men are heroes, who go to foreign lands to uphold the virtues of a civilised society and keep us safe, and free from tyranny," she cried. "So courageous, all of them. One can only admire their dedication."

Gus had to smile at that. "In Gil's case, it is less a matter of devotion to King and country, and more a question of galloping about with a sword in his hand as much as possible. He has joined a Hussar regiment, and is wild to see some action, but he may feel differently once he gets there."

"But he would not shirk his duty," she said, straightening her back. "Just as my husband would not, and paid the ultimate price for his country. I wish your brother good fortune, and I shall pray for him and hope that God will protect him, my lord, but I wish he will not rush to join the fray. My husband was a careful man, who took no undue risks, yet that did not save him."

Gus said nothing, wondering whether Gil's love of risk would count for him or against him in war. He had heard tales of men whose reckless daring was legendary, yet they survived battle after battle unscathed while careful men like Mr Walsh fell in their first skirmish. There was no accounting for it.

Shortly afterwards, he deemed it proper to leave. But as they cantered back to the stables, Edgerton grinned lasciviously at him.

"A widow, eh? What could be better! You are well set there, Gus, for she would be in your hand without the least exertion."

Gus was so annoyed that he spurred Jupiter to a gallop and left Edgerton far behind.

~~~~~

Gus had discovered, on his first Sunday at Castle Morton, that Mrs Walsh did not attend the castle's own chapel. He decided, therefore, that she must attend one of the town's churches, and why should he not also venture outside the walls of the duke's domain for his weekly dose of preaching? He wondered a little at his own interest in the lady, for he had never been in the petticoat line himself, and if asked would certainly have said that he was too young to be thinking of matrimony. He was but four and twenty, with an empty title and not a penny to his name, except for the small allowance his brother made him and the even smaller amount he made from his work at Tattersall's. That would be more profitable in time, but he could certainly not afford to consider taking on a wife who brought nothing but charm to the marriage.

Nevertheless, his second Sunday saw him ensconced in a pew at St Peter's Church, not far from the castle gates, and looking eagerly about him for a certain face. The office began before he had seen her, but when he left the church, he was rewarded by a glimpse of her. He positioned himself so that she would have to pass him by, she saw him and curtsied, he bowed and she moved away. Not a word spoken, but his spirits were lifted by the sight of her. He was beginning to be concerned for the state of his own heart. Was this what it felt like to fall in love, this keen interest in her welfare and a desire to see her? He had not yet dreamt of her, but he felt gloomily certain that such an event could not be far away and then he would be truly sunk.

"You are acquainted with Mrs Walsh?" said a voice at his ear. He turned to see Lady Darrowstone beside him, as ethereal as ever in pale muslin, with an exotic little cap to match.

"Slightly," Gus said, hoping he did not look too conscious. "I ride past her lodge almost every day."

"One might ride past a place a thousand times without ever striking up an acquaintance with the occupant," she said archly.

"My horse nearly ran her down at our first encounter, and on my return I naturally enquired after her wellbeing," Gus said rather huffily, for he did not like this line of questioning. He had no obligation to explain himself to Lady Darrowstone, after all. "I have exchanged pleasantries with her once or twice since then, no more than that."

She laughed and tapped him playfully on one hand. "I do not mean to quiz you, Lord Augustus, but the lady intrigues me. Why does my father-in-law support her? Who is she?"

"A relative, perhaps?" he hazarded.

"Not that I have been able to find out. No one knows the least thing of her origins or history. She just arrived one day and settled in the empty north lodge, from which she never emerges except for church. Who is she and where did she come from?"

"Why, she is from Drifford," he said, surprised. "Her husband was a soldier who was killed in the Peninsula."

She laughed in delight. "And already you know more of her than I have been able to determine in the three years since she arrived. Although — that is a convenient tale, is it not? The soldier husband, who died in the war. Many a woman uses *that* story."

"I have no reason to disbelieve her," Gus said, not at all pleased with the suggestion that the husband was an invention.

She laughed again. "Oh, Lord Augustus, I do believe you are sweet on her! Well, you may think of her as you choose, I am sure."

"Thank you, I shall," he said stiffly, with a bow. She smiled, shook her head and moved on, leaving Gus seriously ruffled by the encounter. Was it possible that the soldier husband was no more than a convenient fiction? Yet she had seemed so sincere as she talked of him. He was certain that she had been close to tears. No, her husband was real enough. But still, there was some mystery about her, and he would love to find it out.

~~~~~

Amaryllis Walsh hurried back home, her head down, her mind filled with thoughts of Lord Augustus Marford. Such an awkward problem! If he were just a flirt, like his captain friend, there would be not the least difficulty, for she could deal with *his* type easily enough. But a serious man who looked at her in just that way... that was trickier, for such men were apt to become persistent, as she knew only too well.

Still, he was only here for a little while and once his business was concluded he would go back to London and leave her in peace. She could only hope he was not too curious about her history, for if he found out the truth, all her comfort would be destroyed. Yet, how could he find out? She would never tell, and the few other people who knew would certainly never reveal it. She was safe, surely she was safe.

6: An Accident

The following day was too wet even for Gus to venture abroad. He stayed in the little parlour he shared with Edgerton, practising his neglected violin, replying to one of his sister-in-law's long, chatty letters, and trying without success to read one of the three books he had brought with him. Edgerton had gone into town straight after breakfast, and Gus began to think that might have been a better way to pass the time. By the middle of the afternoon, his boredom has reached a critical threshold, and he threw on his greatcoat and braved the rain. He would take his letter to the post office himself.

The rain was a little less heavy, but even so, he was drenched by the time he had splashed his way to the little room at the inn and back to the main square. There were a few shops down one side, and he idled his way past them, gazing into the windows, although not taking much notice of what he saw, for his mind was elsewhere. At a certain lodge, to be precise, for no matter how much he remonstrated with himself, his thoughts would keep straying back there.

When he came to the street where Lady Darrowstone lived, a quick glance showed him that lady progressing directly towards him. He was not minded for conversation, so he ducked hastily into the nearest shop. It turned out to be one of those shops so common in small towns, a mixture of cast-off furniture and household ornaments, some books, sheet music and instruments — the detritus of house sales, items of no interest individually and sold as a job lot by impatient owners. There were a few good pieces, and Gus lingered over a small but pretty pianoforte, his fingers running over the keys, since its position in the window meant that he could observe Lady Darrowstone pass by.

"You play, sir?" enquired an elderly man in neat black.

"The violin only. Do you have any suitable music for me?"

"A few pieces, sir. We do not get much call for it, but... this one might do. Or this?"

Gus chose three pieces and paid for them, and then, satisfied that the danger from Lady Darrowstone was over, hastily left the shop and slunk back to his quarters in the castle.

~~~~~

The next day was wet again, and saw Gus industriously working at one of his new musical pieces, but the day following dawned clear and bright, and he was at the stables on the stroke of eight.

"He's a bit frisky, today, milord," said one of the Carsons.

"Good, for so am I," Gus said. "A fast ride will be just the thing for both of us. Stand away, there."

Jupiter shot out of his stall, hooves skidding on the stone slabs, and was almost at full speed before he was well out of the stables, grooms leaping out of his way with oaths, buckets clattering. The horse no longer needed any guidance, for he now always headed straight for the northern gate. That suited Gus very well too, so he settled down to enjoy the ride, hoping the gate would be open. It was, and they sailed through without any reduction of speed. Gus laughed for joy, and lay low along the horse's neck, letting the creature have his head.

They had not gone far when something untoward flashed upon Gus's awareness, a flicker of something on the track ahead of them that should not be there. Almost at once, they were upon it. Jupiter reared high, with a whinny of alarm, his hooves thrashing the air. Gus could only hold on tight, but the horse veered sharply aside, then kicked wildly with his rear hooves, only to jink again and jump so abruptly that Gus was tossed into the air.

He landed hard on his back, crashing into a bush of some kind. Jupiter whinnied again, then his hoof beats settled into a rhythm and faded into the distance. After that, there was no sound but Gus's own laboured breathing—

—and someone screaming, a high-pitched, long-drawn-out wail that chilled his blood.

Gus rolled over, with a grunt of annoyance as thorns tore at his face. But although he was winded, there was no great pain, and he seemed to be more or less intact. Pushing aside the last fronds of the bush, he saw the last thing he expected...

A child.

He was very young, perhaps four or five, curled up into a muddy ball and screaming his head off. That seemed like a good sign, for surely he would not make so much noise if he were seriously injured? There was no blood, in any event.

Gingerly Gus rolled onto his hands and knees and then pushed himself to his feet. Everything worked, thank God. Still nothing terribly painful, and no limbs dangling uselessly, although he would feel the bruises in a day or two, no doubt. He had the greatest fear of broken bones, for no matter how competent a surgeon might be, an injured body never got put back together quite the way it had been before.

The child was still screaming.

"Are you all right?" Gus said, realising immediately that this was probably the least sensible remark he had ever uttered. He knelt down beside the boy. "Are you injured? Hush, now, I am trying to help you. Are you in pain?"

But the child only screamed all the harder.

"Hmm. I do not believe you could howl with so much vigour if you had sustained a major injury, young man. Your head is not broken, and your arms and legs appear to be in working order. But I wonder where you are from? The only habitation nearby is Mrs Walsh's house."

Perhaps it was the sound of that lady's name, or perhaps it was just the reassuring rumble of an adult voice, the child's sobs slowed.

"Mama," he said.

"Yes, a very good idea, young man. Shall I take you to find Mama? Can you walk or should you like me to carry you?"

A small nod, so Gus scooped the child into his arms. "There! Are you comfortable? No pain? Very well, so which way is home, young man?"

He pointed towards the lodge, so Gus began to walk. The child began to whimper, and since he seemed to be soothed by talking, Gus said, "You know, it seems a little rude not to introduce ourselves after we have been thrown together in this unfortunate way. I shall begin, shall I? My name is Gus. What are you called?"

"Ned."

"Ned, eh? A fine name. You remind me of my young nephew, for you must be much of an age. He is four years of age now, and I guess that is about your age, too, am I right?"

The child nodded.

"You are well grown for four, Ned. You are a little larger than my nephew, I think, although his lungs work just as well as yours do when he falls down. His mama is a very pretty lady. Is your mama pretty, Ned?"

Another nod.

"Of course she is. All mamas are pretty to their children. My mama was pretty, too…" He stopped, trying to remember her face, and realising that he could not bring it to mind any more. It was seven years since she had died, and even before that she had faded, seeming less and less substantial with each passing month. Nor had she ever sat for her portrait, so there was no reminder gazing down at him from the wall. Catching his breath, he remembered the child in his arms, gazing up at him with wide blue eyes. "What about your papa — is he handsome?"

But the child made no answer.

They had not quite reached the lodge gates when a voice could be heard, crying, "Ned! Ned! Where are you?"

"He is here!" Gus called, as loud as he could. "He is safe!"

She entered the woods at a run, and he was not surprised to see the anxiety of a mother writ large on her face. Who else around here might have a four-year-old child but Mrs Walsh?

"Oh, Ned, what have you done? Oh no!"

"He is quite safe, and, as far as I can tell, unharmed," Gus said. "He was on the path in front of me, and startled my horse, but I do not believe he was struck. Jupiter jumped to avoid him. However, you will want to send for a doctor to be quite sure."

As they emerged through the gates, three others converged on them, a man and woman of middle years, and a younger woman, servants to judge by their clothing.

"John will take him from you now, my lord," Mrs Walsh said.

"No, you will want him to fetch the physician. Allow me to carry Ned into the house for you. Do you have a sofa where he may be examined?"

"Yes, yes, in the parlour here. John, run at once to Mr Lassiter's house. Thank you, my lord, lay him down on here. Lucy, fetch cloths and a bowl of warm water, with a little lavender in it. Maggie, some brandy."

"You would give the child brandy?" Gus said, in surprise.

She smiled. "The brandy is for you, my lord. You look as if you need it."

"Oh." Gus was aware for the first time of his bedraggled state, his coat and shirt torn, his buckskins and topboots coated in mud, and pieces of bramble everywhere. "I beg your pardon, madam, I am not fit to be in your parlour."

"You are very fit to be here when you bring my son back to me, my lord, and I thank you from the bottom of my heart." All the time she was loosening clothing and surreptitiously feeling arms and legs, and running her hands over the child's skull. "It seems by some miracle that he has escaped injury. But you, my lord — you must have been thrown, I think. Are you hurt?"

"Only my pride," he said, with a laugh.

"And your coat," she said, with another smile that made his treacherous heart spin. This would never do! She went on, "But what of Jupiter? He is not injured?"

"As to that, I cannot say. He ran off while I was extricating myself from the brambles. I shall send my grooms to look for him. Is the physician far away? You will want to be reassured that Ned has taken no injury."

"Mr Lassiter's house is only just outside the castle gates, no more than ten minutes' walk away."

The maid entered with the water and cloths, and the older woman with the brandy, and Mrs Walsh insisted on spreading a cloth on one of the chairs so that Gus might sit down and drink his brandy. He knew perfectly well that he should leave, but he was too contented watching her fuss over her son, cleaning the boy's face and hands and gently soothing him, the very image of tender motherhood.

But eventually the doctor appeared, and Gus could no longer delay his departure. Mrs Walsh accompanied him to the door, with many expressions of gratitude for his care for the child.

"May I call tomorrow to see how he goes on?" he said hopefully.

"Of course, my lord," she said, with a curtsy, and he thought she blushed.

But even as he walked back to the castle, longing for the hours to pass until he could call there again, he knew it could not go on. Since he could not offer her marriage, it would be cruel to continue to meet her. Tomorrow must see an end to it. But his heart ached at the thought.

~~~~~

Having dispatched as many grooms as could be spared in the hunt for Jupiter, Gus partook of a hot bath and a change of clothes, followed by a substantial breakfast. Edgerton eyed him with interest, but said nothing until Gus sighed, and pushed away his plate.

"Ah, there is nothing like breakfast for setting a man up for the day."

"Dinner is better," Edgerton said. Then, after a pause, "Well? Are you not going to tell me about it?"

"You have heard the story already," Gus said, frowning. "The child appeared, Jupiter reared and threw me, the horse ran off, and I took the child back to his home. What more is there to say?"

"Oh, Gus, for shame! A great deal! What of the lady? Was she suitably effusive in her gratitude? Did she gaze into your eyes and clutch your arm, while expressing her undying admiration for your bravery?"

"You are overly fanciful, Michael," Gus said shortly. "She was grateful to me for bringing the child home, naturally, but it was my horse which nearly killed the boy."

"Ah, but ladies do not think in that logical way. She saw you carrying her son to safety, so naturally her emotions towards you will be the warmer for it. As are yours for her, I wager."

Gus knew he should give Edgerton a set-down, but he had not the heart for it. His own feelings were too complicated. He decided in the end that the plain truth would serve as well as any other story. "Neither her feelings nor mine should become in the least warm," he said. "It would be catastrophic for both of us. I cannot afford to marry a penniless widow, Michael, and it must never come to the point where I am obliged to. I am determined to stay away from her from now on."

"Cannot afford to?" Edgerton exclaimed. "Why, your brother is one of the richest men in the kingdom, Gus."

"He is not, for there has been some mismanagement of his estates over the years, and the vast income of earlier generations is nowhere to be found. As for me, most assuredly I cannot lay claim to any wealth at all, beyond a small allowance and anything I can earn from Tattersall's. It is far from adequate to maintain a wife. The time may come when... but it is useless to speculate. I must be prudent, and ensure that my behaviour arouses no expectation in the lady."

"Hmm. I had not realised your prospects were so dismal, Gus. Perhaps I should distance myself from you, for I have my reputation to consider, after all. If you cannot increase my consequence—"

Gus laughed. "You are nonsensical, Michael. I am very good *ton* as all the Marfords are. An impoverished son of a marquess is still several rungs higher on the social ladder than a captain of the East India Company Army, you may be sure."

Edgerton shrugged, not in the least put out. "A lowering thought, although undoubtedly true. However, unlike you, I can afford a wife, and perhaps your little widow would be just the thing for me, eh? If *you* cannot make a play for her, maybe I should try my luck. What do you think?"

It took every ounce of self-control Gus possessed to say, "Why not? If you think she would have a rattle like you."

But Edgerton just laughed.

7: A Morning Call

There was another letter from Connie that morning, and Gus settled down to read it with pleasure. But this missive was not the usual outpouring of trivia about the children.

'My dear Gus, Reggie is at last away to Lincolnshire to be married, with Lord Carrbridge, Humphrey and Monty to support him, for nothing of significance may be accomplished by any Marford without two or three of his brothers by his side. I am not to go, for my dear husband fears the jolting of the carriage would overset my health in my present condition. To speak truth, I am glad they are gone, and on such pleasurable business, for we are all in uproar here and Lord C in a towering rage these two days past. With Mr Sharp vanished, there is no one here who knows how Lord C may obtain any quantity of his own money. His bank account in Sagborough is empty, and he was obliged to borrow from Mr Merton to be sure of paying his shot at inns and the vails to the servants in Lincolnshire. So now Mr Merton and the lawyers are attempting to find where Mr Sharp kept the money. Mr Sharp was last heard of in Northumberland, inspecting some Marford properties there, for there are bits and pieces scattered all over the country that the eighth marquess won at cards or on some wild bet or other. Mr Merton wonders if you have the time to go to these properties and enquire if Mr Sharp has been there, or where he may be found?

There is a note from him enclosed, with details of the properties. But not, of course, if the duke requires your attendance. Do write again, and in more detail, of the duke and anything that has been happening. You make it sound so dull — nothing but work and cribbage with the duke every night. I am sure you must be making some new acquaintance, so do tell me all about everyone you have met. Yours in anticipation, Connie.'

The note from Merton was briefer, and far more to the point.

'Lord Augustus, I should be very grateful if you would enquire at the following properties for any information on Mr Sharp, in particular, whether he employs any agent or lawyer locally, or has accounts at any bank nearby, as well as his whereabouts and movements. Hexlowe Hall, near Galthwaite; Hexlowe weaving mill, ditto; Gillingham House, Church Road, Galthwaite. Much obliged, yours, D Merton.'

This was so timely that Gus could not but think it the very hand of Providence acting on his behalf. Here was the very excuse he needed to absent himself from Castle Morton for a few days, and thus wean his mind from all thoughts of Mrs Walsh. He sent a brief note to the duke, asking if he might take advantage of the delay in dealing with the stud to attend to some family business, and then went to the stables to enquire about Jupiter. The horse had been found none the worse for his misadventure, and not half a mile from the gates.

"Lucky he didn't fall into a ditch, milord," said one of the Carsons.

"Nonsense," Gus said briskly. "He is an intelligent animal, so he would have got over his fright soon enough. He has no scratches on him?"

"None, milord. Looks to be in good shape."

"Well, Jupiter, you did well, my friend," Gus said, stroking the creature's soft muzzle, and receiving a whicker of response. "And tomorrow, all being well, we shall go a little further afield. Fred, Nick, I shall need one of you ready for a journey tomorrow at eight. One pack horse should be sufficient. We will be away for... three nights, perhaps four."

"Will Cap'n Edgerton be travellin' with us, milord?"

"No, just ourselves."

When he returned to his rooms, he found a grudging agreement from the duke — *'Go if you must, but do not dawdle, for I shall want you here when this Frensham woman arrives'*.

Gus sat down to write a response to Connie.

'My dear Connie, Tell Merton I shall go to Galthwaite. The duke graciously grants me permission to leave, for I have nothing else to do here at the moment, as the ownership of the entire stud is in doubt. This dramatic situation came about because Capt. E and I were invited to dine with Lady Darrowstone, who is three months widowed but wears not a scrap of black, not even gloves, but instead is fashionably pale from head to toe. She lives in the town, not at the castle, and in simple style, but entertains all the good burghers of the town with novelties newly arrived from London, like ourselves. The captain repaid her amply with tales of tiger-shooting ladies and the like. I was a sad disappointment, and disgraced myself by telling her the purpose of our visit, thereby provoking her to exclaim that the stud was hers, not the duke's at all. So now it is with the lawyers, and I daresay will take a twelve-month to resolve and I shall never be invited to dine there again.'

He stopped here, chewing the end of his pen thoughtfully. Some part of him wanted to keep Mrs Walsh to himself, but at the same time he had a burning desire to talk about her to someone — someone other than Edgerton, that is, who was not a satisfactory listener in this regard since he responded by expressing his intention to pay court to the lady himself. The worst of it was, he could well afford to do so and Gus could not, and so he could not in all conscience object. But he could not quite relinquish all claim to her, not yet, for if he shut it all away in his mind and never spoke of it again, as he must do if Edgerton were to make good on his resolve, then it would be as if it had never happened, just a dream in his head that had died unborn.

Besides, Connie was such a romantic, that she could not fail to sympathise with his predicament, and she might even think up some clever ruse to enable Gus to marry Mrs Walsh. But he caught himself at this point. His feelings were yet too nebulous for there to be any question of marriage, even if he had the income to consider it. He must not jump too far or too fast. But he could at least pour out his heart to Connie, and perhaps by forming the words, he could reconcile himself to whatever destiny awaited him.

'*I have another matter to confess to you, and this a most unexpected one. I am on the verge of falling in love. There! Are you not excessively diverted, Connie dear? Would you ever have thought to hear such words from me? And the worst of it is that nothing can ever come of it, for I am an impoverished younger son and she is an impoverished widow and thus it is a hopeless case. So I am determined to avoid her company in the future, both for my own peace of mind and for hers, for I am so easy in her presence that she must notice it, and I should not wish to give rise to any hopes that I am entirely unable to fulfil. So now you may write me long, consoling missives, and tell me that I am being foolish beyond endurance even to entertain the idea of love in my position, and I shall try very hard not to die from a broken heart. Your affectionate brother-in-law, Gus.*'

After this, he went into town to leave his letter at the post office and make a few purchases, returning just long enough to change into a smarter coat. Then he set off on his final visit to Mrs Walsh.

~~~~~

Amaryllis knew she should not look forward to his visit. He was nothing to her, after all, and after this one time she would discourage him from calling again, for no good could come of it. She had seen the way he looked at her, and she knew well enough what that meant. But it was useless, and he was wasting his time with her.

Still, the prospect of company was so uplifting. For so long she had been alone, just her and Ned, and the servants, who were very good and discreet, but were not company. No one else had come near her. John and Maggie went twice a week to the castle, once for the laundry and once for supplies of food, and if she wanted anything from the town, one or other of them would go for her. Naturally, she went to church. But otherwise she was entirely cut off from all society, and that was as it should be. It was both a punishment and a blessing.

But today she would have a guest in her house, and since she knew he was coming, she had the pleasure of anticipation. Also the pain, of course, for it must never be repeated, and she would have to tell him so. She could not risk it.

Ned saw him coming first, for from the nursery window there was a view above the trees to the castle and the road leading to the lodge. "Gus! Gus!" he shrieked, clattering down the stairs with Lucy in pursuit, laughing.

"He's that excited, ma'am. Never saw him so excited before."

Amaryllis laughed too, her own excitement every bit the equal of her son's. "We so seldom have visitors. It is a treat for all of us."

"Yes, ma'am. I'll tell Maggie to be ready with the tea."

She disappeared down the passageway to the kitchen, and Amaryllis led the bouncing Ned into the drawing room to await the knock on the door. She would answer it herself, as she always did, having never maintained the sort of dignity that must wait for a servant to emerge from an inner fastness to admit visitors, or perhaps turn them away with the dread words, *'The mistress is not at home.'* Amaryllis was always at home.

Ned had no dignity at all, so he was at the door, yelling, "Open it! Open it!" long before the visitor arrived. By the time she gave in to his pleading, Lord Augustus was striding up the garden path. Ned flew out of the door, yelling, "Gus! Gus!" at the top of his voice. Lord Augustus laughed and swept the boy into his arms.

"Well, this is a fine welcome indeed! Good day to you, Ned, and I need not enquire as to your health, for I can see that you are fully recovered from your ordeal." He had reached the door by this point, Ned beaming happily from his arms. "Good day to you, Mrs Walsh. Forgive my inadequate bow, but I should not like to drop Ned."

She smiled as she made her curtsy. He was so easy about it! Some men would have set the child down at once, or would never have picked him up, being too conscious of their dignity, but he was not in the least stuffy.

"I beg your pardon, my lord. He has been talking about you ever since you left us yesterday. It has been *Gus this* and *Gus that*, and I cannot persuade him to be more formal."

"And why should you, indeed? That is how I introduced myself to him, and I believe we are fast friends now, so why should we not be on first name terms?"

She took him into the drawing room this time, and he looked around with obvious interest. That was understandable. The rest of the house was very much as it had been arranged when she had moved in, but this room was hers and contained everything she had been able to bring with her — a few small pieces of furniture, the portraits of Papa and Mama, one of herself with her long-dead brother and sister, her music and books, the ormolu clock that was all that had been saved from Aunt Winnie's house, the Turkish carpet that was a little too large for the room. But he asked no questions, accepted the offer of tea and sat on the sofa, Ned on his knee, allowing the boy to cling to him, to the imminent danger of his cravat. He was a little more formally dressed today, his riding clothes set aside for a well-fitted coat of superfine, clearly made by a London tailor. He looked every inch the gentleman of noble birth.

"Ned, will you not come and sit beside Mama?" she said, but Ned shook his head, and buried his face in Lord Augustus's coat.

"Please, do not take him away, for I am not usually so popular, I assure you. It is very good for my esteem to be so well-liked, and most unexpected after I ran him down and almost killed him yesterday."

She laughed, shaking her head. "It was Ned's fault for running off in that foolish way. He should not have been there, and is very fortunate that he was not injured. But what of your horse? We saw him go past with your grooms, but I trust he has taken no hurt, or you either, my lord."

"Jupiter is uninjured, as am I, although much chastened by my valet's reproofs. I am never again to return to him in such an unspeakable state, for he has his reputation to consider, you understand, and I bring great shame to him when I roll about in mud and brambles."

She had to laugh at the serious tone with which he spoke.

"Now Ned," he said. "If you will sit beside me here, you may help me unpack the presents I have brought you."

"Presents!" he yelled. "Mama, Gus has presents."

"By way of an apology for all the upset I caused yesterday," he said, bringing forward his bag and opening it.

She felt herself blushing, but she could not be angry with him, murmuring, "You are too kind, my lord. Ned, please speak lower, or you will deafen us."

"What are the presents?" Ned said in a dramatic whisper which made the adults laugh.

"A bottle of brandy," Lord Augustus said in exactly the same whisper. "To replace that which I drank. And a book of poetry for your mama. Does she like poetry, do you think?"

"She does indeed," Amaryllis said, flushing with pleasure. A new book! What a delight. "Thank you, my lord."

"And this parcel is for you, Ned."

Ned grabbed the bundle and began tearing at the brown paper and string. "Scissors!"

"No, no," she said. "You must unpick the knot. Shall I do it for you?"

But Lord Augustus took the bundle and carefully teased apart the knot and made no comment on the degree of economy where the saving of every piece of string was a necessity. Ned sat down on the floor and with one sweep shook the wrapping open. Out tumbled a number of tin soldiers. Ned shrieked with delight and began to arrange them all on the low table that sat nearby.

Lord Augustus watched him, smiling. "My brothers and I had so much fun with our toy soldiers as boys, and my nephews love them too, so I knew you would enjoy them, Ned."

But the child was too much engrossed to answer, and Amaryllis had to make thank yous enough for both of them.

The tea arrived and Amaryllis poured and cut cake for him. Lord Augustus drank, and munched his way through three large slices of cake, and all the time they talked, not as new acquaintances, but as if they had known each other for years. He talked about his home at Drummoor and his brothers and their foibles, and she told him a little about her father and their life at Drifford and his last, lingering illness. He noticed her sheet music and so they talked of music — he played the violin, he told her, and sympathised when she explained that she no longer had an instrument — and then of books, and when she asked, he talked of London and horses and society balls and hunting and his family's financial difficulties and how they were struggling to manage on only five thousand pounds a year, an unimaginably large sum. And yet, for all the grand titles he dropped into the conversation and his wealthy life, there seemed to be no gulf between them at all. In that room, at that time, they were equal and friends and she was glad of it.

He stayed for an hour, until, catching sight of the clock, he jumped to his feet. "Forgive me, I have overstayed my welcome, and must go." He made for the door, but then turned back. "Mrs Walsh, you must tell me if I am being unforgivably impertinent, but there is a pianoforte for sale in a shop in the town which would fit perfectly against that wall there, and I should be deeply honoured to buy it for you, as a gesture purely of friendship, you understand, with nothing more implied. But you must say at once if you feel it would be improper."

An instrument! Oh, the joy of being able to play again, of losing herself in the music, of forgetting, just for a while, all her grief. If only she could! If only she dared!

"I beg your pardon, I have offended you. Pray forget that I spoke."

"Oh, no, no! I am not in the least offended. Who could be, at such a kind… such a *thoughtful* suggestion?" Her eyes filled with tears of gratitude. "It is only that I do not see how it might be contrived without raising comment or affecting your reputation. People would wonder greatly at it."

"It is *your* reputation which concerns me," he said gently.

"Oh, I have no reputation to lose. But I do not see how it may be done. If you give instructions at the shop to have it delivered to me, well…"

"Quite. But the castle servants know about you, I take it? You must have dealings there. So I shall have the instrument delivered to myself, at the castle, and then I will instruct the butler to have it delivered here. Would that do?"

"Oh, yes! That would do it! You are too good, my lord, and I know I should protest that I cannot accept such a gift and I should worry that you might overspend yourself, but I cannot. I am too happy! So thank you, thank you, a thousand times thank you!"

He bowed, and murmured some reply but she was too delirious with joy to know what he said. She hardly knew what she said herself. It was only as he stood on the doorstep, she offered him her hand, and he raised it to his lips with a look of such warmth that she was shocked at herself. To accept such a gift from a man! And now he would expect more from her, he would visit more often and she could not now send him away. How stupid of her.

But then he said, "I shall be going away for a few days on family business, and by the time I return here I expect to have instructions to return to London. Most likely we shall not meet again. I wish you the greatest joy of your pianoforte, Mrs Walsh. I shall always look back on our acquaintance with the fondest of memories."

She hardly knew what she said, but as she watched him walk away down the path, her feelings were more confused than she could ever remember.

8: *Galthwaite*

The pianoforte was bought and paid for, the butler given his instructions, and Gus rode off the next morning confident that Mrs Walsh would from now on have a somewhat happier life on account of it. Yet his heart ached for her. She had talked so artlessly of her home and her father, and said little of her mother, and her older brother and sister, dead of a fever, and was there an aunt who had died as well? And her husband, the most recent grief, was not mentioned at all, as if the sorrow were still too heavy for him to be a matter for idle conversation. He had so longed to know more about him, and whether he had Ned's nose or chin, so unlike his mother's, but he dared not ask. Such a sad, solitary life she lived.

Gus's thoughts ran in this gloomy vein for some time as they passed through High Morton and on southwards, and then west on a smaller road that ran across moorland as wild and bleak as any he had yet seen. The wind, a light drizzle and the lowering clouds were all of a piece with his mood. But by degrees, as they rode at an easy pace away from High Morton and its difficulties and towards a new adventure, his spirits lifted. For a few days at least, he would have his hours and his mind filled with other matters entirely, and he could perhaps begin to put Mrs Walsh into the past. And he tried not to think of Edgerton, left behind and perhaps even at that moment paying court to the lady.

By the time they stopped at midday to rest the horses and eat a bowl of indifferent broth, Gus was feeling much better.

"Did they tell you anything of this Galthwaite in the stables?" Gus asked his groom as they ate.

"Lots o' mills and such like," Fred said.

"That sounds dismal," Gus said. "Did you get the name of an inn?"

"Aye, the Running Boar. It's on the main street, apparently. Used to the quality." He grinned.

"That just means it will be expensive," Gus said with a frown. "I shall not leave Jupiter there unless I am quite satisfied that the stables are well-managed."

The groom shrugged. "Just have to wait and see, won't we?"

By the middle of the afternoon, they had come to a major route between north and south, with carriages and wagons visible in both directions. When they turned south, they found themselves constantly moving aside to allow passage to coaches with four or even six horses, pelting along at a great rate. But before long they saw the haze of smoke ahead, then one or two tall chimneys belching black clouds, and gradually the roofs and buildings came into view. Galthwaite was indeed a town of mills and manufactories, but the high buildings, the gleaming paintwork and the well-paved streets suggested that there was a great deal of money to made from such trade.

The Running Boar was indeed expensive, but an inspection of the stables reassured Gus that the inn was a worthy recipient of his custom. He saw Jupiter settled and then bespoke himself rooms and dinner before enquiring of the landlord regarding the properties he was to visit.

"Hexlowe Hall? Oh, that'll be Sir Roger de Ferrers, milord. About ten mile or so from here, bit less across the fields, but the road is good, and the weaving mill will be there too. Hexlowe's not a big place, milord, you'll find it quick enough, I'll warrant. Gillingham House? No, don't recognise the name, but Church Road is just a little way along the London road, milord. Maybe ten minutes to walk it. Fifteen, at a push."

Suspecting that *'fifteen, at a push'* was more than likely twenty or more, which would not leave him time to talk to the inhabitants and return before his dinner was cold on the table, he decided not to attempt it until he had fortified himself with the best comestibles the Running Boar could offer. The inn was indeed superior in that regard, and even Captain Edgerton could have found no fault, had he been there.

But after dinner, the skies had cleared and the evening was set to be a fair one, so Gus set out to walk off the landlord's best mutton, and find Gillingham House. Surprisingly, it was indeed no more than a ten minute walk. Church Road was wide, and lined with some fine old buildings on one side, all jutting eaves and red brick, and on the other a line of more recent houses, with the clean stone and simple lines of some eight decades ago.

It was in the midst of the newer houses that Gillingham House was to be found, a large detached house of some four storeys, not counting the basement and attics. It was a distinguished house — or it would have been, were it not for the peeling paint and overgrown garden. Gus would have thought the place uninhabited, but for the three small children tearing round the garden, pausing every now and again to throw lumps of earth at each other. Amongst its neighbours, exuding wealthy gentility, Gillingham House was a dramatic exception.

As Gus stood, wondering how best to proceed, a woman with untidy hair emerged from the front door of Gillingham House, yelling at the top of her lungs.

"'ere, you mis'rable lot! Inside, ri' now or I'll wallop you so 'ard, you'll not sit down for a month!"

The children, with one final flurry of earth, ran inside on bare feet, and the door slammed shut behind them.

Directly opposite, in the midst of the older houses, was the church that gave the road its name, a fine medieval building promising the peace and quiet to ponder this interesting situation. Inside, his footsteps echoed hollowly around the high roof. Dust motes spun in shafts of evening sun from high windows. Gus found himself a pew, and settled there, puzzled.

Gillingham House was a property owned by Carrbridge, and presumably managed by Sharp, as agent for the marquess. So why was it seemingly so uncared-for and occupied by a family quite out of character with their neighbours? Apart from the hair, the woman looked otherwise respectable, for her gown was unremarkable, but the accent could not be disguised, and the children looked like urchins. If he had seen them at a rough farm labourer's cottage, he would not have spared them a second glance, but here in this sedate neighbourhood, they were a mystery.

Footsteps down the aisle brought a man of about forty, wearing the sober black of a clergyman, to his side.

"May I offer you any assistance, sir? Naturally, if you are here for private prayer—"

"Oh, nothing of the sort, sir. Thank you for your kindness, but—" He was about to dismiss the man, but it occurred to him that the family from Gillingham House must naturally attend church here. "Actually, perhaps you can help me. The house across the road, Gillingham House—"

"Ah, the Carters," the parson said with a heavy sigh. "Rather a thorn in our side, I fear. You will forgive my frankness, I am sure, for you cannot possibly have any connection to such a family."

Gus laughed. "Only in the most distant manner possible — my brother owns the property, but I assure you, he would be as horrified as I am to see it in such a state."

"Then how is it that it comes to be in such a state?" the parson said gently. "Does your brother not tend to property in his care?"

"He has an agent, but... you know how it is sometimes with agents."

"Indeed, indeed. They are not always as diligent as one might wish. And so your brother sends you to inspect the property?"

"To track down the agent, if I can. Do you think these Carters would have any information?"

"If they have, they will not reveal it. A more obstructive set of people I have yet to meet. I rather fear that your journey has been wasted. Have you come far?"

"I was in the county already on business for the Duke of Dunmorton—"

"Oh!" said the parson, visibly adjusting his view of Gus's position on the social ladder.

"—so it was a good opportunity to see the place. Several places, in fact, which came into the family at different times."

"Oh," the parson said again, clearly readjusting again. "Your family is not from Northumberland, I collect?"

"From Yorkshire. I beg your pardon, perhaps I should have said — my brother is the Marquess of Carrbridge, and I am Lord Augustus Marford."

"Oh!" Another, even larger, readjustment. "Then he still owns it?"

"Still?" Gus said, confused.

"We assumed Lord Carrbridge must have sold the house. Perhaps I should also introduce myself, my lord. I am Terence Grayson, and *my* older brother is Viscount Grayson, who lost Gillingham House to your father in a wager sixteen years ago. I believe he would very much like to meet you. He is at my house even now."

Gus agreed to it, for to meet the original owner of the property was more than he could have hoped for. The parson's house was modest, tucked unobtrusively into a quiet side street, but, he explained, it suited him well since he had never married. The viscount and viscountess were staying with him at present so that Lady Grayson might receive treatment from her physician.

Viscount Grayson was a taller, bluffer version of his brother, although not much older than him.

"You must understand, Marford," he said when they were settled in the parson's comfortable book room with Madeira to hand, "that I came into my honours most unexpectedly. One year I was just an unnoticed cousin, the next a peer of the realm. It goes to a man's head, rather. At least, it went to mine. I became rather wild for a time, and tried to run with the London crowd. I drank, I gambled, I... well, I did a great many things of which I am now heartily ashamed. Not surprisingly, I lost a great deal of money, and when my funds ran low, your father suggested I should wager a property or two. He himself did so, and I saw him lose several. I even won an estate from him one evening, although he won it back the following night. Such a charming man, Charles Marford! So much fun, you cannot imagine. For a man like me, unused to high living, it was enchanting and a great privilege. But then he persuaded me to wager Gillingham House, and when it was lost—"

He paused, and for a moment the room was quiet, the only sound the low crackle of flames in the hearth.

"I realised at once that I must stop, before the madness consumed me entirely. That house was intended for my brother, Marford. The living was to be his, in time, and the house with it. Yet it was gone, and I have never forgiven myself."

"It was never of the least consequence to me," the parson said. "Having no wife or family, my needs are modest."

"But it was of consequence to *me*," his brother said. "However, there was nothing to be done about it, for I was in very deep water by then. I was very fortunate in my wife, however, whose good sense and faith in me brought me through a dreadful time of remorse. My father-in-law advised me, and there were some lucky investments, and within three years or so I had come about. I wrote then to your father, but received no reply. When he died, I wrote to your brother, but again was not honoured with a reply."

"I can say with some confidence that your letters never reached the intended recipients," Gus said. "I should imagine the agent, Mr Sharp, intercepted them both. But he has vanished, and my brother now has an excellent secretary, so I venture to suggest that an approach now would receive the attention it deserves. Indeed, my brother may be very pleased to sell, under his present circumstances."

"This agent, then... he has been lining his pockets?" the parson said.

"We cannot at all tell *what* he has been doing, except that there is less money than there ought to be, and a great confusion about where it has gone to. The marquess did not even know of Gillingham House or Hexlowe Hall or the weaving mill until recently, still less that he owned them."

"Hexlowe Hall? Sir Roger de Ferrers?" the viscount said, in surprise. "I am sure you must be mistaken about that, for the Hall has been in the de Ferrers family for generations. He is an old friend of mine. If you mean to visit him, I should be happy to accompany you. He, at least, is an honest man and will not fob you off as these Carters will do. If indeed the Hall is owned by your brother, he will say so."

Gus thanked him with sincerity, and a time was fixed for the following morning when they would ride to Hexlowe Hall.

Having seen Gillingham House, Gus was unprepared for the splendour of Hexlowe Hall. A sweeping drive past woodlands and lakes led by degrees to a fine house in the classical style of a hundred years earlier, with a massive pillared portico and a roof edged with statuary. A butler and two footmen emerged from the house to greet them, and grooms appeared from nowhere to tend the horses. Gus had brought his own groom, naturally, to take care of Jupiter, but he noted the smart uniforms and efficiency of the resident grooms and was impressed.

Inside, the butler led them in stately procession across a tiled entrance hall, lined with busts in the Roman style, and into a large book room, or perhaps a small library. There Sir Roger de Ferrers and his wife waited to greet them. He was a man of perhaps seventy, physically robust but with eyes that turned unseeingly towards them. Lady de Ferrers was no more than forty, and a beauty still. How dreadful to be married to such loveliness and yet be unable to see it! But then she would live on in his mind just as she was in her prime, unspoilt by the years. Gus could not decide whether that would be any compensation or not. If he were to have the inestimable good fortune to be married to Mrs Walsh, he would—

But that was a fruitless line of thought.

The courtesies were exchanged, refreshments were brought and as he sipped Madeira and nibbled macaroons, Gus wondered why it was that polite society insisted that two or three people could not meet together for rational conversation without there be food and drink presented.

Eventually, Lord Grayson came to the point, and Gus told again his reasons for visiting, and Lord Grayson related his own story, which clearly his friend of many years' standing had not heard before. What had they talked about, over all their long acquaintance?

Sir Roger listened quietly, asking only an occasional question, but eventually all was told. Still he was silent. Even his wife expected some response from him, for she said, "Roger?" in a puzzled voice.

He sighed, but still said nothing. Eventually, it was Lady de Ferrers who said, "You are correct that the Hall — indeed the whole estate — is owned by Lord Carrbridge, and we must pay rent to live in our own home. Roger never speaks of it, but he lost it in a bet many years ago. I do not know what the bet was—"

Sir Roger coughed, and for a moment his wife was distracted by the need to attend to him.

"No one knows of it but us," she went on. "Even our son does not know, and will not, until he decides to look for a wife. Then he must be told that our fortunes depend on him marrying well."

"It has not been easy," Sir Roger said. "With the loss of the estate, we live on my small investments and my wife's dowry. It is difficult to maintain the appearance of wealth when one is not at all wealthy, but we must, of course."

"Must you?" Gus said at once. "Why not move somewhere smaller?"

"Because the de Ferrers have lived at Hexlowe Hall for two hundred and fifty years," Sir Roger said, in ringing tones. "First in the medieval manor house, and then this one. This land is where the de Ferrers *live*, Lord Augustus, it is our place in the world. Would your brother give up Drummoor, hmm?"

"I beg your pardon, I meant no offence."

The old man chuckled. "None taken. Are you like your father, young man? Do you take after him in ways or looks?"

"In looks, perhaps, but in ways, not a great deal," Gus said, smiling. "I have had my wild moments, it is true, but Father was positively ramshackle, if even half the rumours be true."

Sir Roger guffawed. "Aye, that he was, but such a charming man. Feckless, of course, as they often are when they have seemingly limitless riches at their command. Wagered huge sums on trivial matters — whether a log would shift on the fire before the clock struck, for instance, or whether a servant would enter through one door or another. Beetle racing — that was one of his inventions. You would not believe the guineas that changed hands over beetles. And he wagered property as well. Everyone in his set did, and some of those places went round and round. One of Camberley's changed hands about twenty times one year. It was Dunmorton's originally, but he dowered it to Camberley to get rid of one of his daughters. Camberley never liked the place above half — trade, you see. Some mill town or other. So he wagered it, and it became a game, anyone who won striving to lose it as soon as possible. Carrbridge held it three or four times, as I recall. I had it once, but lost it again. Ah, but that was such a long time ago — more than thirty years, it must be. But as to the matter in hand, I shall give you the name of the attorney who collects the rent from me and—"

He stopped, for there was some commotion out in the hall, with one loud voice intermingled with the low murmur of the butler.

The door burst open and a young man of about twenty raced in, the butler wringing his hands helplessly behind him.

"—such nonsense in my life, Gripp! Why should I not go in? Papa, why is Gripp trying to stop me from seeing you? Oh!"

The room froze into a little tableau, the newcomer just as taken aback as the others. He stared at Gus, and Gus, shocked, stared back. There, looking back at him from the young man's face, quite unmistakably, was the Marford nose.

"Lord Augustus," Sir Roger said, as blandly as if nothing untoward had occurred, "may I present to you my son and heir, James? James, this is Lord Augustus Marford of Drummoor, brother to the Marquess of Carrbridge."

"But…" the boy said. "But… I do not understand."

9: Family Secrets

The butler crept out of the room, closing the door with a soft snick. The silence in the room was absolute as they stared at one another. It was Sir Roger who spoke first.

"Come now, James," he said, not unkindly. "You are not deficient in intellect. Surely you can work it out?"

The boy's eyes drifted to his mother, and then back to Gus, then to his mother again. "No," he whispered. "No. It cannot be."

Gus had not taken his eyes off the boy, but now his gaze was drawn to Lady de Ferrers, hands to mouth, tears pouring down her cheeks, rocking slightly.

"You must not think badly of your mother," Sir Roger said firmly. "I put her in an impossible position, but I was very happy with the outcome. I have always been happy with the outcome, which was exactly what I wanted."

"You knew!" she cried. "You have known all along."

"Of course. But it is time everyone knew. Grayson, my old friend, I can see that this is no surprise to you, so you do not need to make for the door. And Lord Augustus, this concerns your family, too. Please, all of you, sit again. Lord Augustus, may I trouble you to pour some brandy for my son. Fanny, will you take a little brandy, too? Let me recount my story, and then you may judge *me*, if you will."

He took a sip of Madeira, and it was wonderful to see how skillfully he managed to raise and set down the glass when he could see nothing.

"I married young, since I was an only child and it was my duty to ensure the succession. My first wife — ah, poor Dorothea! Her horse threw her into a wall, and broke her neck. Three years we were married with no sign of a child, but within a year I had married again, and a widow this time, with two children already. Surely she would give me a child or two? But no. In twenty five years, there was no sign of it, and I had resigned myself to the inevitable — my dim-witted nephew would inherit everything. But then fate intervened, and Lucy died too. A third chance! So I married my lovely Fanny, and surely God would smile upon us? She came from a large family, so there were bound to be children. But no. In three years, there was nothing. And now I was desperate, for my dim-witted nephew had by this time married a wife as pea-brained as himself, and produced a brood of unpromising children, and I did *not* want them in my house, ever."

He paused for another drink, or to collect his thoughts, perhaps, since for the first time there was agitation on his face.

"So I devised a plan. Amongst my less reputable friends from my youth was one who was wilder than most, Charles Marford. I suppose he was the marquess by then, but to me he was always Charles Marford, handsome, charming, irresistible to women. Fanny was drawn to him, too, I could see that. So I threw a party, a month-long house party, and in the middle of it, I arranged an emergency that took me away for a week."

"You planned it all!" Lady de Ferrers cried. "You *wanted* me to... But why did you not just ask? An arrangement between friends — it has been done before."

"Because if I had suggested it to you openly, you would have been insulted, and proclaimed your unbreachable virtue and sworn always to be true to your marriage vows. And if I had asked *him*, he would have refused to besmirch the wife of a friend. In fact, I was not sure he would surrender to the temptation at all, so I devised the wager to make sure of him. I pretended to be entirely certain that no one could seduce you, not even Charles, and so certain was I, that I staked the Hall on it. I made my calculations first, naturally, to ensure that we would still have enough money to live on. Charles could never resist a bet, so..."

"But you were certain *I* would surrender to the temptation," she said sadly. "You needed no trickery to ensure my compliance."

"My dear, I was not at all certain, but I stood to benefit either way. There were only two outcomes. If you resisted him, I would have known I had a virtuous wife and been glad of it, and if you did not, then I would perhaps have a child to inherit the Hall and could be glad of *that*. As I am, my dearest, as I am. You and Charles have given me an incomparable gift, and I am truly grateful to both of you."

"Then I am not your son at all," James said, his voice low.

"You are my son in the eyes of the law, and in every other way that matters," Sir Roger said. "You may have Charles Marford's blood, but *I* have given you all that makes you a man, James. Do not let this change you. I had hoped you would never know of this, and that is why I sent you to the farm today, and told Gripp to keep you away from my visitors, for Grayson warned me of Lord Augustus's coming. But now that you do... I hope you will not judge me harshly.

All I have done is to preserve my family and bring happiness to my old age, and there was no harm in that, was there? Was there?"

~~~~~

'My dear brother,' Gus wrote, 'I came to Galthwaite to find Sharp, and ended up finding something quite different. How generous Father was! For he has spread his charity liberally over the north of England, even into the family of Sir Roger de Ferrers of Hexlowe Hall, whose son and heir has as fine an example of the Marford nose as I have seen. The father is pleased about it, having no other child, and the boy, being not yet twenty, is bemused and distressed and angry by turns, as the wind changes. He professes a wish to meet you, but I leave you to determine the wisdom of that.

'As for Sharp, I can find no trace or rumour of him. The rents from the Hall and the weaving mill are paid to an attorney in Galthwaite, who deposits them to an account at the bank there in the name of a Mr Harcourt, who is a very fine gentleman, well dressed in the London style, arriving on horseback accompanied by two grooms. The bank manager and attorney are horrified that you are not receiving the rents due to you, and if you will supply the title deeds to the properties, all will be corrected. The occupants of Gillingham House pay no rent that I can find, and are excessively disreputable. I have a buyer for the property if you are minded to sell it.

'I return to Castle Morton tomorrow, so do not reply to me here. I daresay I shall be returning to London very soon, and I shall be glad of it, for apart from this visit there has been little enough entertainment, and what little pleasure there has been is best to end anyway. You may apply to Connie for more information on that head, for she knows all my little secrets, although they are trivial when compared with some others. Ah, secrets! Is there a family in the kingdom that does not have these long-buried mysteries? We *have our share, but it appears we are not alone in that, and perhaps such matters are best left buried in the past, where they belong.'*

He set down his pen thoughtfully. Was that true? The human mind was naturally curious and liked to know all that might be known of its fellow humans, but perhaps a man might be happier not asking too many questions. Especially about a lady with a heart-shaped face and wide blue eyes. So many questions… Why did she live in such isolation, excluded from society? What was her connection to the duke? And why, when she held her husband in such clear affection, did she speak of him so little? It was puzzling, but he had no right to seek answers and certainly it would be better for his peace of mind if he did not.

Gus dined with the Grayson family that day, the talk all of the events at Hexlowe Hall.

"What a risk he took!" Lady Grayson said. "Imagine if there had been no child at all — he would have thrown away his home and his wife's virtue for nothing."

"I imagine he would then have taken matters a stage further," her husband said. "Having established the willingness of both parties to fall into sin, he would undoubtedly have approached them more directly, and persuaded them to repeat the offence until a child resulted."

"Goodness!" the lady said. "That is… unorthodox. And if it had been a girl? Would they have been expected to try again?"

"The knighthood dies with Sir Roger, so a male heir is not essential. For a daughter, there would be a marriage in due course to a wealthy man prepared to change his name to de Ferrers. That is done all the time. But Marford, this was no shock to *you*, I think. Your father had something of a reputation as a rake."

"Indeed, and Lady de Ferrers is far more in line with his usual tastes, although we have recently discovered the fruits of his dalliances with less lofty females."

Lord Grayson chuckled. "He liked a roll in the hay with a milkmaid, eh? He would not be the first."

Gus glanced at Lady Grayson, rather shocked at this plain speaking with a lady in the room, but she laughed easily, not in the least discomposed.

"I cannot speak to the hay, and the milkmaid was in fact a parlourmaid, but the principle is the same," Gus said. "The boy grew up to be a light-fingered rogue, and would undoubtedly have been hanged or transported if Humphrey had not rescued him. He is carving a career for himself in the theatre now, where his plausibility is an asset."

~~~~~

Gus left Galthwaite early the next morning. The viscount had told him of a different route back to High Morton, one which veered further to the north but ran through quiet minor tracks to a pretty little vale where lay an excellent inn, one which would cater even for Jupiter's fastidious requirements, if Gus should choose to stay overnight. The vale was indeed pretty, the inn perfect, the stops along the way, also supplied by the helpful viscount, excellent, and Gus was in mellow mood by the time their journey brought them back to the main road some miles north of High Morton.

The road to the south forked at that point, so they stopped at the small inn there to rest the horses, while Gus enquired of the innkeeper for the correct road to High Morton.

"Either will get you to High Morton, sir," the innkeeper said. "T'road to t'right be more direct, is all. Tak' t'road to t'left, and you be going through Drifford first."

Drifford. Gus was seized by a powerful urge to see the town, with its place in Mrs Walsh's history. So as soon as the horses were ready, he led the way down the left fork, his groom and valet trotting along uncomplainingly in his wake. They were used to his sudden starts.

The road passed through good farmland, and then a belt of trees before emerging to a surprising sight — an army camp in all its well-regimented glory.

"Ah, the army," Gus murmured to himself. "I had forgotten the army."

He would have pushed on at once for a closer view, but his valet called out to him. "My lord! My horse — I think he may have lost a shoe."

A quick examination confirmed this assessment.

"Well, we must enquire at the army camp for the whereabouts of the nearest farrier," Gus said, not at all displeased to have an excuse to visit the camp. He did not even have to give his name, for the soldiers manning the gates recognised him as a gentleman by his appearance alone. They were directed to the farrier, and it was the work of a few minutes to replace the missing shoe and set them on their way again.

They were halfway back to the gate, and Gus was trying to think of an excuse to linger and perhaps make enquiries about the mysterious Edward Walsh, when a troop clattered past, led by a pair of officers. One of them gave an exclamation and wheeled his horse about.

"Jupiter? By George, it *is* Jupiter, I am certain of it! I would recognise that proudly arched neck anywhere. How are you, old boy?" He leapt from his horse and began stroking the horse's neck, as Jupiter whinnied in return. "And unless I miss my mark, you must be Lord Augustus Marford."

"I am indeed," said Gus, laughing. "I have been recognised by many different characteristics in the past, but never by my horse before."

"Ah, but I have known this fellow since he was a foal. I even have the honour of being thrown by him on several occasions, before I decided that he had bested me and retired from the fray. Lord, but he is beautiful! And it gives me the greatest pleasure to see him ridden by one of the few men in England capable of it. Why, you make him look almost docile, my lord."

"He is not, I assure you, but if he is ridden hard every day he graciously pretends to be amenable. You must be one of Haverley's brothers, I suppose?"

"Kit, the youngest. But do come in and have a chat. We see so few fresh faces here, and yours is a most unexpected one. You will be able to tell me all the London *on-dit*, I daresay."

Gus was by no means unwilling. The horses were safely stowed in the stables, Carson and Willett were led away to be filled with army beer, and Gus followed Kit Haverley into the officers' quarters to be plied with a very good Madeira and an array of pastries. In return, he told Kit and his fellow officers as much town gossip as he knew, which was not much. Then he remembered his own family, and tried the tiger lady on his listeners, which went down very well. Astonishingly, they had already heard the tale.

"Ah, such a glorious story cannot be kept hidden," Kit said. "I wish your brother the greatest joy of her, for she sounds like quite a handful. And so he is to open a gaming house in York? It will be a great success, in his hands. I like Lord Humphrey — he once told me never to play cards for money, for I should surely lose. I have not the brains for it, he said. Play dice for small amounts, if the ivory be not loaded, and you might win a little sometimes, but do not attempt anything requiring skill."

Gus laughed. "That sounds so like Humphrey — he is no diplomat."

"Oh no, he was quite right," Kit said. "I always lost at cards, and everyone says, do they not, that one's luck will turn if one but keeps playing? But at whist or piquet or anything of that nature, my luck never turned. So I stopped playing for money, and only a little at games of chance, like dice or faro, and I have been much happier for it."

Eventually, enough gossip had been proffered and wine consumed for Gus to ask the question burning in his mind.

"There is a widow in High Morton whose husband was here for a while. It would have been perhaps five years ago now. He went to the Peninsula not long after and was killed there. I should be glad to know what sort of man he was. His name was Edward Walsh."

"Edward Walsh?" Kit said. "Not ringing any bells. Was he an officer?"

"That I cannot tell you," Gus said. "I would imagine so, for his widow is a lady, but one never knows."

"Rickard, be a good chap and go and look the fellow up, will you? So what are you doing here, Marford? It is a long way from Drummoor to High Morton, widow or no widow."

Gus explained about the duke and the stud, and the discussion that ensued filled quite half an hour. The pastries were long gone and the Madeira was running low when Rickard eventually came back.

"No Edward Walsh," he said. "In fact, no one by the name of Walsh at all. Not amongst the officers, nor amongst the men. Whoever he was, he was never here, that much is certain."

Or perhaps he did not even exist, Gus thought sadly. Perhaps Lady Darrowstone was in the right after all, and Mrs Walsh's story was just the age-old one, of a woman making a mistake and paying a very high price for it. Abandoned and alone, who could blame her for inventing a dead husband to add a veneer of respectability to the situation? Poor lady! His heart was heavy, but he was powerless to help her.

10: The Duke Has Visitors

Gus and his groom and valet rode on in rather better spirits after their refreshments at the army camp, and, after a sharp descent through woodlands, entered the town of Drifford. A narrow river valley was crammed with mills and weaving halls and manufactories of many sorts, tall buildings shading the only road. But as the valley opened out and a bridge crossed the river, the town proper emerged, with warehouses and neat rows of cottages for the workers, and many shops and artisans' yards. Then another, grander, bridge, leading to a fine church and other stone buildings clustered around a large square, with wide streets leading off. All of it looked prosperous and well kept, and the streets were thronged with people and wagons, a couple of goats being led somewhere and men on horses trotting about purposefully, while the river was crowded with barges plying up and down to the warehouses.

In the centre of the square was a statue of a lady in a hooped skirt, bearing the inscription, *'Mrs Charles Ballard, Patroness of Drifford'*.

Intriguing, to see a woman so honoured. But there was no time to linger to find out more about her, for Jupiter was getting restless in the traffic. After he had kicked out at a cart with a pig in it, and attempted to bite one of the goats, Gus pressed on out of the town back to the main road, and eventually back to High Morton.

~~~~~

There were three letters waiting for Gus. Two were from Connie, but the other was from Tattersall's, and was brief and to the point.

'Pray stay at Castle Morton for the time being. We are sending a legal expert to advise.'

He balled it up and threw it on the fire in disgust. Now there was no escape, and what was he to do with himself? Or, more to the point, how was he to avoid Mrs Walsh?

Connie's first letter was even briefer. *'Tell me your widow is not Lady D — she is poison, Gus!'*

The second was more in her usual style. *'Dear Gus, pray forgive my moment of hysterics. On rereading your letter, I see that your widow is impoverished, which Lady D cannot be and I am very thankful for it. Not thankful that she is impoverished of course because think how delightful it would be for you if she had a fortune at her command, for you could marry at once. If you wished to, I mean. Oh dear, I am not at all coherent, am I? It is only that I was in such a state of alarm in case you had fallen in love with Lady D, for you must not, I implore you! She is a most unpleasant woman, she was in London when her husband died and she did not go home at all. Everyone in her set is just as bad, for they hate their husbands and their children, and that is despicable, is it not? They all sneer at me whenever we meet, and although I am not a duke's daughter, Papa was perfectly respectable and I do not like to be sneered at, and especially not in my own house. So I am determined not to invite any of them again. Horrid women! They like to draw young men in and then abandon them when they are quite in love. It is too cruel, so you must never fall in love with Lady D, promise me that! Oh, but you are not, are you? It is the other widow. Gus, dear, you must write and tell me all about her — I want a proper description of her hair and eyes and height and figure, and whether she likes books or anything of that nature. For you are quite bookish yourself, so it would be very comfortable to have a wife of that type, for look how happy Belle and Mr Burford are, and they are both terribly bookish.'*

Gus stopped at this point, laughing at the idea of himself as bookish. But then to Connie, anyone who was occasionally seen with a book in his hand was bookish.

'I have heard from Lincolnshire, and the wedding went off charmingly. Reggie and Robinia are gone to Melton for a week or two, but Robinia is very keen to be settled in her new house, so they will not—"

A knock at the door heralded the entrance of the butler.

"Ah, Bedford, good afternoon. All is well here, I take it? His grace in his usual spirits?"

"His grace requests your presence, my lord."

"Yes, yes, dinner at five. I understand."

"No, my lord, immediately."

"Oh." That was curious. "Anything up?" But the butler said nothing. "Hmm. Very well, but I must change out of all my dirt, you know. Pray tell his grace that I will be there directly."

"Very good, my lord."

In an unusually rapid half an hour, Gus was washed and changed into more respectable attire, and was striding across the bridge to the keep. His curiosity was piqued, for what could cause this unprecedented summons? Perhaps there was some news on the ownership of the stud, which would be excellent, if true, since it would allow him to escape to the south within a few days. He tried resolutely to suppress the pang of regret that assailed him.

A footman outside the duke's drawing room threw open the door and announced him. He stopped on the threshold in astonishment.

The room was full of ladies. That was his first impression, although in fact there were no more than half a dozen or so. But in that austerely masculine environment, filled with heavy furniture and dark wood panels, their frothy muslin dresses and feathered caps seemed to be everywhere, and the duke himself, cowering in his chair, looked like a black spider surrounded by fluttering moths.

"Ah, Marford! At last! What took you so long?"

"I was still in my riding clothes, Duke, so I—"

"No, I mean this business of yours that took you away. I have been expecting you back for days. But look who is here! You know everyone, I take it?"

He did, but the names were as insubstantial as thistledown in his mind. Lady Darrowstone's supercilious sneer was easy to remember, and there was Lady Emma Frensham lurking in a corner, and her aunt, Lady Prudence Frensham, dozing by the blazing fire. But the other three — they were Emma's sisters, but what were they called?

Emma laughed, seeing his difficulty. "Come, your grace, my sisters have been living quite secluded for years. It would be a miracle if Gus could remember their married names. Maria is Lady Delacross now, Gus. Lucia is Lady Carey and Arabella is Lady Graceton."

Gus smiled his appreciation, and made his greetings, but all the time wondering at their presence there. Emma had been invited, and Lady Prudence would naturally chaperon her, but why were the other three there? Was it a family effort to see Emma wed to the duke? And why was Maria here, so recently widowed, yet the only signal of it her black gloves? And sitting a little aside, Lady Darrowstone, another widow, but with not a scrap of black, watching the scene with amusement.

"Is this not delightful, Marford?" the duke said. "It is quite marvellous how ladies' minds work, for one need only invite one, you know, and here are a whole gaggle of them, and I am sure I did not invite them all. No, I am positive of it. And Edith is never invited at all, but here she is, as if I wanted her here, which I do not."

Lady Darrowstone only smiled the more at this insult, but Emma's younger sisters twittered in mock indignation.

"Now, Duke, you know that four minds are better than one — five, if one includes Aunt Prudence," Maria said. "I do not know why you asked Emma for help, for she is so bird-witted she will not be of the slightest use. But Arabella and I — we can help you find a wife, I am certain of it. I have any number of ideas already, you know. I am so full of ideas, I hardly know where to begin."

The duke tittered, but Gus thought he looked a little uneasy all the same.

"Whatever are you thinking of, Emma?" Gus whispered to her when he had a chance to move towards her. "This will not help your cause."

"Bringing my three prettier sisters with me, you mean? I am aware of it, but they *would* come. Lucia and Arabella were at Maria's too, you see, and the butler most unfortunately brought my letter from the duke into the parlour when everyone was there, so there was no hiding it. But there is no difficulty, because Lucia and Arabella are married, and Maria is so recently widowed…"

She broke off unhappily, and Gus saw her eyes stray to her sister, the black gloves, the only sign of her widowhood, now resting in her lap. Maria had always been a flighty type, and perfectly capable of snaffling a duke from under her sister's nose, if she felt like it. And she *was* pretty, there was no denying it. Maria was small and dark and appealingly plump, while Emma was tall and pale and inelegant. Emma's frizzy mountain of hair was transformed on her sister into charmingly becoming curls. It was hard to see much advantage to Emma from Maria's presence.

At dinner that evening, Maria and Arabella raced for the seats next to the duke, until he shouted at them and insisted that Gus sit to one side of him and, after some dithering, Lady Prudence the other.

"At least that way I shall have rational discourse on one side of me." Raising his voice, he turned to Aunt Prudence. "And you, madam, will please me best by remaining silent."

"I have nothing to say to you, old man," Lady Prudence said cheerfully. "I am only here to chaperon my niece, and very tedious a business it is, too, and hardly necessary with her sisters here. I hope your cook is better than your manners. Footman! Wine here, if you please."

Lady Darrowstone had gone back to her own house, but it was still an uncomfortable meal. Maria was determinedly cheerful, leaning round Aunt Prudence to talk to the duke.

"Do you like your women fair or dark, Duke? It would be helpful to know."

"Oh yes, it would be most helpful to know *that*," Arabella said. "Ask if he prefers tall or short, Maria."

"Do you prefer tall women or short, Duke? We must have all your preferences arranged, you know."

"Oh yes, all his preferences. We can do nothing without those."

And so they went on, while the duke ignored them, talking resolutely to Gus about his visit to Galthwaite, although too distracted to attend to the answers. Meanwhile, Lucia sulked from being left out of all the scheming, and Emma sat quietly at the furthest point from the duke, watching and not eating much. Lady

Prudence ate her way through a prodigious amount of food, with a footman stationed behind her chair ready to replenish her wine glass the instant she clicked her fingers.

When the ladies withdrew, the duke sighed. "Thank God! Heaven preserve me from all women. Whatever possessed me to consider marrying again, Marford, answer me that?"

"You have taken an aversion to the attorney from Cheshire who will otherwise follow in your footsteps," Gus said with a smile. "And if you dislike having them around, why, send them away. You did not invite the sisters, after all, only Emma herself. I am not even sure why she needs a chaperon, so you could dispatch Lady Prudence, too, if you were so minded."

He chuckled. "She will empty my larders and cellars, that one! Ah, but earl's daughters, you see, every one of them. Hardly the thing to toss them out into the night, is it? And who knows, they might turn up some pretty little creature to warm my bed. Begun to think about that, I cannot deny it, and there is something very appealing in the idea. What about you, Marford? Any plans to get leg-shackled? Although you are young enough and active enough and handsome enough, dammit, that you hardly need to bribe them with a trip to the altar."

"Not rich enough to marry," Gus said, "and not foolish enough to get entangled otherwise."

The duke cackled. "Aye, you are a downy one. Although a little bird told me you seem to like to ride past the north lodge. Ah, you look conscious! But you had better stay away from her, if you know what is good for you, that is all I have to say about it."

"That is… very cryptic," Gus said, his curiosity piqued. "I have no skill at reading hints, Duke, so if you know something against the lady, you had best say so plainly."

The duke grunted, and looked at him through lowered eyebrows. "Do you play me for a fool or are you really as naive as you pretend to be? I cannot tell."

"I beg your pardon, your grace. No offence was intended."

"Now you are on your high horse. Too sensitive by half, you young men these days. In my day, we were a deal more robust. But let me speak plain, then, Marford. That woman is not a suitable match for the son of a marquess. There! Is that clear enough? Do what you came here to do, and then take yourself back to London, and leave me in peace. And now let us rejoin the ladies, for I tire of your company."

They played a round game of vingt-et-un, everyone joining in except Lady Prudence, who declared she was too old for cards, ordered the fire built up and promptly fell into a sound sleep. The duke was the banker, and a lively job he made of it too, ribbing everyone unmercifully when they went bust, gleefully collecting his coins when he won and sulking when he lost. Maria and Arabella chirruped like songbirds at first, and only began to grow quiet when their losses started to mount. Emma played at random, and lost heavily. Gus played as he always did, steadily, for one could not have Humphrey as a brother without acquiring some skill at cards. And Lucia played silently but with great skill and annoyed Maria and Arabella by winning a great deal of money.

Abruptly, the duke's liveliness dissipated. They were all abused roundly for their lack of amusing conversation and dispatched to their beds. The ladies drifted in a gaggle of shimmering silk across the bridge to the outer castle, but Gus lingered on the bridge to smoke. He had never taken to snuff, but liked an occasional pipe or cigar when he was in contemplative mood.

Tonight he had a great deal to think about, not least his discovery about Mrs Walsh. Her husband was fictitious, which was a common ploy for a woman finding herself in an awkward situation. Yet why had the duke taken her in, when he disapproved of her sufficiently to warn Gus away? Not that he intended to disobey, in this case, for he saw his own danger with the lady and had no desire to become entangled. There was still time for him to step back, and that was what he must do. There would be no more rides through the cool northern woods. From now on, he would take Jupiter south and stretch his legs on the stud's gallops on the cliff top. But he had still to attend church, and there could be no harm in returning to St Peter's, could there? He need have no conversation with her, but to see her face on a Sunday would get him through the long dreary days of the rest of the week.

He had barely turned his thoughts, with some effort, to Emma and her problem, when the lady herself appeared at his side, wrapped in a voluminous shawl.

"I am not at all ready for my bed," she said. "Since you have the same problem, perhaps we might keep each other company? But if you wish to be alone with your thoughts, pray say so at once. You need not be gallant with me, you know, Gus. We are old friends, are we not?"

"Indeed we are, which is why your company is always a pleasure, Emma."

"Shall we walk?" she said, pointing towards the outer castle.

"By all means. Shall we rouse Lady Prudence to chaperon you? Or one of your sisters, perhaps?"

She laughed merrily. "I am an old maid, and hardly need a chaperon at my advanced age. I am not sure why Aunt Prudence is here, except from greed and nosiness. Besides, I believe my reputation is quite safe with you, and there need be no fear that you will take advantage of me as soon as we are alone, and ravish me. Although I have always wondered if ravishment is quite such a dire prospect as maidens are told. It might be rather fun, who knows?"

"Do not wish for it!" Gus said sharply, as they entered the castle.

"Oh, so serious!" she said, turning enquiring eyes on him.

"It is a serious matter. Having seen the distress of a lady who was almost a victim of such an event, I can assure you that it is no fun at all. Although dealing with the scoundrel *was* quite fun. We tossed him in the river eventually. Where are you leading me, Emma? I do not know this part of the castle at all."

"No more do I," she said with a laugh. "I do so love exploring, however, and especially at night, when one is least likely to encounter the butler. Other people's butler's are so censorious, do you not find? Do grab that lamp over there, Gus, for we must have some light. Ah, that is better. Now then..." She opened a door, only to find all the furnishings shrouded in holland covers. "Oh, how disappointing. Let us try that one... Oh dear, are none of these rooms used?"

In this way she progressed along the corridor, finding each room filled only with ghostly shapes. But eventually, one that was not. It was a long gallery filled with marble busts on plinths, each one labelled.

"Look! The first duke... and the second... Quick, quick, where is the present duke? Hurry, Gus, bring the lamp. Ah, there he is! So handsome, is he not? This is how he looked when I first saw him, you know. I must have been eight or nine, peering down from the gallery at the dancers in the ballroom, and there he was. The handsomest man in the room, and the best dancer. He was quite magnificent." She sighed. "I suppose there was never much hope that he would ever notice me, and now there is none."

"He is an irascible old man, and would make your life a misery, Emma."

"Oh *no*, that is not how he is, not really. It is his gout, you see. He is in constant pain, and that would make any man irascible, for he does not want to take laudanum. It clouds the wits so. But I have some little tricks which might help him, if I could but get him to attend to me. But who are these faces? Henry, Edward, George... his sons. All dead now, poor souls."

"Oh, *Edward!*" Gus said, realising. "The soldier who died in the Peninsula. Of course."

So that was why the duke had taken in Mrs Walsh and her son. A charity case, indeed. Ned's father was the duke's son, Lord Edward Winfell. No wonder the duke had warned Gus away from the lady, when she was raising the last reminder of the duke's dead son.

11: A Matter Of Law

Gus had no prospect of sleep that night. After Willett had left him, he sat up in bed and pondered all he had learnt. So Mrs Walsh's case was indeed the age-old one of a woman seduced by a handsome face. Perhaps he had even promised her marriage, eventually. *'When I return from the Peninsula...'* or perhaps it was more *'When my father will look favourably upon the match...'*. For the duke would not have countenanced a marriage between his son and a woman of no consequence, not when the succession was so insecure. Henry was the heir then, but he had no sons, and Edward, the spare son, was very much needed. Yes, his father would have expected him to make a noble match.

Poor Mrs Walsh! Left alone, with her lover dead and no prospect of marriage, and a babe to raise alone. Lord Edward had acted shamefully to put her in such a position, a respectable woman with no friends or relations, it seemed, and left with her reputation in tatters. What was it she had said? *'I have no reputation to lose?'* So typical of the arrogant duke and his family! They took what they wanted, without a thought for the consequences, as his own father had done in his youth. It was despicable.

And yet... presumably she had not been forced, or *ravished* as Emma had it? She must have been complicit in the shameful event. It had been foolish of her, and somehow it seemed out of character.

She appeared to be the epitome of respectability, yet she had been weak. Not that she was alone in such weakness, but he had thought her better than that. Poor, yes, and alone and struggling to survive, but *respectable*, at least. And she was not. It was disappointing.

Yet perhaps it was for the best, for now that he saw her in a different light, he could not quite esteem her as once he had. It would be too strong to say that he was now indifferent, but the warmth of his feelings towards her was now tempered with disillusionment. She was not what he had thought her, she was not respectable and no fit wife for the son of a marquess, or any man of good character, as the duke had pointed out.

And with that sorrowful thought, he lay down and tried to sleep. But it was not until close to dawn, not long after he had heard Edgerton creep into his room next door, that he finally drifted into a disturbed slumber.

~~~~~

He was woken late in the morning by Willett rapping on the door, followed by the sound of the door opening and closing, and brisk footsteps across the wooden floor. The shutters were flung open with a clatter, then the bed curtains pulled apart, admitting brilliant sunlight to Gus's dazzled eyes.

"Good morning, my lord. I trust your lordship slept well. Your bath awaits you in the dressing room, my lord."

"Good God, Willett, what are you trying to do to me? Leave me be until I send for you, or you will be out on your ear, I warn you."

"Chocolate on the table over there, my lord. Bath ready. Also a gentleman from London. Been here since eight o'clock, awaiting your pleasure. Told me if you wasn't up by noon, he was going straight back to London and you could explain it to Tattersall's yourself."

Gus groaned. "Oh, the lawyer. Very well. But what about Captain Edgerton? Is he not up and about yet?"

"Gardner's working on him, my lord, although like as not it will involve a jug or two of cold water. He's the very devil to rouse. Whereas *you*, my lord — normally up long before this."

His tone was so offended that Gus could only laugh. "Very well, Willett. Go and tell the impatient lawyer that I am on my way."

Even with Willett's assistance and a rather hasty attempt at a cravat, and not at all his usual style, it was a full hour before Gus deemed himself presentable enough to face the world, or the portion of it that contained the lawyer from London. He was not surprised when he entered the parlour to find that gentleman red in the face with anger, his pocket watch in hand. He was not as old as he had expected, being about Gus's own age, and rather ostentatiously attired in the style favoured by pinks of the *ton*, who aspired to the height of fashionable dress. Edgerton, in a rather splendid dressing gown, was watching in amusement from an armchair.

"Are you Augustus Marford?" the lawyer said.

"I am, and—"

"Whatever time of day do you call this, eh?"

"I have not the least idea, but you could enquire of your watch, I daresay."

Edgerton spluttered with laughter, but the lawyer grew, if anything, even redder. "Oh, a fine wit! You find this very amusing, I daresay, Marford. But your rudeness is not only offensive to *me*, but a great impertinence to his grace the Duke of Dunmorton, who awaits our attendance even now."

"Really? He seldom rises so early."

"I daresay it is in compliment to me. Allow me to introduce myself, Marford. I am the Honourable Pettigrew Willerton-Forbes, son of the third Earl of Morpeth, and brother to Viscount Dillington. I daresay you have heard of me?" Edgerton was laughing openly now.

"I regret to say that I have not. I—"

"Oh, you are more ignorant than I had supposed. You horsey types are all the same, no idea how to deal with those of rank and consequence. I have no idea what his grace the duke sees in you, but according to Edgerton here, his grace will not see me without you in attendance. So come on, come on, make haste, and let us have no more delay."

"As you wish, Willerton-Forbes," Gus said easily.

"*Mr* Willerton-Forbes to you. Or sir, if you wish to be absolutely correct."

"Oh, by all means let us be absolutely correct," Gus said, trying not to catch the eye of Edgerton, who was positively rocking with laughter in his chair. "You may address me as Lord Augustus. Son of the eighth Marquess of Carrbridge, you see, and brother to the ninth. Sorry."

Willerton-Forbes's mouth opened and then snapped shut again. He wisely decided to make no further observation on the matter of rank, and gestured for Gus to lead the way out of the room. Edgerton's laughter followed them all the way down the corridor.

"Captain Edgerton is exceedingly rude," the lawyer said, in more moderate tones. "I am relieved that he is not to accompany us into his grace's presence. Men of rank and consequence should have as little as possible to do with those of humbler origins, or so my father always says."

"The duke would agree with him," Gus said. "No one enters the keep or his presence except they be of noble blood. It is the only reason I was selected to come here, for in truth Edgerton is the man with the skills needed, and could have managed the business without any involvement from me, had the duke not been so particular. For myself, I would not be so fastidious. Edgerton is very good company, especially when he is plied with decent claret. He also plays an excellent hand of cards, if you are so minded."

The lawyer was silent, and Gus wondered if he had the wit to deduce that he, too, had been selected for his blue blood rather than his legal skills. But he must be tolerably competent, for Tattersall's had sent him alone, and not with an older, wiser lawyer to advise him.

As Gus had suspected, the duke was far from ready to receive them, and they were left kicking their heels in an ante-room for a good half hour before they were finally admitted to the duke's presence. This time, they were shown into the library, a room no larger than any other at its lowest point, but with walls soaring upwards all around, and every inch covered with shelves of books. Spiral staircases and narrow galleries allowed access to the upper stacks. Far above them, a painted ceiling was filled with winged cherubs of the most preposterous kind. The lawyer looked around him with wide eyes before remembering that he was an earl's son and therefore need not be impressed.

"The Lord Augustus Marford, and Mr Willerton-Forbes," the butler intoned, as they entered.

The duke stood behind a large mahogany desk, flanked by two bewigged gentlemen in coats of the old style, whom Gus had no hesitation in identifying as lawyers. It was the first time he had ever seen the duke on his feet, and now that he did, he understood just why Emma's childish self had been so impressed, for the duke was a head taller than his two legal advisers, and several inches taller than Gus himself. He felt the young lawyer at his side shrink away at the sight, which was, of course, exactly as the duke intended.

"Ah, Marford!" the duke said. "Pray introduce your friend."

"With pleasure. Duke, may I present to you my esteemed colleague, Mr Pettigrew Willerton-Forbes, son of the Earl of Morpeth. His grace the Duke of Dunmorton, Willerton-Forbes."

The lawyer made a low bow, while the duke grunted, and introduced his own lawyers. Then, with an audible sigh of relief, he heaved himself into the massive carved chair behind the desk. Gus wondered at the effort it must have taken to stand when he was clearly in considerable pain. And then he wondered why he bothered, for a mere business meeting. Was this so important that he must not show his own physical weakness to a rival lawyer? Yet the matter would, ultimately, be decided by the law, and not by his height or the impressiveness of his room or the number of lawyers he brought to the table.

Gus was not quite sure why he himself was there. Willerton-Forbes could certainly have seen the duke without him, being the son of an earl and therefore meeting the duke's personal criteria for admittance, and Gus could contribute nothing to the discussion. The duke's lawyers talked at great length about the stud and the duke's claim to it, but as far as Gus could see, it all came down to two simple facts: the stud was located on the duke's own land, and had been paid for by the duke, by way of his allowance to his son, for it seemed the marquess had had no income of his own.

Willerton-Forbes said little. He took a few notes, asked one or two perceptive questions regarding the allowance, but otherwise was silent.

"There, you see?" the duke said eventually. "It is quite clear, is it not? The entire stud is mine, beyond question. You do understand, Willerton-Forbes, do you not?"

"I have understood what I have heard, yes, your grace," he said. "I shall, naturally, wish to discuss the matter with the other claimant."

"Her!" the duke spat, his face clouding. "She is a witch! You must not believe a word she says, for she will poison you against me."

"The matter will hinge on the ownership of these items, and the proof thereof, your grace," the lawyer said. "I shall not be swayed by what anyone *says*, you may be sure."

"So you are to decide and we are to accept your decision?" the duke said, his brows snapping together ominously. "Your decision might be challenged in the courts."

"Hardly so, your grace. I act only for Tattersall's. If I determine that you have title to the various properties, then Tattersall's will arrange the sale on the terms already agreed. If I do *not* so determine, then there will be no sale. And if I should decide in your favour — *if*, mind you — then my decision will be so firmly rooted in law that there will be no possibility of a challenge. If there is any question at all, however slight, in the matter, such that might give rise to a legal dispute, then I shall recommend Tattersall's withdraw from the case."

The duke's face grew purple. "Get out, you insolent little jackanapes! Go on, get out of my sight! At once! Bedford! *Bedford!* These miserable specimens of humanity are leaving."

"Yes, your grace," said the imperturbable butler. "This way, my lord, this way, sir, if you please."

The lawyer, white-faced, made a hasty bow and scuttled away behind the butler, with Gus following in his own time.

"He does not mean any of it," Gus said as they crossed the bridge from the keep. "He likes to shout at people. I suppose he thinks it keeps them on their toes, but it is a good sign."

"A good sign?" the lawyer squeaked, coming to a dead stop. "A *good* sign? To be thrown out by the duke after the first meeting?"

"A very good sign," Gus said, amused. "He hates to be bested, and you had the better of him in there, so he became cross and threw us out. If he is affable, that is the time to worry."

"Oh." He pondered that. "I had the better of him? You really think so?"

"Certainly. He cannot proceed without your agreement, and you made it very clear that you will not simply roll over for him. It was well done, Willerton-Forbes, very well done."

"Oh," he said again, his face brightening. "Well, thank you, my lord."

Gus sighed. "Your father must have come into his honours recently, I surmise?"

"What has that to say to anything?" he said testily.

"Nothing at all, except that if you wish to be taken seriously by the duke and others of his ilk, you must address them as equals."

"How dare you!" he spluttered. "I need no—!" Then he stopped, working it out. "As equals?"

"Those of noble blood call him Duke or perhaps sir. Only inferiors call him your grace. And only inferiors call me my lord. You should call me Lord Augustus, if you want to be formal, or Marford, otherwise. When we are both drunk, I shall not mind if you call me Gus."

"I am not your social inferior?"

"You have lower precedence, but all those of noble blood are equal."

"I shall never get into the way of it," the lawyer said sorrowfully. "Papa was only a distant cousin to the second earl, and we had no idea... at least, my father knew, I think, but my brothers and I did not. So now Wilbraham is a viscount and the rest of us are honourables, and... it is so *difficult*. In the law, I know exactly where I stand, and everything is easy, but mingling in such company... I have never met a duke before."

"You will get used to it. Now let us go and harass Edgerton, for he is inferior to both of us, and so we may sneer at him as much as we choose."

"Oh. Now you are teasing me."

Gus laughed. "Just a little. I rather liked how you handled the lawyers in there, so I am treating you as a friend and ally, and not as the rather pompous prig you appeared to be at first."

Willerton-Forbes gave a rueful laugh. "Pray forgive me! I was nervous and... even the butler terrifies me."

"The butler! Good God, you are in worse case than I had supposed. Butlers are very inferior socially, but you must never be rude to them, because they have the power to make your life miserable. If you want your bath water on time, and decent fires in your room, you must be very polite to the butler, but in a superior sort of way, you understand."

"Not really. Ah..."

They were still standing on the bridge, but now the door from the castle opened and Emma appeared. Gus could understand why the lawyer stood, frog-eyed, gazing at her in wonderment, for she was almost as tall as a man, and the hair piled on top of her head gave her extra height. She was dressed in a serviceable brown morning gown, with a heavy shawl chosen more for warmth than style, and a basket over one arm.

"Good morning, Gus," she said cheerfully. "Is the duke up yet? I have some medicaments for his gout which I should like to attempt, if he will allow me. Who is your friend?"

Gus made the introductions, and Emma chatted amiably to the tongue-tied lawyer before rushing away to see the duke.

"What a striking lady!" Willerton-Forbes said. "Who is she, again?"

"Lady Emma Frensham. Frensham is the family name of the Earl of Huntsmere. You need to invest in a copy of Debrett's if you are to make sense of all these families."

"I have one. I shall look up the Earl of Huntsmere at once. She is unmarried, then, Lady Emma?"

"She is," Gus said, amused. "But do not get your hopes up. She has no dowry to speak of, and she aspires to marry the duke."

"The duke? *This* duke? Oh!" The lawyer became thoughtful, and they walked the rest of the way back to Gus's parlour in silence.

12: Inheritance

Gus was rather at a loss to know how to fill his days. There was no knowing how long it would take the lawyer to reach a determination of ownership, and he was already tired of writing to Connie and walking aimlessly around the town, poking about in shops and then feeling obliged to buy something when the shopkeeper started to become restless. Nor could he enjoy his long rides through the woods any more, for he was determined to stay as far away from Mrs Walsh as possible. If that was even her name.

Leaving Jupiter to rest after the journey back from Galthwaite, Gus found his steps drawn towards the stud. He had not yet completed his task of reading the late marquess's notebooks, and that was something that could occupy his time usefully, for at least it was about horses and that was a domain where he felt comfortable. Just as Willerton-Forbes was at ease within the dusty realm of the law, so Gus was at ease with horses.

He found Johnny Waterbury, the stud's head groom, with a broom in his hand, mucking out some of the stalls. He looked up with a grin, leaning on the broom handle, as Gus approached.

"Help you, my lord?" Waterbury said.

Gus pointed to the broom. "Is this a penance, or do you enjoy the work?"

Waterbury gave a bark of laughter. "Enjoy it? Ah, if only that were true! Indeed, it is a penance, in a way, for I have been obliged to let two of the under-grooms go, and now we have not enough hands for the work."

"Happy to help, if you need me. I can be changed and back here in ten or fifteen minutes. I am very much at a loose end just now, until the lawyer has completed his investigations."

"Are you serious? Because what I need most just now is someone to exercise the faster horses."

Gus broke into delighted laughter. "There is nothing I should like more! You are the most excellent of fellows, Waterbury! I shall be back directly."

He raced away to change, and although it required a little more than fifteen minutes, for Willett was nowhere to be found and Gus had to make do with Edgerton's man, Gardner, he was back at the stud in his buckskins and topboots in not much more than half an hour.

Waterbury had found him a very pretty little filly to ride, a docile enough creature as she trotted with delicate steps down the gravel drive to the southern lodge, but once he had followed the track up to the grassy clifftop and set her onto the long oval marked out with rails, she needed no further urging and flew as if the wind carried her forward.

"That was tremendous fun," Gus said to Waterbury, as he dismounted in the yard. "Have you raced her yet?"

Waterbury's face clouded. "His lordship had thought he might try her soon, but... ah, he *talked* a great deal of racing this one or that one, but somehow there was always some reason why not. I suspect he was afraid his horses would be outclassed and all his dreams would come to dust."

"Never know unless you try it," Gus said with a shrug. "Have you another one for me?"

Waterbury had, a larger mount, one of the stallions, which was almost as keen as Jupiter to be off and running. And then a charming little grey mare, which was not quite so fast as the others but ran on and on for more circuits than Gus would have thought possible, before she slowed and turned for home of her own accord.

"What next for me, Waterbury?" Gus called across the yard, as soon as he was within earshot.

"I should think the duke is next for you, my lord. It is gone four o'clock."

"Good God, is it really? I was enjoying myself so much I had no idea of the time. May I come again tomorrow? I am quite happy to muck out, as well, if that is what you need most. What time would suit you?"

"We start work about six," Waterbury said, grinning.

Gus blinked. "In the morning? Is there such an hour? Well... I shall do my best."

~~~~~

Dinner was very different that evening, for the duke had Willerton-Forbes on one side of him and Gus on the other, and ordered Emma and Lady Prudence to take the seats next to the gentlemen, thus insulating himself from the chatter of Maria, Arabella and Lucia. The three ladies pretended not to be offended, and talked loudly to each other, with much raucous laughter, pausing often to see if the duke was observing how splendid a time they were having. He, meanwhile, studiously ignored them.

As soon as the ladies withdrew, the duke sighed with relief. "It is very pleasant to have so many ladies in attendance, but they do chatter so. Not Prudence, of course, for she is still not speaking to me since—" He broke into a cackle of laughter. "Well, well, that was a great many years ago. Such long memories these ladies have for an insult. And the other one is tolerably quiet, too — what is her name, Marford? The fright with all the teeth?"

"Lady Emma, Duke."

"Emma… hmm. As I was saying, a pleasant, quietly-spoken girl. Does not plague one with a lot of useless chitter-chatter. She changed the bandages on my feet, you know, and applied some noxious unguent or other, and made me drink some foul potion, but I am persuaded that the pain is a little better as a result. My medical man is useless. Lassiter, his name is. Cups me and leeches me, and tells me to drink less port, then sends me a bill for twenty guineas, if you please. Twenty guineas! He must think me a gullible fool if he expects me to pay exorbitant fees of that nature. I swore I would not send for him again, and I always keep my word. If you see him come into my room, you will know I have gone to my maker at last, for while I have breath in my body, he is not coming near me again with his evil leeches. Drink less port, indeed! Pass the decanter, Marford. How are you getting on with the legal business, Forbes? I hear you have been bothering my secretaries, instead of putting that daughter-in-law of mine in her place, which is what you are here for, after all."

"I am clarifying the details of the allowance that was paid to the late marquess, Duke."

"I do not see why you need to know anything about that."

"It is because your claim to the stud—"

"My claim! My ownership, you mean."

"That may be so, but in law one does not quite like to prejudge the outcome. Your *claim* is based upon the allowance paid to the late marquess, and once I have the correct amounts and so forth, I shall be able to approach the marchioness fully armed, as it were."

The duke grunted. "So you will have to go through her financial affairs, will you?"

"Most certainly, sir. Only by a thorough examination of the accounts shall I be able to determine whether the stud was indeed paid for by you."

"Well, just so long as she is thoroughly inconvenienced by all this, for that will make it all worthwhile. Shall we have some whist later? With three of us, we should be able to find a tolerable fourth from the ladies. Prudence, perhaps?"

"Lady Prudence likes to sleep after dinner, Duke," Gus said. "Perhaps Emma?"

But in the end they played vingt-et-un again, with the duke once taking the role of banker. Where Lady Prudence fell into somnolence after a good dinner, the duke seemed to be enlivened by the consumption of large quantities of red wine, and was in playful mood. Emma sat in near-silence, and the two younger men said little that did not relate to the game, but Maria, Lucia and Arabella flirted outrageously with the duke, vying for his attention, and he laughed and teased them and sat on long after the game had palled for Gus. It was Emma, in the end, who broke up the party.

"You will forgive me, Duke, but I am too tired to play any more. I shall go to bed."

And that reminded the duke that it was indeed late, and past his usual hour for sleeping, and perhaps reminded him that his gout was still painful, and so the party broke up, the duke yelling for his manservant, Lady Prudence, still half asleep, on Emma's arm, and the three younger ladies in a whispering huddle.

Gus and Willerton-Forbes followed the ladies across the bridge, and then back to Gus's parlour for a brandy before bed. Gus was not at all surprised to find that Edgerton was absent, and judging by the ashes in the fire, had not been there all evening.

"He has made a few friends in the town," Gus said, in answer to Willerton-Forbes's raised eyebrow of enquiry. "Lady friends, in particular. He rolls home shortly before dawn."

"Ah," said the lawyer. "Lucky fellow. So tell me about the ladies, Marford. Lady Emma I know about, and Lady Prudence needs no explanation. But what of the other three?"

"They are all Emma's sisters. Two are married — Lady Carey and Lady Graceton — and Lady Delacross is recently widowed."

"Which is Lady Delacross? And how recent is the widowhood?"

"The very pretty, plump lady with the blue and gold gown. Her husband died some five or six months ago, and if you take an interest in a woman so recently bereaved, who wears no black and has no problem going out into society again, then you have less sensibility than I do, Willerton-Forbes."

"You are inclined to be censorious? I take your point. It shows a want of delicacy, I feel."

"I would put it more strongly — it is unconscionable," Gus said, with feeling.

"You are quite right. Why then would she do it?"

"Because there is a duke to be ensnared, I should imagine. Maria has never had the least qualm about pursuing her quarry. Concerns about propriety do not weigh with her, I believe."

"Ah." The lawyer swirled the brandy in his glass, gazing down at it with a solemn expression. "Is he serious about remarrying, the duke? He must be sixty if he is a day."

"I cannot vouch for the seriousness, but his heir recently died without male issue, his other sons are dead and his heir presumptive is an attorney from Cheshire. Not that there is anything wrong with being an attorney," Gus added with a smile. "Nevertheless, it does not fit one to inherit a dukedom."

The lawyer gave him a wintry smile. "Perhaps not. Yet that is how the rules of inheritance stand at present. And who is to say that the present duke is so much better suited for his honours than the attorney from Cheshire?"

Gus could not give any satisfactory answer to the question.

~~~~~

The whole of the next day was spent at the stud, riding, tending the horses, sweeping and cleaning, carrying buckets of oats and water, and generally making himself useful. Gus did not quite manage to be there by six, but he was busily engaged from eight until four in the afternoon, cheerfully sitting down with the grooms for a noon dinner. When there was nothing else for him to do, he sat in the marquess's office, reading through his meticulous notes and growing increasingly impressed by his clarity of vision and careful planning.

"Same again tomorrow?" Gus asked as he left.

"Fine by me," Waterbury said. "Do you want a permanent post? I have a vacancy for an under-groom — twenty pounds a year, board and lodgings included."

Gus laughed. "Do you know, sometimes I wish I had been born to that sort of life instead of being the son of a marquess. Simpler, you know? A man knows where he stands."

"It is only simpler because there are fewer possibilities," Waterbury said grimly. "One starts as a stable boy and gradually works one's way up to head groom. At that point, with care, one might be able to consider taking a wife. Not much of a life, I should say."

Gus could not entirely agree with him. Sometimes the difficulties of his own life weighed heavily on him and he rather yearned for fewer possibilities, and nothing more complicated than a recalcitrant horse to worry about.

His plan for another blameless day amongst the horses was foiled when he was summoned by Willerton-Forbes to accompany him to Lady Darrowstone's house the next morning. "You do not mind, do you, Marford?" he said anxiously. "It will help to have you present, in my opinion, since you know all these people so well."

"You place too great a regard on my acquaintance with the lady, for I barely know her. She is not part of my set in London, and we are certainly not on visiting terms elsewhere. But I have no objection to hearing how she defends her claim to the stud."

There were no lawyers in evidence, and Lady Darrowstone had clearly decided to approach the matter with friendliness rather than ceremony. They were shown into her private sitting room, and she poured tea for them with her own hands.

Lady Darrowstone got down to business briskly. "Here are all the papers relating to my husband's purchase of the horses," she said, hand resting on a high pile of documents. "You will see that each one was bought by my husband, the purchase recorded in his name and the title transferred to him, and to him alone. This is a letter from his bank, confirming that funds were transferred on his authority from his bank account for each purchase. And this is his will, which leaves everything he owned to me. Well, to his eldest son, should there be one, but failing that, to me. So you see, it is all perfectly clear."

She leaned back in her chair with a satisfied smile on her face.

"Thank you, that is most helpful," Willerton-Forbes said. "I shall need time to examine these papers, and—"

"Of course."

"—also the household accounts, and any other account books you or your husband may have kept."

"The *accounts!*" She jerked sharply upwards. "What does my expenditure on candles and tea have to do with anything? I own those horses, and no one can dispute it!"

"The question at issue, Lady Darrowstone," the lawyer said smoothly, "is who paid for the purchase of the horses? The duke claims that he did, since his son's income derived solely from the allowance made to him."

"And the interest from my dowry," she said haughtily. "Besides, once money is in a man's hand, it is his to spend as he pleases, is it not? And anything he buys with it is his. My husband bought me gifts of jewellery from time to time — will the duke claim those, too? Will he take the very clothes off my back and the plate we eat from?"

"There is no jewellery, apparel or plate under discussion at present," the lawyer said calmly. "Only the horses, and I must determine where the money came from to purchase them, and the *intent* behind it. It might have been a loan, for instance—"

"Such nonsense!" she said in exasperation. "But I have nothing to hide. You may examine the account books until your head swims, for all I care."

Gus left Willerton-Forbes rubbing his hands with glee at the mountain of account books produced for his inspection. He was as bad as Daniel Merton, Carrbridge's secretary, for liking nothing better than burying himself in piles of dusty old documents. Gus could not quite understand why a man would shut himself away with pen and paper all day when he could be out in the open air, with a horse under him, and trees and walls flashing past. It was time to release Jupiter from his post-journey rest and let him stretch his legs a little.

The horse was wild, of course, as he always was when he had been left in his stall for a couple of days. He kicked and snorted, and tried to bite the two grooms holding his head. Twice he got away from them, and had to be coaxed back to a degree of quietness before Gus's own grooms could saddle him. As soon as Gus was mounted and the stall gate opened he shot forward, legs pounding. A hapless under-groom tripped trying to get out of his way, but Jupiter sailed majestically over the prone figure and on his way.

He headed north, as Gus had known he would. He wanted to go that way too, but he dared not, for his own peace of mind. So he wrestled and heaved, and the horse fought him every inch of the way, but eventually he got Jupiter turned around and pointed towards the southern lodge. It was the exact match of the northern lodge, except that there was no aproned figure running to open the gate, for they stood open all day, as did the eastern and western gates. It was only the northern gates that were closed, to stop Ned from wandering away from his mother, he supposed.

The wave of grief that overwhelmed him at the thought of her caught him unawares. Was he really so far along the road to love that the very image of her in his mind could make him crumble into helpless dust? He was in a bad way. Yet the obstacles were no less immovable. He was still an impoverished younger son. She was still an impoverished widow — no, not a widow. She must be a spinster, still, and Ned would be a formidable obstacle to any attempt to introduce her into society.

Yet with a shock of dismay, he realised that for himself, he did not care. She was still the same person, her mind and form every bit as beautiful as when he had thought her a widow, and he would marry her tomorrow if he could.

13: A Walk After Church

Ned woke crying again. It was still dark, and Amaryllis had to light a candle before she could go to him. She met Maggie in the passage outside the boy's door, bent on the same errand.

"I'll see to him," Maggie said. "You go and sleep."

"No, it is quite all right. I am awake now."

"Tsk. You'll take him into your bed, I daresay, like you always do."

"And why not?" Amaryllis said. "He will sleep again if I do that. Hush now, no more argument, I beg you."

She opened the door, and went into her son's room, the flickering candle driving the shadows to the furthest corners. "Now, now, little man, what is it?"

"Where is Gus?" he sobbed. "I want Gus! Where is he?"

"He has business elsewhere that takes him away," she said. "Men always have business that takes them away."

"When will he come back?"

"I cannot say."

It was a careful answer. She would never lie to Ned, and she already knew that Gus was back at Castle Morton, but he had not come to see her, nor had he ridden past the lodge. His last words to her had sounded so final. *'Most likely we shall not meet again. I shall always look back on our acquaintance with the fondest of memories.'* She understood him — he intended to see her no more. He was drawn to her, that much was clear to see, but he had decided not to travel further down that road, and she could hardly blame him for that. She was not a fit person for him to visit.

Taking Ned back to her own bed, she settled him down and sang his favourite lullabies until he drifted into slumber in her arms. Ah, what would she have done without Ned! Such a comfort to her, for all the difficulties surrounding him. Without him, she would have been quite alone in the world. She might have no family or husband, but at least she had Ned to care for and protect and love. And he had her, his mother, and that must be enough for him. If only he had a father to look up to, as well. Someone like Gus... but Gus was gone.

For herself, she could bear the loss of his company, or so she told herself. She had been alone for a long time, after all, and she had John, Maggie and Lucy to talk to. They were like family, in a way. But still... it was not the same as being with those of her own kind. Gus was educated and knowledgeable about the world, a man she could talk to about music and books and philosophy and a thousand other things beyond the domestic sphere. But she was determined not to regret him. Naturally she would miss him, but she would not repine, she had made up her mind to it.

But for Ned, it was different. He had never had a man to look up to before, not a *gentleman*. John was all very well and a good sort of man, but he was only a servant, and could not teach Ned how to behave, the little nuances that distinguished the high born from the lower ranks. She did not want Ned to grow up thinking of John as an equal, and yet how could he learn, if he were never to meet men of his own rank? Perhaps she should consider going into company a little. The parson at St Peter's could perhaps introduce her to one or two people. Yet she quailed at the thought. It would be necessary to hide behind so many lies, and if anyone from Drifford should find out... No, it was not to be thought of. If only Gus would come! That would be ideal, and even when he went back to London, Ned would have the memory of him fixed in his mind.

Her thoughts chased each other round her head until she fell into a troubled sleep.

"Shall I stay with Ned today, Amaryllis?" Maggie said over breakfast. "Lucy hasn't been to church for several weeks."

"If you wish," Amaryllis said.

"You know, the child's old enough to go to church with us," Maggie said. "There are plenty younger than him that go, even babes in their mothers' arms."

"You know my reasons. The fewer people who know of his existence the better. Too many questions would be asked, and rumours travel."

"Aye, but half the castle staff know about him already, and they guess who he is, too. There are no secrets here."

"And there is no point inviting further speculation by parading Ned about in public."

"Can't keep him hidden away forever," Maggie muttered, collecting the plates in an angry clatter.

Amaryllis took no notice. They had such a discussion at least once a week, and since Maggie had been Amaryllis's own nursemaid, and had stood in place of her mother after the tragedy that had torn their family apart, she was allowed to say what she liked, without reprimand. Maggie knew Amaryllis as well as she knew herself, but in this one matter they disagreed.

Sunday was Amaryllis's favourite day. It was the one day of the week when she went out into the world and mingled with humanity for an hour or two. She could even pretend she had acquaintance in the town — the Farmer family, who shared her pew, or the two elderly spinsters who always smiled and exchanged a few words with her. The parson, too, shook her hand as if she were just another parishioner, and not someone disgraced and alone. And the walk through the park invigorated her, too. She walked a great deal, but only into the woods where she could be alone with her thoughts and would encounter no one. But on Sundays she walked through the castle gardens and admired the bright tulips or buried her nose in sweet-smelling roses or collected chestnuts for Ned, according to the season.

On this particular Sunday, the walk was less pleasant than usual, for a sharp wind tossed the last of the roses about and tore the first browning leaves from the trees. Amaryllis joined the throng entering church, nodding at the two spinsters as she passed their pew. They were always there before her, no matter how early she was. The Farmers were already seated when Amaryllis took her own seat, John and Lucy beside her.

And then a shock, for who should she see striding down the aisle to a prominent pew but Gus? She recognised his coat, the same one he had worn when he had called on her. And he must have been close behind her as she entered the church, so close that they might almost have met. Why was he here and not at the castle chapel? She had wondered at it when she had seen him there before, but then he had not been avoiding her. Or had he thought better of that policy? Her heart beat a little faster at the thought, but then she chided herself for it. Lord Augustus Marford was not a man she could ever think of in that way.

All through the service, her eyes sought him out. It was fortunate that he was tall, so that she could catch a glimpse of his head between the waving bonnets of the congregation. It was fortunate, too, that she knew the words of the liturgy so well, for she was not attending in the least. A daring plan was forming in her mind, and she could think of nothing else. It was so forward of her that she could hardly conceive of acting in such a way, but for Ned she would do anything. Besides, she had no reputation left to lose.

So when the congregation was dismissed, and the important people from the front pews made their way down the aisle, Gus included, she held her gaze on him so that if he looked her way at all, he must notice her. He saw her, she bobbed a curtsy and he made her a small bow, all that could be managed within the crowded confines of the church. But he looked so serious! That was not a good sign.

Nevertheless, she hurried outside as quickly as she could, hoping he had not rushed away at the sight of her. There he was! Thank goodness, he was still there, loitering a little apart from the chattering crowds, head down. So sad, he looked, standing by himself in that way, a stranger in the town, just as she was, even after three years.

"My lord." She dipped a proper curtsy.

"Mrs Walsh." A respectful bow. "How are you? And Ned? He is well? No repercussions from his accident?"

"No, he is perfectly well, but…" Oh, how difficult it was! She had not had time to rehearse to herself what she might say to him, and now her mind was empty.

"May I escort you home?" He offered her his arm. "Then you may tell me all about him as we walk."

She stammered her thanks, and, blushing, took his arm. How kind he was! So gentlemanly. He made her feel like a lady again, although she could not say a word.

They walked slowly down the church path, and she saw one or two people staring at them, wondering. Gus walked on past them, and they passed under the lych gate, across the road and through the gates to the castle grounds before he spoke.

"You must think me very rude," he began. "It is the height of bad manners to whisk you away from your friends in that way, and then not offer a word of conversation. It is my great weakness, that I can never think of the proper thing to say, although I realise I should say *something* — the weather, perhaps. One always talks about the weather."

She giggled. "There is no need to say anything, if you had rather not."

"Oh, I wish to. I very much wish to, for if we talk about the weather for a while, then you will be comfortable enough to tell me what is worrying you about Ned. But my head is empty of weather-related thoughts just now."

That made her laugh out loud. "You are very kind, my lord. It is only that the pleasure of walking about on a gentleman's arm is not one that has come my way for some time. Perhaps... if we walk this way, there is a small arbour where we may sit for a while."

"An excellent idea, and you would be sheltered from this cold wind, too."

"Ah, now you have made a weather-related remark," she said. "Well done."

"There is hope for me yet," he said, smiling. "Perhaps next time we meet we may progress to the prospects of rain?"

Next time we meet! Was there to be a next time? Her pulse raced again, and this time she did not try to suppress it. Why should she not enjoy his company for a while? He would be gone soon enough, after all.

They sat in the arbour, and Lucy and John, who had been following them, walked on past. Lucy continued on, but John stopped a little further down the path, leaning against a tree, staring into the distance, watching over her. They took such good care of her, John, Maggie and Lucy.

"Now, will you tell me about Ned?" he said.

So she told him about the bad dreams, and how he woke calling for Gus, and nothing she did could comfort him. "He never knew his father, who died before he was born," she said. "It would be good for him, I think, to get to know you, to understand what a gentleman is."

"Nothing would give me greater pleasure," he said at once. "However, I shall not be here for long, only until the difficulties with the stud are resolved. Then, whatever the outcome, I shall be going back to London."

"I know," she said easily. "At least he would have the memory of you." She leaned forward, suddenly intense. "You are so *good* with him, as few adults are with children. Even the doctor is brusque with him, and Maggie sometimes... whereas you just treat him as a person."

"Which he is, of course," he said, smiling, but she could not quite smile back. Ned was too serious a topic for the least degree of levity. He went on, "Adults I find difficult sometimes, for they are complicated and subtle, and I am neither. But children — children are just like horses."

"Like horses!"

"Of course. One always knows where one stands with them. They both kick and scream and bite when angry, take every opportunity to run away, and are all docility when fed copious amounts of sugar."

That made her laugh, her gloved hands raised to cover her mouth.

His smile died away as he looked at her thoughtfully, his face sympathetic. "You must be aware, Mrs Walsh, that the very best thing you could do for Ned is to take him into company, to mix with other children and see other families. That is how he would learn the ways of his class."

"I cannot," she said firmly. "My life must be one of seclusion, Lord Augustus, and therefore Ned's also. That is how it must be."

"I beg your pardon," he said at once. "It is the height of impertinence for me to be offering you advice. You must be the best and only arbiter of how Ned should be raised."

Then she felt guilty for rejecting his advice so peremptorily. "If only I could do as you suggest! But there are reasons — good and sound reasons — why I must avoid society, for Ned's sake. My life is dedicated to my son, my lord, and everything I do, however odd it may appear to those who do not know my circumstances, is for his benefit, now and in the future."

He nodded, his face serious. "Forgive me, it is not my concern. Let us talk about the weather instead."

That made her laugh again. For all that he was so serious sometimes, he was easy to talk to. "Tell me about your journey. Was your business concluded successfully?"

"Yes and no. I did not find what I sought, but I found something quite unexpected instead, for I unearthed a natural son of my father's. In this case, however, he is being raised as the legitimate heir to another man."

"Oh," she said, diverted. "But how is that possible? Oh!"

"I see that you have worked it out," he said, turning to her with a gleam of amusement in his eyes. "An affair with the wife... but seemingly with the complicity of the husband, who would otherwise have had no heir at all."

"How... how *complicated*."

"It is now, for they were all going about their business quite happily, the son in complete ignorance, until I turned up with my nose an exact match for his. It is a wretched hindrance to cuckoldry, the Marford nose. There is no disguising one's misbehaviour."

She giggled, and all the constraint between them was gone. No matter what was said between them, she realised with sudden joy, he would not fly into sudden anger, or sulk, or take offence. He was such a refreshingly straightforward man. She could have sat all day in the arbour with him.

But then he said, "I came through Drifford on my way back to the castle. It interested me greatly, since it was your home for some years. It looks to be a fine, prosperous place." He paused but there was nothing she wanted to say about Drifford. "That is a fine statue in the main square. *'Mrs Charles Ballard, Patroness of Drifford'*. She must be a very great lady, to have a statue raised in her honour."

He paused again, looking at her, and surely he must wonder why she made no response! It was absolutely necessary to exert herself. "She is the most important person in Drifford," she said at length, in a low voice. "Mr Ballard owns the town, but Mrs Ballard manages it."

"Ah, I see," he said. Then, the moment she had dreaded. "You must have known them, I imagine? What sort of people are they?"

Could she talk calmly about them? She must! "Mr Ballard is a kindly gentleman, although not often at home. He owns many businesses over the county and some in Cumberland, Westmoreland and Durham too. Mrs Ballard is... she is..."

"You did not like her," he said gently. "Was she unkind to you?"

Her breath caught in her throat. Unkind! Oh, if only that were all. "No indeed, but she is... a strict taskmistress. She expects hard work and total loyalty from those she employs. In return, she has instituted many improvements for the town. She has raised a fine new church, for instance, and established a school and many new shops."

"I should like to see this paragon. Does she ever come to High Morton?"

"Oh no, never! She never leaves Drifford, but she has friends here who tell her all that happens." Friends? Spies, she would have called them.

He fell into silence, and she could see him thinking it over, trying, perhaps, to read between the lines of her bland comments and find the real history behind her words. That would never do! She must turn his thoughts elsewhere at once. "Lord Augustus, will you come and see Ned?"

"It would be my pleasure, Mrs Walsh."

Smiling, he rose and offered her his arm, and as she rested her hand on it, there was a rightness to it that brought her an unaccustomed degree of serenity. It was if they were meant to be together, and for a while she could forget Drifford and Mrs Ballard altogether.

14: Arrivals

Gus took the greatest delight in strolling through the park with Mrs Walsh on his arm. He had long since made a resolution that he must stay out of her life, but somehow that was all forgotten. He had thought, as he had walked to church that morning, that he would not approach her, but if they should happen to meet, then common courtesy would require an acknowledgement. A bow, perhaps. An exchange of greetings, at most. But she had come to him! And he could hardly refuse to speak to her, and then he was obliged, as a gentleman, to allow her to say what she wanted. His conscience was screaming that he should take the first opportunity to run away from her, but his heart was singing so loudly that he could not hear his conscience at all.

So he tried very hard not to smile with joy as they walked sedately along the path towards the north lodge. It was curious, what she had told him of Drifford. There was such constraint in her manner that even he, poor as he was at understanding people, knew that there must have been some quarrel with this Mrs Ballard. But Mrs Walsh clearly did not wish to confide in him, and he must respect that. He had no wish to make her uncomfortable, and so would say nothing further to her about Drifford.

When they emerged from the sheltering trees and were visible from the lodge, a small figure burst out from the house, the maid in pursuit.

"Gus! Gus!" he shrieked at the top of his lungs. "You came back!"

Gus had never been so popular before. His nephews and small cousins had such an array of nurses and doting parents and aunts and uncles, that one lone man was of no great significance. When they started to learn to ride, then Uncle Gus would become a great deal more interesting to them, but usually small children found him dreadfully dull. But here was one who thought he was quite wonderful, and Gus would not have been human if he did not respond with delight to such overtures.

Releasing Mrs Walsh, he squatted and held out his arms, and the boy ran straight into them. Gus swept him up, and hugged him tightly. "Well, hello, young man! Are you quite recovered from your encounter with Jupiter?"

And then, as was so often the way with small children, Ned became shy and refused to say a word, burying his face in Gus's cravat. Gus laughed, and carried the boy into the house, where Mrs Walsh directed him to the drawing room.

The first sight to meet his eyes was the piano, nestling against the wall as if it had always been there. It was closed today, being Sunday, but his heart somersaulted at the thought that one day soon he would hear her play it.

"It fills that space on the wall admirably," he said to her, with a smile.

She blushed — how charmingly she coloured up! — and made some attempt to thank him again, which he waved aside.

"Instruments are made to be played," he said. "They are no use sitting in a shop for month after month. Now, young man, are you allowed your soldiers on a Sunday, or must we read the Bible?"

"We could perhaps read the battle of Jericho?" Mrs Walsh said. "Ned could arrange his soldiers in a suitable manner."

So she read the Bible verses, while Ned and Gus, both sitting cross-legged on the floor, tried to re-enact the battle. In a corner, the older maid sat mending one of the child's shirts as chaperon. Then there was another Bible story, which Gus read with the child sitting on his lap, eyes drooping. Before long he was asleep.

"Poor little fellow! He must have been tired," Gus said.

"He has not slept properly since— for a while," she said, and he guessed what she was about to say — *'since you left'*. Well, he was back now, and he would find some excuse to see the boy every day from now on. And the child's mother, his heart whispered.

"We have dinner at two today," she said, whispering so as not to disturb Ned. "It would be the greatest pleasure to us if you would join us, Lord Augustus."

How much he wanted to! Yet an extra plate at table today might mean bread and dripping for them later in the week. "It is kind in you to offer, but your servants will only have cooked enough for your usual number."

"We have a haunch of beef large enough for twenty," she said, smiling. "The castle keeps us well supplied with meat."

So Gus accepted the invitation, and sat down to dinner at the unfashionably early hour of two o'clock with Mrs Walsh, Ned, John, Maggie and Lucy, and enjoyed it a vast deal more than any of the duke's elaborate meals. He stayed until four, and accounted the day one of the most enjoyable of his life. He went to his second dinner of the day humming, his head full of her, counting the hours until he could visit again.

~~~~~

The next day brought Lady Rachel Medhurst, daughter of the Duke of Wedhampton, to the castle, accompanied by a long train of carriages bearing her luggage and many servants. She was quite open about her intention to marry the duke.

"I owe it to the family name not to marry anyone of lesser rank," she said haughtily, when she was shown into the drawing room before dinner. "Yet so few of our dukes are available at the moment. I nearly got Camberley once, but he slipped through my fingers and one of those devious Linford girls got him instead. But this time I am quite determined to succeed, and I do not mind your age or infirmity, you know. I am not so young myself, these days." And she brayed with laughter.

"You will hardly do for my purposes, in that case," the duke said testily. "How old are you, madam?"

"Not so old that I cannot give you an heir or two," she said archly.

"Why would I not choose a pretty little debutante, eh?" he said. "Seventeen or eighteen, with soft, smooth skin... not sure why I should choose you instead."

But she laughed, not at all discomfited. "An older, more experienced woman is a great deal more fun, Duke." And she winked broadly.

He grunted, but his eyes gleamed, and Gus saw the Frensham ladies exchange glances. They had not expected a rival!

"Who is she?" Gus whispered to Emma. "How did she know about all this?"

"She is a friend of Edith's," Emma whispered back. "No doubt she has written to all her set, and we shall have half the spinsters and widows in the country scampering up to Northumberland to simper at the duke. Although Rachel is not the simpering type, I grant you. Good heavens, Gus, this is turning into a veritable circus, and most unseemly in a man of his years. Look at him smirking at her."

"It has quite ruined your chances, I fancy, unless you are prepared to elbow your way to the front of the queue."

"It is to be hoped I have a little more dignity than that!" she said acidly. "Ah, we are going into dinner at last. Can you contrive to sit with me, Gus? I am desperate for some sensible conversation."

"If the duke will allow it," he said. "Goodness, look at him go! He is very sprightly today, and not the least sign of gout. You have worked a miracle, Emma."

"Oh, gout comes and goes all by itself. If my little attentions have helped, then I am glad of it, and I rather enjoy my half-hours with him each morning. He is great fun, you know, when he is not in pain, or being foolish over women. He has the sharpest sense of humour." She sighed. "I shall miss him when I have to leave here."

But Gus was summoned to the head of the table again, and Emma was left to find a place further down, sitting silent and still, toying with her food.

When Gus returned to his parlour, he found he had a visitor of his own. Daniel Merton, Carrbridge's secretary, was listening politely to one of Edgerton's lengthy tales. Gus introduced Merton to Willerton-Forbes who then diplomatically disappeared. Edgerton sat on, and would have lingered if Gus had not stood and held the door open for him.

"You will forgive me, I am sure, Michael, but Merton is here to talk family business."

Edgerton smiled and bowed, and went off without demur.

Merton sighed. "Thank you! He is entertaining company, but a little wearing after a while."

"The ladies would probably disagree with you. More brandy? Now then, tell me what brings you here."

"Galthwaite," Merton said, with his slight smile. "I have had some most satisfactory dealings there. Lord Grayson and Mr Terence Grayson have been very helpful, and, with their assistance, the Carters have been given notice to quit Gillingham House. Lord Grayson is to buy the property as soon as the papers can be drawn up. He is also to buy Hexlowe Hall from Lord Carrbridge, and lease it to his friend for a peppercorn rent until his fortunes are restored. The weaving mill also is to be put up for sale. Best of all, the bank manager and attorney have been most obliging. Having been shown the title to these properties, they very readily agreed to make over the balance of the account to Lord Carrbridge. It is but a modest sum, but better in Lord Carrbridge's pocket than anyone else's. In all, his lordship will be some fifteen thousand pounds better off as a result."

"And what of Sharp? Or this Harcourt fellow?" Gus said.

"No sign of either while I was there. No one has heard of Mr Sharp, although when I mentioned the name in Mr Carter's hearing, it seemed to me that he looked conscious. My guess is that the Carters are relatives of Sharp's. I can think of no other reason why they would be permitted to live in Gillingham House without the payment of rent."

"But where *is* Sharp?" Gus cried. "He has vanished into thin air. And who is this Harcourt?"

Merton set down his brandy glass and steepled his hands. "Do you not think that Harcourt and Sharp must be one and the same?"

"Impossible! Harcourt is a very finely-dressed man, an exceedingly well-set-up gentleman with an excellent horse, and accompanied always by a pair of grooms. Whereas if Sharp wears a single item of clothing made in the last twenty years, I should be astonished to hear it. And that old tricorn hat! No, it cannot be!"

Merton smiled and raised an eyebrow. "I asked several people in Galthwaite for a description of Harcourt. He is some sixty years old, his back a little bent but otherwise in good health. He has greying red hair, which he wears in a queue. Does this sound familiar?"

"Oh. That does indeed sound like Sharp. But the clothes!"

"A man who wishes to present a certain appearance to the world may choose to wear one set of clothes, and when he wishes to present a different appearance he will wear another set. It always seemed to me that Sharp's choice of attire at Drummoor was rather contrived. What man of business, after all, faces the world wearing clothes from twenty or more years ago? No agent would be taken seriously in such garb."

"So he wears old clothes at Drummoor, and elsewhere dresses like a rich man? But why?"

"Now that is an interesting question," Merton said, his eyes gleaming. He leaned forward. "One can only speculate, of course, but consider what we already know. The man is absent from Drummoor a great deal — far more than is necessary for an agent. There are properties scattered all over the country which the eighth marquess won at cards or dice or wagering how high a frog would jump."

"Truly? A frog?"

"Indeed. There is a very pretty little dower house a few miles north of York which changed hands on just such a wager. The nobility marches to a different drum from the common folk, that much is certain. Your father and his cronies would bet on any event, and lay any wager on it. It was not all estates, for horses changed hands, too, and a coat or two. A valet, once. Oh, and a girl on one occasion, but I cannot at all find out who it was or what became of her."

"A girl!" Gus exclaimed.

"Drake's daughter, according to letters sent to your father, but who Drake was I cannot tell. They all had nicknames — Hawk, Foxy, Wolf, Boar, Rat. Your father was Hawk."

"The nose, I suppose. What a wild crowd they must have been. I feel very tame by comparison."

Merton smiled. "There is nothing wrong with living one's life prudently, and with regard for the future of the family. Not all of those men grew out of their wild years with their fortunes intact, I imagine. Your father was lucky, or clever, perhaps. But to return to Sharp, the interesting aspect is that all these properties that your father won were not regarded as part of his estate. More than once, his letters of the time talk of his ownership as a guardianship, so that he would look after them until such time as the original owners could recover them. The titles were not kept with the lawyers in London, or in the Drummoor safe, but were given to Sharp to look after separately. And only some of them were mentioned in the accounts and other records. It was not until we retrieved all Sharp's papers from his cottage that we learnt about the Galthwaite properties, for instance."

"So Sharp kept those to himself."

"Exactly so."

"And you have a theory as to why?"

"Clearly he has been managing all the properties to his own benefit — pocketing the rents, and allowing his disreputable relations to live rent-free in empty houses. He kept Lord Carrbridge supplied with funds, and found extra when he was asked for it, but otherwise he held onto every penny, and has been amusing himself by living like a lord on the proceeds."

"But not at Drummoor," Gus said.

"No, his domain is clearly to the north. But we are closing in on him. I am convinced that Harcourt and Sharp are two sides of the same man, and if we find one we find the other. And the bank manager has given me an address for Harcourt, at a place called Churlswade. It is, so I am told, half way between Galthwaite and York, and a very convenient location for a man to change his appearance when travelling between the north and the south."

"Ah! How soon can we go there?"

Merton smiled. "I had hoped you would be able to accompany me. If my horse is rested sufficiently, we can go tomorrow. A day each way and a day at Churlswade should do it."

~~~~~

Gus was up and dressed not long after dawn the next morning, and striding into town. The shop he wanted was not open, but he roused the shopkeeper by banging loudly on the door, and shouting at the upper windows until a bleary-eyed woman opened a window.

"We're not open! Go away!" She closed the window firmly. He banged and shouted even more loudly until the window flew open again. "We're *not open*, are you deaf? Come back in an hour."

"I shall pay you very well to open early." Gus rattled his purse of coins at her.

She paused, and then, perhaps noticing his expensive clothing, grunted. "Ten minutes."

It was a little more than that, but eventually a rattling of keys and grating of bolts heralding the opening of the door, and Gus was admitted to the rather dishevelled presence of the shopkeeper.

"I am greatly obliged to you," Gus said. "Business takes me out of town, and I cannot leave my young friend without some recompense for the loss of my company. I should like to buy some more of your excellent tin soldiers, and I shall pay twice the usual price, by way of apology for dragging you from your warm bed at so unreasonable an hour."

The man's face brightened. "Ah, of course. I remember you now, sir. Here we are, sir, here we are. My entire supply, for the moment, although I can get more in a few days. What was it you'd be wanting, sir? Infantry? Cavalry? Some archers? Or pikemen?"

"How much would you want for all of them?"

The man trembled so violently that Gus feared he might fall over. He suggested a price, Gus agreed to it without demur and within minutes the transaction was complete. Gus left, a neat parcel under his arm, and wondered if the harridan at the window might be getting a new bonnet soon, or perhaps, if he had overpaid by a wide margin, a small piece of jewellery. Or would it be put to buying beef for the table, or a chaldron of coals, or new boots for the children? He had no idea what it was like to live on a small income, and have to weigh the burning of every candle, and perhaps not drink tea at all. Was that what Mrs Walsh's life was like? She had her own chickens and vegetables, and no doubt the castle supplied meat and game, but there must be a great need for economy. Yet there was no sign of it, and he supposed she must be a good manager.

Back in his parlour, Gus sent for more brown paper and string, and divided the soldiers into three separate parcels. Then he sat down with paper and ink.

'Dear Ned, Family business which I cannot shirk takes me away for three days. As soon as I return, I will come to see you again. In the meantime, I am sending some reinforcements for your troops. I hope you like them. Your very good friend, Gus.'

Folding and sealing the paper, he wrote on it, 'Master E. Walsh'.

With a second sheet, he wrote, 'Bedford, Pray see that one parcel and the letter are delivered to the north lodge today, a second parcel tomorrow and the third the day after. Augustus Marford.'

Then, smiling to himself, he made his way to the stables, where Willett and one of the Carson brothers awaited him. They collected Merton and his groom from the Dunmorton Arms, and headed south.

15: The Kings Arms

Merton was pleasant company on the road. He was not amusing, in the way that Edgerton was, but he was a thoughtful, educated man, and not a chatterer, and Gus was grateful for that. Since he was not a chatterer himself, there were long stretches when neither man spoke. Behind them, the murmured voices of the two grooms could be heard, with Willett occasionally joining in, but Gus watched the scenery and thought his own thoughts and enjoyed the restful silence of his companion.

They reached Churlswade in plenty of time for Gus to investigate both the inns and determine which of them best met his requirements for the care of Jupiter. He was not entirely satisfied with either, but eventually, after a long discussion with the head ostler and the transfer of silver, he selected the Kings Arms to receive his patronage. Merton, amused but uncomplaining, waited until this process was complete before dismounting.

"If this place is good enough for Jupiter, I daresay it will be adequate for Richmond Lad," he murmured, handing the reins to his groom. "Am I correct in supposing that the provision for humans is of lesser importance in your decision?"

Gus laughed. "You think me over-fastidious, I daresay, but a single inadequate night may render a horse of Jupiter's temperament unrideable for days. It is for my own comfort that I attend to his. Besides, I can eat anything and sleep anywhere, and I am sure you are the same, Merton."

"Indeed I can, but I had very much rather not, if there is any choice to be had in the matter."

But once a parlour had been bespoken, the bed chambers examined and a promise of hot water sufficient for baths extracted from the innkeeper, Merton relaxed in a wing chair and stretched booted feet to the fire.

"Ah, this is better! I was a little concerned that we might have to sleep on bare boards or eat dry bread. It would have been a noble sacrifice, to be sure, in the aid of your magnificent horse, but still I am devoutly thankful not to be called upon to make it. I confess to liking my comforts just as much as Jupiter."

Gus laughed at him and shook his head. "What are humans but parasites upon the face of the earth in comparison to God's most perfect creation, the horse?"

"No horse is perfect, in my opinion, but if mine will carry me where I wish to go, and not try to kill me while he is about it, I shall be satisfied with that. And at the end of a day's riding, I like to be able to hand him over to someone else and not think about him at all for twelve hours or more."

"You have no soul, Merton. Shall you hunt this year?"

"Lord Carrbridge has offered to mount me, and I am to accompany him to Melton, so perhaps... but it is not yet a year since my friend, Sir Osborne Hardy, died and I am not minded for selfish pleasures."

"Only comfortable beds and good food, eh?"

Merton smiled. "A man must eat and sleep, so why not the best provision of each? Ah, our baths must be ready," he added, as a maid bobbed a curtsy at the door.

As they followed her up the stairs to their rooms, Gus found himself wondering rather about Merton, who so liked the best of everything yet paid for nothing himself. A parasite, perhaps, but a likable one, and very clever at what he did.

After bathing and changing into fresh linen, followed by a dinner that met even Daniel Merton's exacting standards, the two men settled down with a bottle of brandy. The parlour was not over-large, but since Willett and the grooms were in the taproom, it was adequate. There was a good fire, with a comfortable chair either side of it, and Gus could not be displeased with the company. After checking that Jupiter was contented, he settled down to while away the evening with brandy and conversation.

Gus had never had a great deal to do with Merton before, but now he was mellow enough to say, "Do you enjoy your work as a secretary, Merton?"

"I do, rather," he said, with that secretive smile that always made Gus wonder what he was thinking beneath the suave exterior. "I enjoy having a desk, and papers to peruse, and money to deal with, preferably someone else's and a great deal of it. There is something very satisfactory in dealing with thousands of pounds at once, which I could never aspire to in the regular way. And of course I enjoy living at Drummoor, for having the Marquess of Carrbridge as my employer increases my consequence enormously."

Gus laughed, taking this as a joke, although one never quite knew with Merton. "Still, it is a dull business, dealing with all the correspondence that a lazy aristocrat like my brother cannot be bothered to do for himself."

"The marquess is too important a man to worry about every little boundary dispute or leaky roof that troubles his tenant farmers," Merton said. "I consider myself as relieving the burden of a man who has weightier matters on his mind, matters which are of the utmost importance to the nation. His lordship has great responsibilities as a peer of the realm."

Gus tried to reconcile this image of a great man with his gentle brother, and failed. "In any event, I am glad Carrbridge has someone like you to help him. He has needed another secretary for a long time."

"Ah, yes," Merton murmured. "The mythical Mr Penicuik, who was struck by some tragic accident shortly after his appointment."

"It *was* tragic," Gus said "Especially the pig…"

"A pig? Oh, pray enlighten me."

But Gus shuddered. "We never speak of it, for it was too horrible for words. Poor Mr Penicuik! But that is all history. He was an adequate chaplain, but never very much of a secretary. It was a kindness to employ him. Whereas you are a gentleman."

Merton sighed, then went on, with his slight smile, "What else should I be doing? As the youngest of five sons, and with no great wealth in the family, there must always have been the necessity to earn my bread, one way or another. My place with Lord Carrbridge gives me greater freedom than I had with Sir Osborne Hardy, to whom I was friend and confidante as well as secretary. It would never have been possible for me to set up my own establishment at Brinford Manor as I have done at Drummoor."

"You have that house arranged very tidily," Gus said. "Mind you, it is a rambling sort of place for a single man."

Merton smiled again, replenishing their brandy glasses. "True, but perhaps I shall marry one day, and then it will be just the right size. But that reminds me — I am charged by Lady Carrbridge with finding out everything I may about a certain widow, for you have not been very forthcoming, she tells me. Or not forthcoming enough for her liking, perhaps."

Gus laughed, rather self-consciously. "Dear Connie! How she loves a romance, however unpromising! But there is not much to tell that she does not already know. Mrs Walsh lives very quietly with her son and three servants on the Castle Morton grounds."

"Oh, a son? But that would not weigh with you, I daresay — raising another man's child?"

"No, indeed, for the boy is delightful, and the more so because he has made me into some sort of hero in his mind. Jupiter nearly ran him down one day, and because I carried the child back to his mother, I am idolised. It is very gratifying, I must tell you."

"I can imagine. But she has no other woman living with her? No sister or cousin? No male relation to offer her protection? How does she travel about?"

Gus laughed at that. "She goes nowhere, except to church on Sundays. She lives very secluded, keeping no horses or carriage, visiting no one and receiving no callers."

"Interesting. Then presumably the duke's patronage is protection enough?"

"No one would dare to cross him, that much is certain. He is a powerful figure in the county."

"Oh, certainly. Well, I will not tease you about the lady. You must be the best judge of your own happiness, and so Lord Carrbridge thinks, also. He has given me the pleasant task of informing you that, now that Lord Reginald and Lord Humphrey are established independently, there is enough money in the family coffers to increase your allowance sufficiently to encompass a wife. If matters should reach that point."

A surge of joy swept through Gus, and so agitated was he, that he jumped to his feet and paced up and down the room once or twice. "And Carrbridge would do this for me? Without knowing anything about the lady?"

"I believe it is Lady Carrbridge who so devoutly desires your happiness, and naturally Lord Carrbridge—"

"—devoutly desires *Lady* Carrbridge's happiness," Gus said, laughing. "He will do anything to please her. In this case, I am to be the joyful beneficiary of her romantic inclinations. How generous of Carrbridge! The practicalities of managing on a very small income had begun to prey on my mind of late, but this is beyond anything. I hardly know what to say. He is the best of brothers — and Connie is the best of sisters-in-law! Now there is nothing standing in my way."

"You will still need to consider your expenses with the greatest care," Merton said. "Lord Carrbridge mentioned the sum of one thousand pounds a year, but that is still not a great amount. I have no doubt he will house you, and continue to supply you with horses, but you will have the expense of feeding and stabling, grooms and farriers, and so forth. You will have to be very careful. Does the lady have any money herself?"

"I... do you know, I have no idea."

"If her husband left her anything for herself, she would likely lose it on remarriage, and the child's inheritance might be tied up until he is of age. But that supposes her husband was a man of some wealth. What do you know of him?"

Gus was lost in thought, too wrapped up in joyous dreams to attend. "Hmm?"

"The husband — was he a wealthy man?"

"Oh, there was no husband."

Merton's brandy glass froze halfway to his lips. With infinite slowness, he lowered it to the table. "No husband?"

"No. Ned is a natural son, but— Good God, man, you are not going to get censorious with me, are you? Mrs Walsh is the same person, regardless of the circumstances."

"But she is not!" Merton cried. "Can you not see that? A widow of good character... that is one thing, and perfectly unexceptional, and the child makes no difference. There will generally be children when there has been a previous marriage. But a woman who has so far demeaned herself as to produce a child outside of wedlock — that is unforgivable, my lord. It is a stain that no subsequent marriage can cleanse. How could Lady Carrbridge introduce such a lady into society? How could she even *visit* such a person? And to be considering inviting such a woman into the Marford family, to be sister-in-law to the Marquess of Carrbridge? It is unthinkable. If you insist upon marrying this woman, then you not only cannot bring her into your own level of society, but you yourself will be excluded from it."

"That might be a small price to pay for such happiness," Gus shot back.

Merton lifted the brandy to his lips and sipped. "Not a *small* price, but it might yet be worth paying," he said quietly. "Only you can answer that, my lord."

They fell into silence, the only sound in the room the crackle of the fire. From the taproom, a voice rose briefly above the hum of conversation into song, followed by a burst of male laughter. Somewhere a dog barked.

Gus kicked frustratedly at a log on the fire, sending sparks flying up the chimney, then collapsed into a chair, head in hands. "Dear God, Merton, what am I to do?"

"I would not normally presume to advise you, my lord, but in this case my conscience compels me to do so. If you are not yet committed to this woman, then you should have no more to do with her. She is no fit wife for you."

"And yet... she seems to me to be everything that is respectable. She is demure, she goes to church without fail accompanied by one of the maids and her manservant—"

"She has a manservant? Interesting. Does she dine at the castle?"

"No, but she is not of noble blood. The duke will have no one of common blood at his table."

"Interesting. And does he take an interest in the child? It is a boy, I believe you said?"

"It is, and the duke takes no more notice of him than of Mrs Walsh herself."

"Interesting."

"Merton, I should like fifty pounds for every time you have said *'Interesting!'* in that mysterious tone of voice."

With a smile, Merton said, "Your pardon, my lord. Curiosity is my besetting sin, I fear, and I confess to a great deal of curiosity regarding a natural child who is being raised within the Duke of Dunmorton's domain. The obvious answer is that his father is Lord George Winfell."

"The youngest son? Why him, in particular?"

"Because I am acquainted with all three of the sons, or I should say rather that Sir Osborne was acquainted with the two older sons, the Marquess of Darrowstone and Lord Edward, and neither of them struck me as the type of man to father a child on a respectable woman. Whereas Lord George... How old is the boy?"

"Four, I believe."

"Ah, then it could not be Lord George, for he fled to the continent some six... no, seven years ago now, after a duel, and then had the ill-luck to fall from his horse. He was very wild. So it would have to be the Marquess or Lord Edward."

"Since the boy's name is Ned, and Mrs Walsh has told me that his father was killed in the Peninsula, my money would be on Edward," Gus said.

"Indeed." Merton frowned. "But such a *respectable* young man. Sir Osborne, you know, would never have anything at all to do with anyone who was the least bit ramshackle, and his instincts were excellent on such matters. It would be very odd in Lord Edward to take a mistress, and if he did, I am sure he would do everything properly, leaving the lady and her child very well provided for. Yet she does not live expensively, it seems."

"She is adamant that she must remain secluded, for the sake of the child," Gus said, and as he repeated her words now, he was struck by how peculiar they were. Why remain secluded? If the child was indeed the grandson of the Duke of Dunmorton, then he might have a respected place in society, and a comfortable career. At the very least, he should be educated, and not abandoned to a remote corner of the estate. "And now you are going to say *'Interesting'* again, I suppose."

Merton gave a bark of laughter. "But it *is* interesting, do you not think? Where did she come from, this mysterious lady?"

"Now that I can answer. She lived at a small mill town some twenty miles to the north of High Morton. Her husband — as she calls him — was at the army camp there. But there was no Edward Walsh there, for I made enquiries. She called him Edward, so that much is certain, but his name was not Walsh."

Merton set down his brandy glass and leaned back in his chair, stretching out his legs. "So she is local — that makes a difference. She met Lord Edward Winfell when he was at the army camp, they fell in love, she succumbed to his advances and— But no, again, I am reminded of the Lord Edward I knew in London, who would never have made advances to a respectable lady, or even to one who was less than respectable. He was a very moral man. Lord Augustus, there is a possibility that must be considered, I believe. Perhaps Lord Edward and your Mrs Walsh were secretly married?"

"But why in secret?" But he knew the answer at once. "Because his father would not have countenanced the match, of course. He would have expected his sons to marry into the nobility. But—"

Realisation struck him like a bolt of lightning, and he saw from Merton's face that he understood the implications, too.

"If that is so, then Ned is the heir to the dukedom. He is the Marquess of Darrowstone."

16: Churlswade

Gus's burst of excitement subsided at once. "No, it is impossible," he said firmly. "Ned cannot be the heir, and the marriage cannot be legal, for why would the duke be looking for a wife himself in such a case? No, we must be mistaken on that point. Perhaps he promised to marry her, but was called away to the Peninsula in a hurry? There would have been no time to call the banns, or to obtain a special licence from London."

"But a common licence is much easier to obtain," Merton said. "A man in a hurry might achieve his object and be married within a day, I should imagine. Even here in the depths of Northumberland, there must be a bishop within a few hours' ride. And I cannot believe that Lord Edward would leave a lady possibly carrying the heir to a dukedom without ensuring that the marriage was legal. He could not depend on returning soon enough to ensure the child's legitimacy. The risk would be too great. There is another possibility… but no, that cannot be."

"What do you mean?"

"No, no, I am mistaken, I am sure."

He looked so uncomfortable, and that was so uncharacteristic of the man, that Gus was alarmed. "You had better tell me at once what is in your mind, Merton," he said grimly. "Do not make me choke it out of you."

"Only this," he said, spreading his hands helplessly. "One possible explanation is that Ned is not Lord Edward's son at all, but Mrs Walsh is claiming he is to obtain shelter from the duke."

"She is lying, you mean," he said coldly, getting to his feet and kicking the log again, which disintegrated under his boot. With a huff of annoyance, he pulled another log from the basket and hurled it at the fire, which collapsed almost to embers under the onslaught.

Was it possible? How well did he know Mrs Walsh anyway? All he knew of her was what she had told him herself, and his own observations. Could he have been deceived in her?

"My instinct is to believe her," he said slowly, considering this new idea. "She appears to be so artless and sincere, it would be a cynical man indeed who would look for deceit. And yet... I know nothing of her. We have no common acquaintance, she has no kin, no one who could vouch for her honesty. Her history may be entirely fabricated for all I know. It is not a strong foundation for marriage, is it? I could not possibly marry her, knowing so little of her. I do not even know her name!" he said, horrified. "She calls herself Mrs Edward Walsh, but there is no Edward Walsh that I have found. Who then is she?"

"Then your task is clear," Merton said. "You must go to this town where she lived and see what may be found out."

~~~~~

Gus made no attempt to sleep that night, for he was quite certain that it would elude him. He sat in his rather shabby room, with its worn furnishings and creaking door, and thought of nothing but Mrs Walsh. Who was she? It was a puzzle indeed. Even if he could uncover the truth about her, how could he marry her? And especially so if she had not been married to Ned's father. He came back to Merton's words: *'It is a stain that no subsequent marriage can cleanse.'*

If only Connie were there! She was not clever, and her education, although solid, had not improved her mind above the commonplace for her station, but she understood people as no one else did. She, more than anyone, could advise him. So he wrapped himself in his robe and went back down to the parlour, coaxed the fire back to life, and sat down with his writing box and a single candelabra to pour his heart out to Connie. All his fears and hopes, his confusion and uncertainties sprawled over five sheets of paper. For an hour or more, he dipped his pen in the ink, wrote, dipped and wrote again, without ceasing. Then, exhausted and despairing, he threw himself into a chair and allowed the ever-changing flames in the hearth to mesmerise him into sleep.

He woke to Merton's concerned face bending over him. Merton was as immaculately dressed as always. He was never ostentatious, yet he never had so much as a single fold of his cravat out of place, even though he had no valet.

"Morning already?" Gus murmured, trying to get his eyes to stay open.

"And has been for some time, my lord. Wait, let me send for coffee." A few steps, the click of the door, a murmured instruction to a servant. Gus closed his eyes again.

The coffee helped a little, although he still felt as if he had been sleeping under a hedge. His mouth was dry, his head was heavy and his eyes would keep closing of their own accord.

"Should you like to go back to bed for an hour or two?" Merton said. "We can visit this house of Harcourt's this afternoon."

"No, I shall be better once I have washed and eaten something," Gus said, although without much conviction. "As soon as I am out in the fresh air, I shall be as right as a trivet. Damnation, but being in love is a ghastly business. Has it ever struck you, Merton?"

"Just once."

"Oh. But nothing came of it, since here you are, still single."

"Indeed. I had the misfortune to fall deeply in love with the wife of my best friend."

"You poor fellow! How did you get through it?"

"One endures," Merton said, with a wry smile. "There is no alternative."

"No, indeed, but a damnable business. Were you obliged to meet often?"

"Every day."

Gus looked up at him sharply, and understanding finally dawned. "I beg your pardon, Merton, I am abominably slow-witted this morning. You are talking, of course, of Sir Osborne Hardy's wife, who is now a widow. And you have a very pleasant house already waiting... I should have worked it out a long while ago."

"How should you, indeed?" Merton said, and his smile this time was full of warmth. "Lady Carrbridge has understood for a long time, for she always knows these things, but I trust that I managed to conceal my affection for Lady Hardy from most of the world. It would be unpardonable of me to expose her to censure on that account. A lady's reputation is a fragile thing." He clicked his tongue in annoyance. "As, of course, you are very aware just now. It is *my* turn to beg *your* pardon, my lord. How unforgivable of me to remind you of your painful situation."

"Oh, Merton, if only I could forget!" Gus burst out. "I have written at ridiculous length to Connie about it, but I know already what she will tell me, for it is exactly what you said to me last night. I must give up all thought of Mrs Walsh, and there is an end to the matter. It must be done, no matter how painful, and then... I shall follow your admirable example, Merton. I shall endure, and the grief will pass, in time."

After a modest breakfast, the two set off in search of the elusive Mr Harcourt, taking only Gus's groom with them, for he trusted no one else with Jupiter. Although Gus was not quite his usual self, the fresh air and the challenge of preventing Jupiter, in one of his rebellious moods, from kicking out at anyone who came unwarily within reach was enough to distract him out of his megrims.

Harcourt's house was not, in fact, in Churlswade at all, but according to the helpful innkeeper was no more than two miles to the south. They rode through grey, drizzling weather, passing few other travellers apart from a mail coach, which went racketing by at a great rate, horn blaring. After two miles they came to the tiny hamlet of Churslwade Cross, where three separate roads intersected. To one side was a small inn, and round about were several rows of cottages, surrounded by the usual clutter of chickens and geese, orchards laden with fruit and a few late beans dangling from their withered vines. On a small hill just beyond the hamlet stood a gibbet, its loop of rope dangling menacingly.

"Cheerful place," Carson, the groom, muttered.

Enquiries at the inn, a rundown sort of place that Gus would not have dreamt of patronising, elicited the information that the White Cottage was to be found just a short distance along the southwestern road. It was easy enough to find, for there were no other habitations nearby, although nothing could be seen of the house itself through the trees that surrounded it.

"My lord, may I make a suggestion?" Merton said. "We need not both go into the house, and it would be very informative to observe what goes on after I leave. If you creep round through the trees, you may watch the back of the house quite unseen, while Carson and I approach from the front."

"That sounds like fun, but do you need Carson too?"

"Just in case of any… difficulty, you understand. Not that I expect trouble, but it is as well to be prepared. A man with a groom is taken more seriously than a man alone."

So Gus walked Jupiter into the trees as quietly as he could and circled round to the back of the house. Loosely tying Jupiter's reins to a bush, he crept nearer until he had a clear view. The house was rather large for a cottage, having three storeys, and an extra low wing to one side, presumably the kitchen. A large barn stood to one side. There were the usual rows of vegetables, a pigpen and chicken run, and a woman in simple clothes was draping laundry over lines slung between trees. She stopped, as if listening, then went in unhurried fashion into the house. In the still air, he heard the clop of hooves on the path, and then a rat-a-tat-tat on the door knocker. Voices, followed by the clunk of a door closing, and silence. Merton had gained admission.

Five minutes later, he was out again. Gus heard his ringing *'Good day to you, sir. Good day, madam.'* Then the horses clip-clopping away, and the door closing. Silence again.

Gus waited. The woman did not return to her washing, so he waited and waited. Then, another door opened at the side of the house, out of his view. Cautiously he moved round until he had clear sight of it. The woman was there, with a man in practical working clothes, and they were having a rapid conversation while he was saddling a horse. Then, shaking his head, he mounted and rode off. The woman went back inside, and did not emerge again.

Curious, Gus crept further round to the side of the house. The building he had taken for a barn he now saw was a sizable stable block set around three sides of a large yard. Through an open door he caught sight of a very stylish carriage of a rather unusual design. Experience told him that stables of such a size could accommodate a dozen horses in comfort, or perhaps more, and he grew very interested in these two people, ordinary working folk who yet had a fancy carriage and perhaps many horses at their disposal. Creeping round to the back of the stables, out of sight of the house, he contrived by standing on a large rock to peer in through a window. He counted seven horses, two most likely for the carriage, and the others rather good riding mounts.

By the time he had made his way back to Jupiter, there were two men out working on the vegetables, and the woman was back at her washing, so he was very glad to make his escape and ride as fast as he dared back to the gibbet, where Merton and Carson awaited him.

"A man rode off on horseback," Gus said. "Rather a good horse, too, and the fellow did not look like the sort who could afford such an animal, nor the seven more in the stables, and certainly not the rather elegant carriage kept there. There are at least two other men living there, and not one of them out at work in the middle of the day."

"Ah!" Merton smiled in satisfaction. "There, you see, it was well worth your while to watch the back of the house, for all I got from the front of it were regretful shakes of the head, and two people who claimed never to have heard of Mr Harcourt, or Mr Sharp either. What sort of carriage was it, would you say?"

Gus was not as well acquainted with carriage styles as with horseflesh, but after some discussion they agreed that it was probably a light travelling carriage.

"Then it is very much as I supposed," Merton said. "Sharp — or Harcourt, perhaps — comes here by carriage with his accompanying grooms, and a valet perhaps, very much the gentleman. Here he changes into his Sharp apparel and rides off alone to Drummoor, leaving the grooms and valet behind. From here, across country, he could reach Drummoor in a day, easily. Whenever it suits him, he returns here, dresses in his finery again, collects his carriage and servants, and heads off to... somewhere. Not Galthwaite, I think, for he was seldom seen there. Probably he has a grand estate in the country, with hordes of servants, and all at Lord Carrbridge's expense. But we shall find him eventually, you may be sure of it."

"The fellow who rode off — should we not follow him? He may lead us to Sharp."

"Unlikely. I gave him a letter for Mr Harcourt, should such a person ever come to the house. Undoubtedly he has gone to the mail coach station in Churlswade to forward it to Mr Harcourt. Or Sharp. Whatever he is calling himself at the moment. It contains an invitation to visit me at High Morton, and I tried to make it enticing — a very subtle suggestion that I would maintain silence about his activities for a consideration. He will probably not bite, but one never knows. It would be a mistake to underestimate the greed of such a man. My very rough calculations suggest that he has pocketed some two hundred thousand pounds of the marquess's money over the years."

"*Two hundred thousand!*" Gus said, appalled, and even Carson whistled.

"It could easily be more," Merton said. "Once we find him, we can certainly recover some of it, anything that is in property, for instance, or held in the banks or otherwise invested. But a great deal of it has undoubtedly gone for good."

"My God!" Gus said, and Jupiter danced with alarm as his hands clenched the reins. "When I catch the villain, he will wish he had never been born!"

"Oh, the law will deal with him, make no mistake about it," Merton said grimly. "He will hang for this."

17: A Walk In The Woods

Gus had never resented so much the daily summons to the duke's presence for dinner. All he wanted to do was to mull over their discoveries with Merton, and perhaps pore over the maps to try to determine where in all the emptiness of Northern England a man like Sharp may have hidden himself. Instead, he had to don his stockings and knee breeches and make polite conversation with an irascible old man and his gaggle of hopeful duchesses.

The gaggle was rather larger than it had been. In the three days he had been away, another five candidates had appeared on the scene, and the old man was distinctly less irascible. When one of his flock glanced coyly at him from behind her fan, he pinched her arm, called her a naughty puss and cackled with glee. When another strolled by to give him all the benefit of her rather splendid figure, he raised a quizzing glass and positively ogled her. And if any of them openly flirted with him, he roared with laughter.

"Whatever is going on?" Gus whispered to Emma. "I had to talk him into this, grumbling every step of the way, and now he seems to be as lively as a song bird."

Emma rolled her eyes. "We shall be inundated with widows and old maids before long. Most unseemly. Let us hope he will make his selection soon, or settle on two or three for a more intensive regime of flirtation and ribald humour, or else the castle will burst at the seams. The poor butler! He has not seen anything like it for decades, I daresay. Did you know that Bedford is some kind of poor relation to the duke? In fact, all the servants in the keep are poor relations, or…" She lowered her voice to a whisper. "*Children*. You know what kind I mean. But have you ever heard of anything so bizarre? One is always beset with poor relations, but one does not engage them to wait at table."

"I daresay it is a form of charity," Gus said, and then, with a pang of sorrow, thought at once of Mrs Walsh, whom the duke had also described as *'a charity case'*. But the information confirmed that she was no poor relation, or she too would be donning her apron to wait on the duke.

The meal was slower than usual, for the ladies liked to remark upon every dish, which would be passed around the table for comment, providing each with an opportunity for boasting about the superiority of her cook, or the tenderness of the game from her own coveys. The duke was unimpressed, but he chortled with delight at every evidence of the competition raging between them.

When the ladies had finally been prevailed upon to withdraw — "Go on, get out, the lot of you, and let the men talk about important matters," he said genially — the duke finally turned to Gus.

"You see how I am situated, Marford. You must not go off and leave me to the mercy of these avaricious women again, do you hear? I had only Forbes to protect me, and he is too terrified of them to be of the least use. Whereas a great tall fellow like you can keep them at bay easily enough, I should wager."

"Should you like me to?" Gus said. "I daresay with a couple of footmen, I can clear them out of the castle in no time at all. Then you could be comfortable again. You have only to give the word."

The duke grunted. "Hmpf. Well. I suppose they are not doing any harm. What do you think of them, eh? One or two pretty ones amongst them, would you not say? And one or two that would be amusing to play with."

"Duke, you are choosing a future duchess and the mother of the next duke, not a toy. And it matters not a whit what I may think of any of them. You must make your own choice."

"Eh! How boring you are, Marford. As bad as Forbes there. He will not give an opinion, either. But how then am I to choose, hmm? They all have their good points and their bad points, and there is not one that seems to be any better than any of the others."

"Then settle it some other way," Gus said, impatiently. "Let them turn over cards — first to produce an ace wins you. Or throw dice. Or… let me see, hold an archery competition or some such, and marry the winner. Lots of ways to decide, if they really are all the same to you."

The duke huffed, and pretended to be annoyed but his heart was not in it, and Gus suddenly realised the reason — the wheeled chair was nowhere in sight. The duke's gout must be very much improved, and his mood with it, just as Emma had foretold.

"So was your expedition successful, Marford? Your note was very cryptic — something about your agent, but in my experience, one does not go chasing round after one's agent, one summons him and tells him to explain himself."

"Ah, if only we could," Gus said. He explained the bones of it, and the duke nodded and soon lost interest.

"Well, well. Unpleasant, but the fellow cannot run for ever," he said vaguely. "What about your business, Forbes? Have you satisfied yourself yet of my ownership of the stud?"

"The matter is still under consideration, Duke, but there is a question I would ask you, if I may."

"You may ask," the duke said. "I may not answer, but you may ask." And he laughed mirthlessly.

"It seems that quite large sums of money were made over to the Marquess of Darrowstone by Lord Edward Winfell. That seems… surprising, for the younger son to subsidise the older."

"What, that Edward was so much richer than Henry, you mean? The money came from their mother, who was a very wealthy woman by the end of her life. Always had a good dowry, but she inherited some money and there were some excellent investments… when she died, the money was to be divided amongst her unmarried daughters and any surviving sons, other than the eldest, since he was well provided for. By then, the girls were all settled, George was gone, so Edward got the lot, the lucky fellow. Well, well, so he was funding Henry, was he? That was like him — always a generous soul. He would not have seen his brother go short. But what has that to say to anything? It has nothing to do with the stud."

"It might have," Willerton-Forbes said, his voice rising to a nervous pitch. "I have not yet tallied all the dates precisely, but it is possible that Lord Edward's money paid for the purchase of the horses, in which case he may properly be said to own them."

"And since he is dead, then all his property reverts to me and I own them," the duke said, chuckling. "You are chasing your tail, Forbes. Chasing your tail."

"Did Lord Edward leave a will, Duke?" Willerton-Forbes's voice was a mere squeak.

There was a long silence. The duke rose to his feet, towering over the two men as they jumped up from their seats. "Let us rejoin the ladies," he said, before sweeping majestically from the room.

And so they moved into the interminably dull part of the evening. Gus was drawn into a game of cassino, and was heartily glad that Humphrey was not there to observe his embarrassingly bad play. He tried his best to concentrate, but his thoughts circled endlessly round this new information. If Lord Edward had been a wealthy man, he would surely have left his wife well provided for. Even if they were not married, he would have made provision for her. Yet Mrs Walsh lived on the charity of the duke. It was a mystery, and he could make nothing of it.

As soon as they returned to their parlour, Willerton-Forbes poured brandy with shaking hands.

"Well, I am in the suds now, and no mistake," he said. "I am tolerably sure that Lord Edward funded all those horses at the stud, and therefore has a claim to them, but unless I have sight of the will I cannot be sure."

"How would the will help?" Gus said, his brain too full of other thoughts to make sense of it.

"I am trying to establish the intent behind the transfer of money," Willerton-Forbes said. "If it was a personal gift, freely offered with no preconditions, then the marquess was free to spend it as he chose. But if it was a loan, or an investment, that would be a different matter."

"But Lady Darrowstone has papers showing ownership of the horses in her late husband's name, and he left everything to her."

"That confuses the issue, certainly, but it is not definitive. The stud itself is composed of more than the horses. There is the land upon which it is situated, the buildings, the equipment and grooms... it is not a simple matter of horses. Tomorrow I shall visit the stud to examine the books there, and see if I may tally the payment from Lord Edward with the purchase of specific horses.

And if, as I expect, I find that it is so, then I must brave the lion's den once more and ask for sight of Lord Edward's will."

Gus laughed. "I wish you good fortune, and offer you my support on the occasion, for I should very much like to see the will myself, if there is one. One has to wonder why the duke is so reluctant to show you." Was it, perhaps, because it mentioned Ned in some way? But no, Lord Edward would have known nothing of Ned. But perhaps he had mentioned Mrs Walsh. Surely he would have made provision for her?

"Indeed," the lawyer said, the brandy glass pausing on its way to his lips. "But I daresay there are mistresses and love children mentioned in the will, and that is why the duke is so secretive about it." He looked conscious for a moment. "And if it should happen that I am granted sight of the will, I shall be sure to convey any information of *particular* interest to you."

He looked meaningfully at Gus, who could not pretend to misunderstand him.

"Your friend Edgerton is a dreadful rattle," the lawyer said, with a slight smile. "He has drawn certain conclusions about your little lady friend and her child. So I shall take careful note of any bequests to mistresses. As to your offer to accompany me, I should be most grateful."

"Excellent," Gus said, trying for a light tone, although his heart sank at the mention of mistresses. "For I should very much like to hear his response. We had better take care there are no ladies present."

"I fervently wish that *I* need not be present," Willerton-Forbes said, refilling his brandy glass. "Indeed, I may very well need to be extremely drunk before I have the courage to make my request."

"Good heavens, man, he is only a duke," Gus said, amused. "He is nothing to be afraid of. He will shout and bluster and insult you and your entire line of ancestors, but in the end he will do what is right. Myself, I should be more alarmed to cross Lady Darrowstone, or almost any of the ladies now assaulting the duke. A lady makes a far more formidable enemy, I assure you. They never, ever forget."

~~~~~

Until she heard Ned's squeal of delight from upstairs, where he had stationed himself to watch for the first sighting, followed by the thump of his feet on the stairs, Amaryllis had not dared to hope that Gus would come back to see them. Each time he went away she became convinced that he was gone for good. Each time he visited she was sure that he would be recalled to London the very next day and she would see him no more. For herself, it was of no consequence, but Ned would feel the separation acutely. It was for her child's feelings that she worried. Or so she told herself. And if a little voice in her head whispered that she looked forward to Gus's visits every bit as much as Ned, she suppressed it firmly.

Her fears were unfounded, for he came with hugs for Ned and smiles for herself, and the glow of happiness inside her burned bright. She could not help smiling back at him, and could only hope she was not betraying an unbecoming warmth in her manner. That would never do! She was right to promote his friendship with Ned, but for herself she must keep her distance and offer him no encouragement. A difficult path to tread. Yet when he had swept Ned into his arms, and kissed the top of his head, he had looked up at her with such a light in his eyes that she had blushed and looked away.

For a while Ned monopolised him, and the talk was all of tin soldiers. The boy's excitement made them all laugh, and even Maggie smiled over her sewing in the corner.

After a while, when the discussion of archery and bows turned to talk of yews, Ned cried, "There is one in the forest! Mama, may I show Gus the yew tree?"

"Perhaps we might all go?" he said. "It is a pleasant day for a walk."

She agreed to it, and Maggie fetched bonnets and cloaks. The air was cool under the trees, and damp still, after the recent rain, but it was not unpleasant. At first Ned ran ahead, and Gus, with his long legs, strode after him, with Amaryllis and Maggie some distance behind. But after the yew tree had been admired, and the discussion of bows exhausted, it was Maggie who went ahead with the child, and Gus dawdled behind with Amaryllis. She was not uncomfortable, though, for even though they lapsed into silence often, they were restful pauses, as between friends who knew each other well enough not to chatter on. If she asked him a question, he answered readily enough, but otherwise he said little.

"How is his grace?" she said.

"Very well," he said, then paused, with a quick glance at her. "Have you heard? He is... planning to marry again. Or so he says, although I am not sure how serious he is, or whether he is just amusing himself."

"I had heard a rumour to that effect," she said. "He is a good age to be considering matrimony, but why not, when there is nothing but a touch of gout afflicting him? I wish him very happy, I am sure."

Again, the sideways glance. "One can understand his problem. Now that he has no heir—"

"He has an heir," she said, amused. "The duke does not like the present heir, that is all. But that is the nature of inherited titles, is it not? Sometimes unexpected jumps occur."

"It is undignified in a man of his age to be scrambling for a wife," Gus said.

"You disapprove? Yet it shows that he takes his position and its responsibilities seriously. If he feels his heir is unsuitable, it is up to him to do something about it."

"That does not mean rushing to produce a new heir. He could undertake to instruct the one he has, take an interest in him and teach him the proper way for a duke to behave. That is how the process is meant to work in a hereditary system. My brother found the burden of the marquessate onerous even after one and twenty years of training for the role. How much more difficult must it be without such training. I have heard recently of two cases where a man came into a title and fortune unexpectedly, and found the change something of a challenge. Better by far to know something of the necessary responsibilities before the need to undertake them."

"If a man has been given sound principles and brought up in proper Christian humility, he should have no difficulty adapting to any change in his circumstances," she said gravely.

"You are correct, of course," he said. "But still I feel it is better for a man to mingle with his own kind beforehand, wherever possible, and grow accustomed to the manners and expectations of the peerage."

"The manners of the peerage ought to be no different from the manners of the gentry," she said softly. "A gentleman is still a gentleman."

"In the broadest sense, that is true," he said, and he was so earnest that she was tempted to smile. "But there are subtleties and nuances... it is not easy. Every society has its own customs and habits, in manner of dress or speech or demeanour. When I walk into an inn, the innkeeper knows at once that I will want the best parlour, several dishes at dinner and a decent claret. I do not have to tell him that, he understands it from my clothes, the way I speak, even the way I walk. And when I go to London, I know exactly how to behave, whether it be dancing at Almacks or playing cards with the Prince of Wales or simply walking down Bond Street, because I have been brought up amongst others who move in those circles. If I were to take *you* to London, Mrs Walsh—" He stopped, and turned to face her, laughing. "No, I do believe *you* would be perfectly at your ease there, and would no more fret over the right way to dress your hair for an evening at Carlton House than my sister would. But for those less composed than you, like Mr Richard Winfell, the duke's heir presumptive, it would be the greatest trial, I assure you. I have seen how such people go on in such society, how their nervousness makes them silent or clumsy or, even worse, gabble unstoppably and behave in the gauchest manner. I have also seen how society derides them for their ignorance. I do not wish it on anyone."

At that moment, Ned came running back towards them, shrieking, and she had no opportunity to frame a response. She was not entirely convinced by Gus's argument, but at least she understood a little better his concern about Ned's isolation. And deep in her heart, where it would warm her through many a lonely hour to come, she buried his charming compliment — that *she* could move in the highest circles. And for the first time she wondered, as she had never dared to before, how it would feel to be part of that world, part of the *ton* and think nothing of meeting the Prince of Wales.

18: A Will

There was a letter from Connie awaiting Gus when he returned from his visit to Mrs Walsh and Ned, his head still in the clouds. So much for his joyous reunion with his friends. For a short time, he had been able to set aside all his confused thoughts about marriage and mistresses and children born out of wedlock, and simply enjoy being with her. Walking by her side through the woods, the newly fallen leaves crisp under their feet and the air sharp with the tang of fallen berries, he had been perfectly content. Now, turning Connie's letter over and over in his hands, her familiar hand a little more irregular than usual, all his fears and worries flooded back in like a storm.

He broke the seal with trepidation.

'My poor, dear Gus, what a coil you are in! I am so distressed by all this, you cannot imagine. Oh pray forgive the blotches on the page, for I cannot stop crying. Francis and I have gone over it and over it, but we cannot see a way round it. If this woman truly has a child outside wedlock, then we can have nothing to do with her, or with you, if you insist on allying yourself with her, not officially. Such a person has cast herself outside all good society, and those who befriend her must suffer the same penalty. Francis would not cut you off, naturally, for you are his brother and very dear to all of us, no matter what, and we would still see you privately, but we could not acknowledge you publicly. So you must choose, Gus dear, either this

woman or your position in society, and whatever you decide will be irrevocable and final. Oh my dear, choose carefully! You must be absolutely sure what you are about before you take this step. Your heartbroken sister-in-law, Connie."

It was as he had expected, so he was not excessively disappointed. And Carrbridge would not cut him off — that was an important consideration. He would still have money to live on, and would not be destitute. He still had the choice if he wished it.

But to see his worst fears spread out on the page in raw, unblinking honesty, the very words sprinkled with Connie's hot tears, was almost more than he could bear. Bear it he must, however. Like Merton, he must endure, for he knew what he had to do.

'My dear Connie, pray do not distress yourself. I have no intention of marrying Mrs Walsh under such circumstances. Whatever my feelings may be, you must not imagine me so selfish as to marry a woman who has thrown away her reputation, nor could I besmirch the good name of the Marford family by so doing. I am not so lost to all propriety as to be able to set it at nought for the purpose of fulfilling my own hopes and wishes. Merton is of the opinion that there may have been a secret marriage, which would render the match eligible, but whatever the truth of the matter, I intend to find it out and will take no final step until I am sure of all the circumstances. Your affectionate brother-in-law, Gus.'

And then, with heavy heart, he summoned a footman to take the letter directly to the post office before his resolve weakened and he changed his mind. The footman was just leaving when another arrived to announce Merton.

"Ah, I see you have received your missive from Lady Carrbridge," Merton said, observing the opened sheet on the table. "I have had a matching one from Lord Carrbridge — very distressed, hopes you will not do it but will continue to support you regardless. I daresay her ladyship gave you the same story?"

"Yes, with ink blots all over the page where her tears had fallen," Gus said. "As if I would do anything to distress them so. I have just written to tell Connie so."

"Ah," Merton said, sitting down in a chair and neatly crossing his ankles. "Then you will not offer for Mrs Walsh? At least until we have determined her precise circumstances?"

"I will not," Gus said. "It would be foolish of me to be so lost in love that I would give up everything for a woman I barely know. My feelings on the matter are still very unsettled. I enjoy her company above that of any other person, but at present I am still getting to know her."

"It is a relief to hear you say so," Merton said. "I must tell you that, in my capacity as adviser to Lord Carrbridge, I shall strenuously represent to him the foolishness of providing you with enough money to live upon in such a circumstance. Rather than assuring you of his support, he should be threatening to cut you off without a penny, for it is the surest way to guarantee your compliance. You would never drag Mrs Walsh into a life of poverty, after all."

"That is very true," Gus said, sitting down abruptly. "But it is a damnable business, Merton, not *knowing* whether she is an eligible match for me or not. I must *know*, one way or the other."

"Have you considered asking the lady, openly?" Merton said gently.

"How can I?" Gus burst out. "What words could possibly frame such a question? *Forgive me for prying, madam, but I must know whether you are respectable enough for me to consider offering for you.*"

"Indeed, it is very awkward," Merton said. "Perhaps the duke—?"

Gus shook his head. "He will tell me nothing about her, and has even warned me away from her."

"That is interesting," Merton said, steepling his hands.

"Is it? What do you read from that? Is it a good sign or a bad one, do you think?"

"I would say bad. If she had been married to Lord Edward and the boy is the legitimate heir, the duke can have no conceivable reason to keep her secret or to warn you away from her."

"He might not want me to marry her and take the boy away from here," Gus hazarded.

"But why? The child will always be his heir, that cannot be changed. Of course, if he is a natural son, then the duke may see her as a scheming woman and be warning you away from kindness. Is it possible she was the duke's mistress at one time? No, I suppose not. The whole story about the soldier husband and living in Drifford is too detailed to be invented out of whole cloth. It is too puzzling, but my instincts tell me there is something unsavoury about the whole business."

The door opened, and Willerton-Forbes crept in, looking so pale and dejected that Gus cried out, "My dear fellow, whatever is the matter? Are you ill? You look dreadful. Merton, some brandy, if you please. Here, my friend, sit down. Thank you, Merton. Here, drink, my good fellow."

"Thank you, I am quite well, but… I have been to see the duke."

"You were to take me with you," Gus said. "Whatever possessed you to go alone?"

"He sent for me!" the lawyer said, waving his hands helplessly. "What could I do? It would hardly do to keep a duke waiting, and you were nowhere to be found. But you were right, my lord. You said he would do the right thing, and so he did. He had the will out waiting for me, and allowed me to read it there and then."

"Excellent!" Gus said. "And what did it say?"

"I cannot answer you!"

Gus sat down abruptly. "Cannot?"

"Cannot!" Willerton-Forbes said, waving his arms so wildly that Merton had to swoop in to rescue the brandy. "I am sworn to secrecy... on the *Bible*, my lord. So I *cannot* tell you anything, even though—" He stopped and put his hands over his mouth, as if willing the words not to spill out. "He made me swear not to tell *you* in particular," he whispered.

"But why—?" Gus began, but Merton waved him to silence.

"What were his grace's *exact* words?"

"Oh!" The lawyer brightened. "You are very clever, Mr Merton. Have you ever thought of taking up a career in the law? You are quite right, I am not to *tell* anyone. Tell, not divulge or reveal." He stood up with a slight smile on his face, and, to Gus's surprise, removed his coat and hung it over the back of his chair. "I was permitted to make a few notes, for accuracy in quoting, you understand. I believe... I will go outside for a breath of air. I shall be back directly."

And so doing, he left the room.

"What was all that about?" Gus said. Merton smiled and began sifting through the pockets of the lawyer's coat. "Hoy, what are you doing?"

Merton pulled out a sheaf of papers, and waved them triumphantly aloft. "He is not *telling* us, you see? Here, there are six pages. You take those three. Oh! Drifford — this must be her! A codecil, apparently. *'To Mr Joseph Cordwainer and Miss Amaryllis Cordwainer of Old Drifford House, Drifford, Northumberland, the sum of—'"*

Gus snatched the page from him. "Amaryllis," he said, enchanted. "Her name is Amaryllis."

He swirled the name around in his mind, beaming with delight, while Merton skimmed through the rest of the pages before Willerton-Forbes returned, nervously, and took up his coat. "I shall be in my room, if anyone is looking for me," he said, before disappearing.

"Are you all right?" Merton said.

"Oh, yes," Gus said, smiling beatifically at him.

"Sit," Merton said, sternly. "Sit down and let me list all the reasons why you should be concerned."

Immediately Gus deflated. "Concerned?" he said in a whisper. Then he realised. "They were not married. She was Miss Cordwainer. They could not have been married."

"Not at that point, no," Merton said placidly.

Gus flared to optimism.

"Now, you must not get your hopes up," Merton said severely. "But look at the dates — the will was written several years before Lord Edward's death, and the codecil is dated... hmm, perhaps five months before his death. When did he leave for the Peninsula?"

"Three months before he died."

"Ah. So he meets her — somehow — and gets to know her well enough to leave money to her father and her. A goodish sum, too — one thousand pounds. That is no trifling amount."

"If she was his mistress..." Gus began.

"Then she would not have been living in her father's house, and the bequest would not have included her father. No, this sounds to me like simple charity, a wish to make life better for two gentlefolk sliding into poverty. Her father was a retired clergyman, and probably had next to nothing to live on."

"He was ill for many years, too," Gus said. "There would have been doctors' fees, medicines..."

"Indeed. So Lord Edward wanted to make their lives better, but I do not think there was any very strong attachment then. But perhaps before he left for the Peninsula they got to know each other better."

Gus frowned. "So... two months later he received his orders, their feelings overwhelmed them—"

"But no," Merton said. "Again I remember Sir Osborne's opinion of Lord Edward as a most upright man. Perhaps it went like this... two months later he received his orders and secretly married her."

Gus was silent for a long time. Then he huffed out a long breath. "It is possible. Anything is possible. Except... surely he would have made another will? I know my brothers all did so before they married."

"If the marriage was secret, then perhaps the new will was kept secret, too, to avoid revealing the marriage. Who knows?"

"Hmm. It is a stretch, Merton. But how might one uncover the truth?"

"We have not officially seen the will, so we are not supposed to know any of this. That means that you cannot ask the duke about it, nor can you press the lady for more details without revealing the source of your information. What we *can* do is to go to Drifford and make enquiries. We have a name now, and an address. We know there was a baptism, and there might have been a marriage, both of which would have been written into the parish register."

"That is true," Gus said. "If there was a marriage, the proof of it will be recorded."

"Indeed. So tomorrow let us go to Drifford and see what we may find out there. It is a small town, and there must be someone who remembers Miss Cordwainer."

With a long breath, Gus sat back in his chair. "Thank you, Merton. You are very good."

He gave one of his slight smiles. "But you must be prepared for any outcome. I have a feeling there is still too much we do not know."

"Yes. I understand. Thank you." Merton was so serious that Gus was subdued, but inside him a tiny flame of hope had been lit and refused to be extinguished.

~~~~~

Amaryllis was restless. She had enjoyed the morning, for what could be more pleasant than a walk through the woods on a crisp autumn day with a gentleman of quality, someone she could talk to as she had not talked to anyone since... well, since dear Papa had finally left her alone in the world. Gus reminded her in so many ways of Papa — his earnest manner, his delight in playing with Ned, careless of his own dignity, and his gentleness. How her heart responded to that gentleness! It was as if she had been walking in the desert these past long years, and now Gus was water to drink and cool shade to refresh her spirit.

And yet in other ways, Gus was nothing like Papa. The way he looked at her, those dark eyes alight with— But no, she must not put a word to it. If she gave it no name, that emotion burning in his eyes, there would be no need to address the question of what it was that he felt. And yet, it reminded her so much of Edward. He, too, had looked at her in just that way, his face aglow, his affection shining. Affection. Yes, let it be affection. Why should a man like Gus not feel affection for her, just as he felt affection for Ned, and for his horse? That was better. She was content to let it be affection, the simple friendship of a man away from home, perhaps a little lonely, towards a stranger who crossed his path.

Yet she was uneasy. He had walked out of her life once, perhaps realising the inequality between them and acknowledging that there could be no future to their friendship. She had been relieved at first, but Ned's distress had led her to bring Gus back into their lives. Now she was beginning to regret it. For Ned, it was wonderful, and perhaps for her too, but for Gus? It was selfish of her to keep him dangling, and if he was truly— No, she must not name it. But perhaps his visits were a source of great pain to him, or would be so when the inevitable separation should occur.

What should she do? Her restless spirits drove her out of doors, to the quiet part of the castle gardens, and somehow her steps led her to the arbour where she had sat with Gus only a few days earlier. It was cool out of doors, but there was no wind or dampness in the air, which often blew in from the sea. So she sat, removing her bonnet so that she could turn her face up to the sun, eyes closed, savouring its warm touch. So much of her life was spent indoors. Even when she went for her daily walk, it was usually into the woods, where there was little danger of meeting anyone. But today, the sun was a welcome companion.

She heard his footsteps on the gravel path. Did she know it was him, or was that just her fanciful mind playing tricks? But when she opened her eyes, there he was. He saw her, stopped, bowed.

"I beg your pardon, Mrs Walsh. I intrude. Let me withdraw at once."

"There is no need, Lord Augustus. Pray, sit down. I should be glad of some conversation with you. There is a matter we must discuss, I believe."

A hesitation. Then a firm nod. "Of course, if it please you, although... you do not have your maid with you?"

That made her smile. "A chaperon? It is hardly necessary."

"Is it not?" he said. Oh, so serious! But he sat beside her, and removed his hat and gloves. "You are well? The long walk this morning did not fatigue you?"

"Not at all, and I am perfectly well, I thank you. My lord, will you forgive me if I speak plainly to you?"

"Oh, please do! I have no skill in interpreting subtlety, so if you wish to tell me something, you will have to say it in the simplest terms."

She smiled again, for it was very much how she would have described him herself. "I am a selfish creature, my lord, and have taken advantage of your generosity abominably. First, in your too kind gift of a pianoforte, which I should not have accepted but I delight in it every day, and cannot regret that."

"Then I cannot regret it either," he said at once. "We need have no further discussion of the pianoforte."

She laughed. "Very well. But my second selfishness we must discuss, I believe." Oh, how hard it was to speak so to him! She could not look him in the eye, so she gazed down at her hands resting in her lap instead. "For Ned's sake, I asked you to visit us, and you have very kindly done as I asked. But..." She bit her lip, wondering just how to express her thoughts.

"But?" he said gently. "But that is an act which you *do* regret, is that what you are trying to tell me?"

"Not for Ned's sake, certainly. For him, your company has been everything I could have wished, and so good for him! But I am not sure that… that these meetings are good for *you*, my lord."

There! She had said it, and let him think her brazen if he would. It hardly mattered.

"Mrs Walsh," he said, in the gentlest tone, "Ned's company — and *yours* — have given me the greatest imaginable happiness. For myself, I have no regrets on that score. But if *you* have concerns on that head… if *your* mind would be eased by my absence, then you have only to say the word and you will never see me again, I promise. *Your* comfort is all my concern."

She looked up then, but what she saw on his face set her cheeks aflame, and she lowered her gaze at once. *Love…* let it be given its true name. In his dark eyes, she saw his unquestioned love shining down on her.

While she was composing herself and trying to frame a reply, he reached across and and took her hand in his, gently lifting it to his lips, so that she hardly knew where to look.

"Mrs Walsh, may I take the liberty of speaking plainly with you also?" Her heart pitter-pattered in sudden fear. Whatever was he about to say? "Will you tell me of your husband?"

Her head shot up. "My *husband?*" Panic washed over her. She tried to speak calmly, but it was so difficult. "There is nothing to tell. My husband was a soldier, he went to the Peninsula just after we married and died there. What else is there to say?"

"His name, for one thing," he said. "For there was no Edward Walsh at the Drifford army camp."

Her stomach clenched in fear. "You asked?"

"Why should I not?" he said gently. "Forgive me, but I know so little of you, and I must, if in the future— No, let me not say too much. But you must be aware that… I wish to know everything about you, everything of importance in your life, and your husband is such a significant part of that. I should like to know something of him."

She jumped to her feet, and now her fear told her what she had to do. "You are impertinent, my lord. There is no *future* — there cannot be! Perhaps it is best if you do not see Ned again."

He rose too, his jaw set. His face worked, as if he were trying to speak, but no sound emerged. Snatching up his hat and gloves, he strode away.

She collapsed back to the seat and burst into tears.

19: Love And Marriage

Gus stormed back to the castle, to his place of refuge in troubled times, the stables. Jupiter whickered happily to see him, and the matched pair of bays for the curricle nosed his coat hopefully.

"*You* will never tell me to go away, will you?" he said, burying his face in Jupiter's mane. "You will still be my friend no matter what happens. You have no secrets, nothing in your nature is hidden away or mysterious, waiting to catch me out. I wish I had never come here, truly I do. I should have asked Connie to find me a pleasant little heiress, then I could have been happy and rich, like Reggie and Humphrey, and not had to worry about who Amaryllis is and whether I can possibly offer for her, and whether she would accept me anyway." He laughed mirthlessly, causing Jupiter to lurch away from him. "But I have an answer to that, do I not? Damnation! Hellfire and damnation, I wish I had never met her!"

But even his horses could not soothe his ruffled mind, churned as it was by too many moments of elation or despair over the last days, and eventually the castle clock struck the hour. It was time to face the duke and his bevy of fluttering attendants, and try to pretend that his life had not just been torn apart.

He strode through the empty corridors, scattering a cluster of footmen who pressed themselves to the walls hastily when they saw his scowling face. At his parlour, his mood was not improved by finding Merton and Edgerton relaxing there, cards and brandy to hand.

"Damnation, Edgerton, where have you been?" he growled. "I have not seen you for an age."

"Oh, here and there. You know me."

"Indeed I do. Did you inflict your presence on Mrs Walsh while I was away?"

Edgerton raised two hands in surrender. "As if I would! The lady is all yours, Marford. She is too demure for me by half. I like my ladies a little more... um, lively, shall we say. Merton, what is your taste? How do you like your women?"

"I like my women to be ladies," Merton said primly.

"Hmpf. How dull," Edgerton said. "But I can give you ladies, if you like. Would you like to dine with me tonight? You must be heartily sick of inn food."

Merton eyed him consideringly. "I confess that inn dinners soon lose their appeal, and if you can offer me some interesting company..."

Edgerton gave a bark of laughter. "Oh, very interesting company. Excellent. Marford, you had better get moving. Willett was looking for you some time ago. Must not keep your valet waiting, you know. Or the duke, come to that."

Gus sighed. "I could wish the duke at the devil tonight, but I must go, I suppose. I wish you could go in my place, Edgerton, and Merton too. You would enjoy it far more than I will."

"You look thoroughly blue-devilled," Edgerton said. "Has she thrown you over, your pretty widow?"

With a huff of annoyance, Gus stamped out of the room. Willett fussed over him even more than usual, so he was late reaching the keep. It hardly mattered, for the drawing room was in uproar, with even more ladies present. Gus made his greetings to the duke, then retreated to a dark corner where he could hope to escape observation and nurse his misery. He could hardly believe how his fortunes had changed. But a few hours ago, he had enjoyed that idyllic walk through the woods with Mrs Walsh — *Amaryllis!* Such a perfect name for her — and now it was all over. She had shut him out, and he would never see her again. How could he bear it? And how had a tiny flame of admiration turned into this great bonfire of desolate love, so intense that it was burning him up from the inside out?

Was it always like this? Did Carrbridge feel this way for Connie, or Reggie for Robinia? And, a lowering thought — did Amaryllis feel this way for her dead husband? Was that why she could so easily summon Gus or send him away, because she felt nothing at all for him? That should make him feel better, for at least she would feel no pain at their separation, but somehow it did not. For if she still loved her husband, then her suffering was deeper and more unending, and only death and the joyful reunion in the afterlife could relieve it.

"Such foolishness!" said a voice at his ear, startling him back to his surroundings. "Oh dear, you look like the ashes of yesterday's fire, Gus. Whatever is the matter?"

"Nothing of significance, Emma," he said, for what else could he say? *'All joy is over, my hopes are dashed to pieces and my life is meaningless and empty.'* For him the world had ended, but to everyone else nothing of significance had occurred. A foolish man with foolish dreams had been brought back to reality, that was all. It happened every day, in a thousand towns up and down the kingdom, as a thousand young men glumly faced a future without the one woman who brightened their lives. Then, he noted what she had said. "What foolishness?"

"Maria has been trying to convince the duke to hold a ball. He would dance with all the ladies, each would have her chance to entice him, then he would make his choice before supper. Such a nonsensical idea, as he told her at once, of course. But now he has agreed to the enticement part of it. Each one who wishes to marry him will have five minutes to draw him in — or it may be six, I do not know. However long his hourglass runs, in any event. She may sing or dance or recite, as she pleases. Five minutes! Or even six! It is the height of absurdity, and so I have told him. If he insists upon it, I shall leave tomorrow and he may bandage his own feet, for all I care!"

But Gus could see the tears trembling on her lashes. "Oh, Emma! That is a foolish notion indeed! What a way to choose a duchess!"

"Will you tell him so? Perhaps he may listen to you."

Gus laughed at that. "I have not the slightest influence over him, but I will certainly represent to him the lunacy of the idea. And how insulting to the ladies, to be reduced to the level of circus performers."

"That is all we have ever been to him," she said. "And I suspect he has already made his choice, no matter what happens tomorrow night. He has been ogling Rachel Medhurst for days. It is too bad of him, when we have had such cosy little chats together over the bandages. He is such a delightful man, Gus, when you remove him from all the sycophants, and treat him as if he were nobody in particular. And I thought he enjoyed *my* company too. But I will not stay here to be laughed at and rejected. If he does not value me as he ought, then he does not deserve me!"

Gus managed to sit between Emma and Willerton-Forbes, and a more silent trio would be hard to envisage. While the duke's flock of admirers chattered and laughed and vied with each other to amuse him, the three at the other end of the table were sunk in their own thoughts. Gus had his own reasons for that, and he knew Emma's, but he wondered quite what was eating away at the lawyer, who toyed with his food and even left his wine untouched. Only when the covers were removed, the ladies had left and the port was set on the table did Willerton-Forbes emerge from his abstraction.

"Your grace," he said, almost before the door was closed behind the servants, "I have resolved the issue of the ownership of the stud to my own satisfaction."

The duke grunted, poured some port and slid the decanter down the table, then grunted again. "I can tell by your face that it will not be to *my* satisfaction. But we can speak of this some other time. It is nothing to do with *him*." He gestured with his wine glass at Gus.

"With the greatest respect, your grace, but this matter does indeed concern Lord Augustus."

"It does not, but he has you in his pocket, so if I exclude him now you will find some way to tell him all. Go on, then, have your say."

Willerton-Forbes coughed, then took a deep breath. "I find that the stud comprises two parts. The first part is the land upon which the stud farm itself rests, and all the buildings thereon, and this part is owned by your grace, as a portion of the Castle Morton estate. The second part is the collection of horses, being stallions, mares, foals, yearlings and older horses residing in the stables and paddocks, and this part was owned by Lord Edward Winfell, who loaned the money for the purchase of each horse to his brother. This split ownership is acknowledged in the accounts and records kept at the stud. The stud was not mentioned explicitly in Lord Edward's will, which means that it passes in the residue of his estate to…" Here he threw a glance at Gus. "… to Lord Edward's legitimate children, if any. And… and, your grace, there is a child, I believe. A son."

The duke took a long draught of port. "You believe that, do you?" His voice was dangerously soft.

"I do." The lawyer's voice was rising to its terrified pitch.

"Then you would be mistaken," the duke said coldly. "Edward left no wife and no son. God knows, I wish he had, but Mrs Walsh is no wife, and I know not and care not who got her with child, but it was not my son."

"But can you be sure he did not marry her?" Gus said, suddenly breathless. "Perhaps a secret marriage—"

"A secret marriage has no legal standing," the duke said, his colour rising. "One cannot simply say a few words before a parson and call it a marriage. There are laws, restrictions, that sort of thing. You can confirm that, Forbes, surely."

"It is true, but—"

"There you are, you see," the duke said.

"But suppose—" Gus began, but the duke waved an imperious hand.

"I know what you want to find out, Marford. A respectable widow, instead of a common whore. Yes, you would like that very much, I daresay. I know how you have been sniffing round her, in defiance of my express orders, and I can see what you want her to be. But I cannot oblige you. Consider my position after Edward died. Two of my sons were dead, and the third could produce nothing but useless girls. I had no heir but this miserable nobody from Cheshire — an attorney, God give me strength! And his wife the daughter of an apothecary! To live here, and wear ermine, and walk just a few steps behind the king! It was unthinkable."

He sipped his port, catching his breath, his expression sombre.

"The will… I confess, I did wonder who this Amaryllis Cordwainer might be. There were any number of small bequests, for my son was a generous man who never forgot good service or those in need, but a thousand pounds is a large sum. When the lawyers were sent out to deliver the bequests, they were instructed to bring me explicit word of Miss Cordwainer and her father. They found her easily enough, living in a low way, with her father very sick and it was clear to me that the bequest was no more than charity."

After a moment, he went on, "And then the woman arrives here with a babe in her arms, and her babe is a boy. A boy! An heir, at last. It was a glorious moment, a moment of hope in my sorry life. Well, she told me brazenly that she had been his mistress but I never believed that for one moment. Edward was not a man to take a mistress, not ever. If he had bedded her, then he had married her first. And…" He looked down at his port. "I am tolerably sure that he *meant* to marry her, for he had been dropping hints about it for weeks before he left. How would I feel if he married some nobody with no family and no name? Well, I told him exactly how I would feel if he ever did such a bone-headed thing. He never spoke explicitly, and at the time I thought nothing of it. It was only later… it preyed on my mind a great deal, for we quarrelled over the matter. Just a few days before he was to leave he raised the subject once more, and we had a terrible quarrel." He paused, and his great hands were shaking at he clutched his glass. "I never saw him again." His voice was harsh.

For a moment, his composure slipped altogether. He pushed his glass away and buried his face in his hands. Gus waited. When Willerton-Forbes would have said something, Gus waved him to silence. And eventually, the duke lifted his head and went on as if nothing had happened.

"So as soon as the woman turned up, I suspected she was his wife, just as you do, Forbes, and you, Marford, even though she denied it. Do you think I did not try to find out? Do you think I would just toss her aside without even looking into it? I moved heaven and earth to prove it, as God is my witness, and not a grain of evidence could I find. Whoever she is, she is not and never was Edward's wife, and the child is none of *my* blood. I look after her because Edward asked me to, in a letter she brought with her, and she has the thousand pounds he left her, and I allow her to cloak herself in the fiction of widowhood, but more than that I cannot and will not do. And now, get out, both of you. And tell those stupid women that you have given me indigestion, which is no more than the truth, and I am gone to my bed. Go on! Out! Bedford! *Bedford!* Get rid of them."

The two men walked in silence through the night-darkened castle passageways, across the bridge and back to the parlour. Willerton-Forbes poured himself a huge brandy and collapsed into a chair beside the fire, hands shaking.

"By God, but he terrifies me," he said, before drinking deeply. "It had to be done, but Lord, he scares me half to death. But Marford, I am so sorry. I just wanted him to acknowledge your Mrs Walsh, to own that she is Lady Edward, but I seem to have done more harm than good."

"It had to be said, I think," Gus said tiredly, running one hand over his face. "I just want to *know* what the position is, and no one would talk to me about it. The duke would not, and she jumped down my throat just for mentioning her husband."

"Oh, Lord, did she?" the lawyer said sympathetically. "Are you at outs with her? Is that why you have been as gloomy as a wet day in February?"

"Partly, but her reaction merely confirms what the duke has said. She allows people to think she is a respectable widow, yet she will not talk about her husband beyond the most commonplace of details. She has not even given him his full name, which makes me think that it cannot be Lord Edward, or at least that if he was her lover, they were not married."

"And yet, you know, I am not convinced of that," the lawyer said quietly. "The duke confirms that Lord Edward was not the man to seduce an innocent or take a mistress. It is very suggestive of a secret marriage."

"Yet the duke looked but found no evidence," Gus said. "Willerton-Forbes, do not get my hopes up. Let me think her a fallen woman, and perhaps I can escape here with my sanity."

The lawyer smiled. "Your pardon, my lord. However, I am charged with determining the ownership of the stud, and in order to do that, I have to establish the truth of the matter. I must investigate whether there was a marriage or not."

"But the duke made his own investigations, and found no evidence, and she herself claims to be his mistress. She has admitted to me that she has no reputation. If she were his wife, why would she hide such a thing, and claim only to be his mistress? "

"Impossible to say, but I cannot accept it without question. Just as in a court of law, every claim must be independently verified."

"How will you do that?" Gus said.

Willerton-Forbes set his brandy glass down on the table beside his chair, and rested his hands on his knees. "There are only three ways to marry — by the calling of the banns, by common licence or by special licence. Afterwards, the marriage must be registered in the parish register. All of those are matters of record. And yet...

forgive me, but there is one other source of information which must be examined."

"You mean Mrs Walsh herself, I presume."

The lawyer nodded. "I would not pain you for the world, or her either, but I must approach her. And since I do not know her, I must ask you to introduce me to her."

20: *Old Drifford House*

They went to the north lodge directly after breakfast, before the proposed visit to Drifford. Since Gus, Merton and Willerton-Forbes had a common interest in uncovering the truth about Lord Edward Winfell's possible marriage, all three were to go to Drifford, if it proved necessary, and Merton was invited to join the others in visiting Mrs Walsh.

"I confess to a great desire to meet the lady," Merton said, "but are you sure I will not be dreadfully in the way?"

"No, no, and you have exactly the right kind of mind for such a visit," Willerton-Forbes said. "You will be able to observe the lady's responses and offer another opinion. Lord Augustus is of no use for such a purpose — forgive me, my lord."

Gus readily agreed that he would not be an impartial observer. Indeed, he was in more dread of the encounter than he could ever remember. A summons by his grandfather, perhaps, had been worse, but that was ancient history, on the very boundary between memory and dreams. But to return to Mrs Walsh only hours after she had sent him away, seemingly for ever... What would she say? Would she be angry, or merely disappointed in him? But it had to be done.

As they approached the house, he heard threads of music drifting on the air, and a wave of grief almost overwhelmed him.

The pianoforte! She was playing the instrument, as he had so longed to hear her do, and yet he could not rejoice in it as he had once hoped. It was now a symbol of all that he had lost.

The music stopped as they crunched up the gravel drive to the front door. Gus rapped on the knocker, and after a few moments there she was, looking up at him, and then at the other two. Bewilderment, that was all her expression told him. Not anger, just bewilderment.

"Mrs Walsh, I beg your forgiveness for disturbing you so unexpectedly, but there is a matter of business that—"

"*Gus! Gus!*" A small figure pelted out of the house and hurled itself into Gus's arms. He laughed, and scooped the child up, planting a kiss on the tousled head.

"And good morning to you too, Master Walsh."

"You brought *friends!*" the child cried, and after that, somehow, everyone was smiling, even Amaryllis, and they were waved into the house and settled in the drawing room, where Ned's soldiers were neatly arranged in regimental order on the floor.

With some difficulty, for Ned was tugging at his arm, Gus introduced Willerton-Forbes and Merton. "A matter of business," he said. "It should not take long. If I stay here with Ned...?"

She understood, and ushered the two men through to the parlour, while Gus settled on the floor with Ned and the soldiers. They were not left alone for long, or perhaps he was so absorbed in the game that he took no notice of the time passing, for suddenly there they all were. He tried to read their faces, but could tell nothing from them. Merton was always a closed book, and Willerton-Forbes had on his lawyer's serious expression. And Amaryllis? She was perhaps a little pink-cheeked, but as composed as ever.

"Now, Ned, I fear that I must leave you to finish the battle yourself," Gus said gently.

"No! Stay!"

"I wish I could, for my troops are in a most commanding position. Unfortunately, there is a matter of business that must be attended to."

"Then come back afterwards."

"That is for your mama to decide."

"Mama! Please, please, *please*!"

Gus held his breath, waiting, watching her.

She looked him full in the face, and said calmly, "Of course. I should be happy to see Lord Augustus whenever he wishes to visit."

He exhaled, and knew he was grinning inanely, but he could not help himself. "Thank you! With luck, I may be able to come back this afternoon, or if not, then tomorrow. But Ned, do not be sneaking your cavalry round behind my infantry, you know. I shall remember how everything is laid out."

Then there were the farewells to be made, and to his delight she held out her hand to him, her ungloved hand, and he had the delicious pleasure of lifting it to his lips. Oh, the warmth of her fingers in his! And she had forgiven him his impertinence in asking about her husband, surely she had. As they walked back across the park to the stables under grey skies heavy with autumn rain, wet leaves swishing beneath their feet, Gus was as light-hearted as a bird trilling the arrival of spring.

"Are you not even going to ask?" Merton said, in amused tones. "But you are too happy to descend to the plane of mere mortals like us, I daresay."

"Of course I am happy!" Gus cried. "Yesterday she told me I should never see her again, and today she has relented. How could I not be happy? But tell me, did she reveal anything of import?"

"Not a single thing that we did not already know," Willerton-Forbes said. "She was very polite, but very, very resolute. So we must go to Drifford and see what we may learn there."

"And what did you think of her?" Gus said.

Merton smiled. "She is in every way a lady."

And upon reflection, Gus could find no fault with this assessment.

Gus and Willerton-Forbes drove to Drifford in the curricle, for the lawyer did not ride, while Merton rode behind them. As the bays were fresh, they covered the distance in no time. The curricle rattled through the newer part of the town, with its fine rows of houses and shops, and into the main square, where the statue of Mrs Ballard in her hooped dress gazed over her people. There were no inns in sight, but there was a small hotel at one corner of the square, where the stables, after inspection, proved adequate to Gus's requirements. Leaving Carson and several ostlers, wide-eyed at the sight of the immaculate pair of bays, to tend the horses, they ordered coffee while they planned their approach.

"Well, this is fun," Gus said, still exhilarated by his meeting with Amaryllis. "I do like an adventure. How shall we begin?"

"Fun?" the lawyer said. "May I enquire, my lord, as to whether you always drive like that?"

"Oh, no," Gus said blandly. "I normally let them have their heads, but you were looking a bit green, so I held them in check."

"Held them in check," the lawyer said faintly. "I see. Perhaps on the way back I shall find a local farmer to drive me at a more sedate pace."

"You did very well," Gus said kindly. "You only screamed once, I believe, when we overtook the mail coach."

"Which was at full speed with four horses," the lawyer said acidly. "And a post chaise approaching from the opposite direction."

Gus grinned. "Nothing at all to worry about, for there was plenty of room. Now, how shall we approach this?"

The lawyer took a steadying breath. "Very well. We do not wish to explain our real reason for enquiring about Miss Amaryllis Cordwainer," he said, "so we shall say only that there is a legacy which has been left to her — which was true enough — and we wish to find her, and the last address we have for her is Old Drifford House. We need to find out where the house is, but we shall not need to call there, since we know she has left."

"No, we should do everything as if our story is real," Merton said, his voice quiet but authoritative enough to compel the lawyer's attention. "We shall enquire as to the whereabouts of the house, and then we must visit it, to enquire if the lady still lives there, or if they know where she may be found. But you must let Mr Willerton-Forbes do the talking, Lord Augustus. It would be very difficult to explain your interest in the matter, so let us agree that you are just a stranger who very kindly offered Mr Willerton-Forbes a lift. An idle aristocrat filling in a few hours between engagements."

"Oh, certainly," Gus said, grinning. "I can play the idle aristocrat to perfection. It is a role I have been playing for four and twenty years, after all. I overheard you enquiring about hiring a post-chaise, Willerton-Forbes, and, being at a loose end, offered to drive you to your destination. How kind of me!"

The first part of this proceeding, to find Old Drifford House, was very easy. Merton summoned the hotel manager, who pointed across the square.

"That there stone cottage is Old Drifford House, sir. Used to be just Drifford House, at first, until Mrs Ballard had the new house built. See that grand new place on the hill across there? That's where Mrs Ballard lives now."

"We are trying to find a Miss Cordwainer who lived at Old Drifford House, but she does not appear to be there now," Willerton-Forbes said.

"Oh, no, she left there a while back, now," the manager said. "Lovely lady, very quiet and shy. She was betrothed to Mr James, until he died, but then she disappeared after that. Grief-stricken, I expect."

Gus was taken aback to hear of a betrothal, for he had never suspected such a thing. But then Amaryllis had told him so little of her past that there might be twenty betrothals for all he knew. And he had died... poor Amaryllis. She had ill fortune with her men, to lose two of them when she was still so young.

"Quite," the lawyer said. "Who is Mr James?"

"Why, Mr James *Ballard*," the man said, seemingly shocked that anyone would not know such a thing. "Such a fine young man. Thrown from his horse, he was. Great tragedy. There were hopes that Mr Richard would marry Miss Cordwainer instead, but nothing came of that, and he married Miss Ellis from Newcastle in the end, and they have a babe expected any day now. Mrs Ballard is very pleased about that, as you can imagine. It is Mr and Mrs Richard who live in Old Drifford House now. Mrs Ballard gave it to them as a wedding present. It should have been Mr James's, but there you are. Such a tragedy. Mrs Ballard was so grieved, it was terrible to see. Never got over it, not in the least. Never goes out now without a veil to hide her face."

Mrs Ballard, everywhere one turned there was Mrs Ballard. Gus supposed that in a small town like Drifford, entirely owned by one man, his wife must be a person of some importance. Amaryllis had told him that Mrs Ballard managed the town, her husband being often away, so no wonder the locals were very conscious of her. She must be a towering presence, dominating their lives just as her statue dominated the square.

The three men walked across the square to Old Drifford House, Gus strutting and waving his cane about, in his role as idle aristocrat, the others more sedately, their sombre black coats a contrast to his burgundy superfine. The house was a good one, pleasingly solid, and large without being imposing, an elegant counterpoint to the rather ostentatious mansion next door, which to Gus's eye was dreadfully vulgar.

There was a knocker and a bell, but Gus rapped on the door with the head of his cane. A footman answered and bore their three cards away to some inner fastness. Gus had expected a 'not at home', but they were admitted, relieved of hats and gloves and Gus's cane, and shown into a very pleasing drawing room, fitted out with exquisite taste, although slightly old-fashioned. Gus knew at once that it bore Amaryllis's hand, for who else would have chosen such daintily feminine colours and furnishings? Certainly not the two ladies who turned to watch them enter. The one lying on a chaise longue was as stout as an ox, her confinement imminent, wearing the sort of violent colours that matrons are allowed to wear but had much better not. The other woman was above fifty, although still handsome, apart from a scar covering most of one cheek. She wore mourning black, and her gown was expensive, but to Gus's London-honed eye, not in the first style of fashion. He did not need to see the hat with its veil pushed back to guess that he was looking at Mrs Ballard, although she was not much like her statue, her face fuller and her figure more voluptuous.

She held the three cards in her hand, which was curious since the other lady was presumably Mrs Richard Ballard, and therefore the lady of the house. But it was the older Mrs Ballard who said, "Lord Augustus Marford? I am not familiar with the peerage, pray enlighten me as to your connections." Her voice was deep, almost like a man's but there was a chill to it that made Gus shiver. Not a pleasant woman, and he understood why Amaryllis had not liked her.

"My brother is the ninth Marquess of Carrbridge, ma'am," Gus said, wondering why she did not introduce herself formally. It was almost as if she expected everyone to know who she was. He was fairly sure he did, but he would have liked it confirmed.

"And he lives where?"

"At Drummoor in the West Riding."

"Drummoor. Interesting. And what is your business with us, Lord Augustus Marford?"

"None at all, ma'am. It is Mr Willerton-Forbes who has business here. I am just his accidental driver for the day. May I have the pleasure of knowing whom I am addressing?"

"Mrs Charles Ballard," she said, her lips compressing as if in annoyance. She did not introduce the younger woman. "Well, Willerton-Forbes?"

"Thank you, madam. I am trying to trace a young lady by the name of Cordwainer who once lived in this house. She—"

"Amaryllis Cordwainer?"

"The same, madam. She—"

"You are too late. She is not here. Indeed, it is some years since she left Drifford, and no one has seen any sign of her since. What is your interest in her?"

"There is a bequest in her name, madam. It would—"

"Who from?"

"I regret I am not at liberty to divulge that information. Do you have any idea where she might have gone to? Did she have relatives? Perhaps she married?"

Mrs Ballard jumped to her feet. She was quite short, although her style of dress and the hair piled high on her head seemed designed to make her look taller.

"She never married," she said, quivering from head to toe. "I can state with some authority that she never married, for she was betrothed to my son, and would certainly have married him had he not been taken from us too young." Her voice shook with emotion. "*Far* too young. Sometimes life is very cruel, gentlemen." She took several deep breaths to compose herself. "We all deal with grief in our own way, do we not? For myself, I rebound stronger than before, and more determined than ever to succeed."

Her eyes flashed as she spoke, and Gus could well believe in her determination. She was a formidable woman indeed.

She went on, "Others grieve by hiding away to lick their wounds, and so it was with Amaryllis. She was weak and foolish, and could not cope with James's death and so she ran away. I looked everywhere for her, as you may imagine. What else could I do for my poor boy but to offer solace to the woman he would have shared his life with? I searched high and low for her, but she escaped me." As she went on, her voice hardened suddenly, "So you will not find Amaryllis Cordwainer in Drifford, Mr Willerton-Forbes, but if you should find her elsewhere, I beg that you will tell me of it, for when she left here, she took something of mine with her, something I value more than diamonds or rubies, and I would have it back."

21: Drifford Church

For a moment, the room was frozen, each of them caught immobile in the spider's web of surprise. Even Mrs Richard Ballard sat, open mouthed, staring at her mother-in-law. Gus had no idea what to make of it. Merton had warned him to be prepared for any outcome, but nothing had prepared him for this deep-seated grief and anger... yes, Mrs Ballard was *angry* about her son's death, angry at Amaryllis and he could not understand why.

"Would you see him? And her, too?" Mrs Ballard said, her voice shifting abruptly to a softer tone. "They are immortalised in the church, and although I thought it an odd whim at the time, now I am glad of it, for every Sunday I may sit and gaze once more at my son's face and that is a vast comfort to a poor grieving mother in her declining years. Will you come?"

She addressed the room at large, but it was at Gus that she looked as she spoke.

"Certainly," he said, aware of a quiver of excitement. He could not guess quite what Mrs Ballard meant when she said that Amaryllis was immortalised in the church, but if he could look on her face there, it would please him greatly.

"You will forgive me, I trust, if I continue my enquiries elsewhere?" Willerton-Forbes said. "I have very little time and—"

"As you please," Mrs Ballard said, with a lift of one shoulder, but her lip curled in disdain. Perhaps she was not used to people who turned her down. She pulled her veil down over her face, took up her cane and left the room without another word.

Gus turned to Mrs Richard, who had said nothing throughout the exchange, and looked now on the verge of tears.

"Good day to you, Mrs Ballard," he said gently, with a formal bow. "Pardon our intrusion. We will leave you in peace now."

"Oh, it is of no consequence. I am always happy to see new faces in the town." She had a high voice like a young girl's, although she must have been twenty five or more. Then, more strongly, with an intense glance at the retreating back of her mother-in-law, "*Always.*"

"You are very kind," Gus said, wondering a little at the strange little family tableau.

He made his way out of the house after Mrs Ballard, and into the square. Willerton-Forbes made his bow, and set off to make enquiries of the various shops surrounding the square and spilling along the main road. Gus followed Mrs Ballard across the square, with Merton silent in his wake. As they progressed, the entire square came to a halt, every wagon was pulled up, every walker stood still. Each one of them turned towards Mrs Ballard, then dipped into a deep bow or respectful curtsy. Heads bowed, they waited until she had passed by before moving off again. Gus had seen less respect paid to members of the royal family.

The church was a fine one, its clock tower soaring high above even the tallest buildings around it. Yet the face of the clock was exactly on a level with the upper windows of Drifford House on its hill opposite, and Gus wondered if that was intentional, if Mrs Ballard put herself on the same level as the high point of the church, and everyone else must go lower. To one side of the church were stones to mark the dead, and on the other side, a single large grave, fenced and roofed, with a carved angel above it and flowers placed before it.

"There lies my poor son," Mrs Ballard said, pausing for a moment. "My firstborn. Ah, it's so hard to lose a child."

Gus and Merton maintained a sympathetic silence, for what was there to say? No words could comfort such grief. Only time and prayer and the steadfast support of those who loved her could bring solace and ease the pain.

With a sigh, she moved on towards the church doors, which stood wide open. A woman scrubbing the steps scrambled to her feet, whisked her bucket aside and dropped into a deep curtsy as they passed by. Mrs Ballard nodded to her, but moved into the vestibule without speaking. It was cool inside the church, their steps echoing on the tiled floor. Unlike the over-ornamented house on the hill opposite, with its decorated porticoes, ornamental arches and domed roofs, the church was starkly plain, its rows of stone pillars and soaring roof devoid of embellishment. Some of the windows were plain glass, but several had been replaced with stained glass images of biblical scenes and to one of these Mrs Ballard led them.

"There," she said. "That is James, and Amaryllis beside him, just as in life."

The window depicted the story of the loaves and fishes, and the benign figure of Jesus was handing out food to a crowd of eager followers, their faces upturned with adoration. And there, as lovely in glass as in life, was Amaryllis.

"Ohhh," Gus breathed, moving closer. Behind him, Merton coughed, and he remembered he was not supposed to know her, and drew back a little, but Mrs Ballard was looking at him oddly. "Which is your son?" he said, his voice a little hoarse. "And... and Miss Cordwainer?"

"This is Amaryllis, and this is James, my eldest son." A handsome man, rather bulky, one hand resting proprietorially on Amaryllis's shoulder. "So like me in ways, and unlike the younger boys, he never went away to school. Here are Richard and Harold, my younger sons, such grand gentlemen they are now, quite above their humble origins. But James never forgot his mother. My girls — Agnes, Emily, Joan, Sarah." She sighed. "I daresay they will marry eventually. Lucia White, the doctor's daughter. Such an unpromising baby, but she married quite well, considering her history, a wool merchant, a very rich man. Janet and Lizzie, the daughters of one of my managers. They are in the Girls' Academy now, and doing very well there. Thomas Leafield, the hotel manager's son." She rattled on, naming them all, knowing every detail about them, their histories and what had become of them. Except for Amaryllis.

"What did you mean earlier," Gus said, "when you said that Amaryllis had something of yours?"

She turned to look him fully in the face, her pale blue eyes as cold and unblinking as a fish. "Why, my grandchild, Lord Augustus. Amaryllis had James's baby and took the child away from me! She took my son from me, which debt she can never repay, but then she took my grandchild from me also, which compounds my loss, for the babe is all that now remains of my son. I shall never stop looking for that child, *never*, for it is *mine*."

With another abrupt shift, she smiled and it was as if the sun had come out from behind a cloud. "Come, let me show you the entry in the register."

She led the way down the side aisle to the vestry, and there, on a plinth, sat a book open at a page edged in black and written in the decorative script of monkish scribes, painted in many colours and embellished with gold leaf.

"There… James Charles Ambrose Ballard. After his father, of course, and his benefactor." For some reason she found this exquisitely funny, and laughed merrily. Perhaps realising how odd it looked, she raised a black-gloved hand to her mouth, and continued more solemnly, "Five years three months and six days ago, my son was killed."

"Killed?" Gus said, horrified. "As in murdered?"

"Oh… not exactly, no. He fell from his horse. But it was *her* fault, all the same. If she had married him when she should have done, he would never have been riding out there, never have fallen, never have been taken away from me. And if she had married him, that babe would have been here now, delighting my old age, and not out there in the world, growing up without knowing its grandmama. Family is so important, isn't it, my lord?"

"Yes, indeed."

"You are very attached to *your* family, I daresay."

"Very much so. However much my brothers annoy me and do the most absurd things, I still love them all."

"Oh, brothers!" She snapped her fingers dismissively. "That is not the family that I speak of. It is *children* who are important, especially when they are small and kneel quietly at one's feet. They grow up to be wilful and disobedient, but when they are young and docile, they are quite perfect."

Gus tried to reconcile this idyllic vision of childhood with the exuberant Ned, shrieking at the top of his lungs and racing about the woods, and shook his head in bemusement. "I cannot recall ever kneeling quietly at anyone's feet. My brothers and I never did anything except at a run, and never spoke but to shout. We must have been a great trial to our nurses."

"At Drummoor," she said flatly.

"At Drummoor, yes. I was born and grew up there."

"It is a great house, no doubt. A fine estate. No neighbours for miles around."

"There is a village nearby," Gus said. "But forgive me, Mrs Ballard. You have been generous with your time to strangers, but I am sure we keep you from more important calls upon your time."

At the *'we'*, she turned to observe Merton, who was leafing through the pages of the register with apparent interest. Her eyes flashed with anger. "Leave that as it was!"

"Of course, ma'am," Merton said smoothly, resetting the book back to the black-edged page.

She stamped her cane against the tiled floor, its thump ricocheting around the room. "You are right, I have wasted too much time on you. None of you are worth it." So saying she strode off into the church and out of sight down the aisle.

Gus watched her go, bemused. "Well, that was an odd thing. What do you make of her, Merton?"

"A strange woman, and one I would not like to cross. But she has been an invaluable help."

"She has told us a great deal about Amar— I mean Mrs Walsh."

"Who is, apparently, still Miss Cordwainer. The register confirms that there was no marriage. Her father's death is recorded, and that of James Ballard, of course, but no marriage and no baptism of the child."

"So he is truly a fatherless child."

Merton raised an eyebrow, and shuffled his feet. "No child is fatherless, my lord, and in this case the line is very clear. Ned must be James Ballard's child."

"Then what has Lord Edward Winfell to do with it? Why does Amaryllis talk about a husband whose name is Edward, and name the child after him? It makes no sense, Merton." He stamped out of the vestry into the church, and down the side aisle. His steps slowed as he drew near to the window, with its so-lifelike depiction of Amaryllis. And there beside her was James Ballard, his hand on her shoulder, claiming her. Her betrothed, the man she should have married yet had not, and she had never mentioned him. "And why did she not marry the fellow, eh? If she liked him well enough to surrender her virtue, why not marry him? Does she strike you as the sort of woman who would be so careless of her reputation?"

"Not at all," Merton said, "but we do not know what she was like then. We only see the face she presents to the world now."

"You are suggesting some deceit or artifice?" Gus said coldly. "I do not like your implication, Merton." He sagged into a pew, and Merton sat in the pew in front, turned round to face him.

"I meant no slur on the lady," Merton said quietly. "But consider her position. She had no mother, no sisters or brothers, no family to advise her, only a sick father. She fell into the orbit of Mrs Ballard, and we have seen how formidable a character *she* is. The son perhaps made strong advances towards her, and Miss Cordwainer was drawn in. He had a pleasing enough countenance, charming manners, let us suppose, so perhaps, in time, she was so enamoured that she surrendered to him. Then he died, and she found herself in a difficult situation. She realised her error, and when her father's death released her from any further ties, she made her escape to Castle Morton, with a plausible tale about Lord Edward. The duke investigated, just as we have done, and realised the true situation, but out of charity he housed her anyway."

"Until that last part, I can believe it all," Gus said. "But the duke is not a man to hand out charity to a woman so wholly unconnected with him. He might give her a few guineas, but then he would send her away. He would not house her and feed her and clothe her if he had no connection at all to her. And she brought the duke a letter from Lord Edward *asking* him to take care of her. No, the child must be Lord Edward's, I cannot interpret this any other way."

Merton grunted. "Perhaps he does not believe her story, but he feels obliged to keep her close just in case some evidence turns up that proves it," he said cautiously. "After all, if she was legally married to Lord Edward, then the boy might be the heir to the dukedom. Better by far to have him on hand if it should turn out to be true, than to have to scour the kingdom for him."

Gus deflated at once. "Damnation, Merton, you are always so *reasonable.* And may God forgive me, now I am using foul language in His holy house. But I am no further forward. She might be… he might be… It is all inference and supposition. Maybe I should just marry her and be done with it. Carrbridge has said he will support me, and for all you will represent to him the unwisdom of such a move, he will not go back on his word."

"No, he will not," Merton admitted. "But have you any idea what it is like to live on one thousand pounds a year, my lord? How many horses do you keep at present? Ten? A dozen?"

"Hmm… fifteen, not counting the hunters." A long pause. "Are they *very* expensive, Merton?"

"That alone would consume half your income, if you were to pay for every part of it yourself. Then there are the costs of coals and flour and tea and candles and soap and gowns for your lady. How much did that coat of yours cost?"

Gus exhaled gustily. "Oh, Merton, you are a good sort of fellow, but this is so *lowering.* So tell me, if Amaryllis were to turn out to be a respectable widow, and I were to take her to Drummoor, Carrbridge would not refuse to keep me, would he? I should not need an independent establishment, and the thousand a year would be enough then?"

"I daresay it would, my lord. Should you like to be the poor relation, always dependent on your brother? Do you think Miss Cordwainer would like to live under another man's roof?"

He was silent for a long time. That was the trouble with Merton, he was always right, and especially so where money was concerned. He sighed again. "It is hopeless, is it not? I should have let Connie find me an heiress, like Reggie and Humphrey."

"You still have your work with Tattersall's, my lord. That will make you independent, in time."

"In a very long time," he said quietly.

Again he fell silent, considering. Would it be so terrible to give up some of his horses? Perhaps all of them? His heart quailed at the prospect. No Jupiter, no Masterful, no Darkling Sun, no Arabian Prince. No curricles with their matched pairs, either. That would be a sorry day for him, to lose so much majestic power. The thrill of a fast drive or a hard gallop, jumping every wall and ditch, would be forever lost to him.

But then, if he could wake each morning to a sweet heart-shaped face, and see her blue eyes gazing at him, it would surely be worth it. A quiet life it would be, but a contented one, with Ned to watch growing up, and, God willing, a few more besides. There would be a joy in that, too, a different kind of joy, but it would be enough for him.

"Suppose..." he said thoughtfully. "Suppose I were to get rid of the horses..."

"All of them?" Merton said, surprised.

"Yes. If all the horses were gone... it could be done then, could it? With care and economy."

Merton blinked. "It could. Many live on a great deal less, and still call themselves gentlemen. My own income is under eight hundred a year."

"And *you* plan to marry," Gus said eagerly. "Such a sum would support a family... Oh, but I daresay Lady Hardy has money of her own."

"She does, twelve hundred and fifty a year, or perhaps a little more next year if my investments on her behalf prove fruitful."

"And two thousand a year will make you very comfortable, I should think, when you are married?"

Merton looked rather conscious. "I do not quite like to be so presumptuous... the lady is still in mourning after all, but I do have hopes, and two thousand a year is a very comfortable income. I could afford to keep a carriage on such a sum."

"But not on one thousand a year?" Gus said.

"A gig, perhaps. Are you serious about this, my lord? For if so, I feel duty bound to remind you that if you marry a lady with a despoiled reputation, you cut yourself off from all good society. It would reduce your expenses, for you would not need to entertain at all, but the change in your circumstances would be dramatic."

Gus nodded eagerly. "I know, I know! I understand what I would be giving up, but Merton, I have been an idle, selfish being all my life, and boredom and too much money to spend have got me into trouble more than once. I buy all these horses because I *can*, not because I need them. Who needs two curricles anyway? Or even one? What rational man needs fifteen horses? I cannot ride them all at once, so they sit about, eating their heads off and keeping who knows how many grooms in employment. It is foolishness. I have wasted half my life, Merton, but I am determined to do better in future. Will you teach me how to manage on a thousand a year?

Teach me the price of coals and candles and… all those other things?"

"I should be delighted to do so, my lord."

"And I shall give up hanging about at Tattersall's, which I only did because it gave me the opportunity to stay in London and stable my horses at Marford House. Lord Longannet offered me four hundred a year to manage his racing stables in Hampshire. That would be a useful increase to my income, would it not? And at least I should get some riding there. I shall write today to ask if the post is still open. My own horses can go — Tattersall's can sell them for me." He laughed at the irony. "And it matters not whether Amaryllis will have me or not, for I am determined to do this, Merton, quite determined. But oh, if she *will!* Oh, how glorious that would be!"

22: *Soup And Bread*

Gus and Merton repaired to the hotel again, where the lawyer met them, his face showing uncharacteristic animation.

"I have some interesting information," he whispered, although they were quite alone in the private parlour Gus had procured. "Miss Cordwainer left Old Drifford House shortly after the death of Mr James Ballard, but she did not leave Drifford. She and her father moved to Holly Cottage in the older part of the town, higher up the river. She had friends there, seemingly. That is where we must enquire next."

"It is of no use," Gus said. "She was not married, for we have seen the register in the church and there is no record of any marriage, or of Ned's baptism, either."

"Oh." The lawyer deflated at once. "The register, of course. I should have checked there first, for even if there had been a form of marriage, you know, it cannot be valid without the event is recorded in the parish register. Even if the banns have been called and the marriage has taken place before the clergyman and witnesses during the proper hours, if it is not registered it is not valid."

"I wonder if that is the way of it," Merton said thoughtfully. "An otherwise unquestionable marriage, completely real to the participants, but without that entry in the parish register, there is no marriage and the child cannot inherit."

"The law can be the very devil sometimes," the lawyer said sadly. "But if we ask her friends in Upper Drifford, we may determine when she left the town altogether, and whether there is any likelihood that she was married elsewhere."

This was a cheering possibility, so they left the hotel and walked some little distance up the main road, crossing the bridge into the old part of the town. At once the fine new buildings and wide streets gave way to a different settlement altogether. Great tall warehouses lined the road, and muddy alleys led to narrow houses where many families lived piled on top of one another, to judge by the lines of washing at every window, or across the street. A few men smoking pipes sat about in groups on the doorsteps, although it was the middle of the day when they should be at work. One had a crying baby on his knee.

But a little further on the valley sides steepened and the warehouses were set closer to the river. On the rocky slopes on either side of the main road were crowded a mass of tiny cottages, thrown together any which way, with odd patches of garden or tumbledown wooden sheds mixed in amongst them. Barefoot children chased each other, and chickens scratched about happily in the dirt.

To one side of the road, where the ground was flatter, an irregular square opened up, edged with small shops and neat little houses with walled gardens.

"There is a tavern over there, Marford," Willerton-Forbes said. "You may want to rest there with a tankard while Mr Merton and I continue our investigations."

"Do you wish to be rid of me?" Gus said amiably. "I can as soon go back to the hotel, if so."

"Not at all," the lawyer said politely, "but you are rather… um, *conspicuous* in that coat and waistcoat, if I may say so, especially in this part of town. I am a lawyer and Mr Merton could easily pass for one, but you, Marford—"

"I look like the idle aristocrat that I am," Gus said with a sigh. "Very well. I am not sure I want to eat in any establishment here, but the beer should be potable, would you not agree?"

So he ambled down to the tavern, cane swishing, and sat in the autumn sunshine at one of the rough tables set outside. The tapboy brought him a tankard of something not too unpleasant, and he stretched out his long legs and watched the poorer folk of Drifford going about their business. The matrons eyed him warily, and one or two men who looked better dressed than mere labourers bustled past on business, but most of those he saw wore thin, well-patched clothes and many were barefoot.

It was the children who showed the most curiosity. They stopped chasing each other and stood and stared at him, fingers in mouths. They were all young, from two or three up to about six, and he supposed that the older children were busy at home, or perhaps they were at school? Had Amaryllis not mentioned a school? Gradually, seeing that he was not about to explode or chase them away with his cane, they began to inch closer.

One boy was braver than the rest, although he was smaller than many of them and as thin as a rail. He came close enough to call out, "Hey, mister, 'oo are you?"

"I am Gus," he said, gravely. "Who are you?"

"Kit Sandwell," the boy said. "Why you only got one name? I got two names. Everyone got two names."

"Oh, you want the whole thing, do you? Very well, I am Lord Augustus Theodore Horatio Marford."

The boy's eyes widened. "You really a lord? What you a lord of, then?"

"Unfortunately, I am not a lord *of* anything, but my brother is — he is the ninth Marquess of Carrbridge. Are you hungry, Kit? You look hungry to me."

The boy nodded, words failing him, although whether this was caused by the prospect of food or meeting the brother of a marquess was hard to determine.

"Boy!" Gus called, and the tapboy, who had been loitering ready to intervene if anyone harassed his noble customer, rushed forward. "Bring something hot for Master Sandwell, if you please. Some soup, preferably with some meat in it. And bread."

"For Kit, sir? I mean, my lord?"

"If you please. Come and sit down, Kit." The boy scrambled up onto the bench, and a few minutes later, a bowl of steaming soup arrived. It looked rather unappetising to Gus's eye, but he guessed that the boy would not mind. Nor did he, for he dived in with gusto.

By this time, Gus had acquired rather a crowd of children, who watched silently and enviously as Kit polished off his soup, and a big chunk of bread. It was one of the girls who dared to speak.

"Please, sir, I want some too."

Gus signalled to the tapboy, who rolled his eyes but went off to the kitchen. And within a very few minutes, some twenty children were squeezed around the tables, as the tapboy was kept busy running back and forth with bowls and bread.

A man with a clerical neckcloth walked by, smiled and diverted to the tavern. He was a dumpy figure, small and solid, with a shock of white hair.

"Good day to you, sir," he said to Gus, doffing his hat. "While I commend your Christian charity in offering sustenance to these ragamuffins, I feel honour bound to warn you of the risk of fleas."

Gus laughed. "I am sure I shall survive the onslaught, although I am not sure my valet will recover from the humiliation if I inflict fleas upon *his* person. But his dignity is more fragile than mine, I fear. Lord Augustus Marford at your service, sir. May I offer you some refreshment? I do not recommend the soup, but the ale is tolerable."

The clergyman laughed. "Mr William Parker, my lord, and thank you, that would be most acceptable."

"Kit, Maggie, move further down and make room for Mr Parker."

Gus passed a pleasant half hour in conversation with Mr Parker. The children lost interest when no more food was forthcoming, and drifted away, but the parson lingered, talking about the town and its history.

"It is much bigger than it used to be, of course. This was the whole of it at one time, and the few mills further up the river. But Mrs Ballard made some great improvements, and built the new town where the managers and merchants live, and this part is half forgotten. Out of sight, out of mind. But this is the heart of Drifford, my lord, with all the mills and warehouses and weaving halls, and the workers who keep the looms moving, sending gold to Mrs Ballard's coffers, and all for a few coppers earned."

"With so many mills here, there must be employment for all who need it," Gus murmured.

"You would think so, but it is a matter of profit," Mr Parker said. "The children are cheap to employ, so once they are old enough they can have as much work as they want. Adult women are paid less than men, so they are preferred for many jobs. Many of the mills have only two or three adult men working there, for the heavy work. The men often have to stay home and care for the little ones while their wives work. And the sick or old are of no use. It is a hard life, my lord, very hard."

"I had no idea," Gus said. "How much do they earn, these people?"

"A few pounds a year, when there is work to be had."

"A few *pounds*. And I was wondering how on earth I was to manage with only a thousand pounds a year."

The clergyman smiled. "And that is the natural order, is it not? That the nobility are sent to rule us, and are given the wealth to sustain their position. A duke or earl should not have to wonder whether he can afford a piece of beef this week, for he has more important considerations weighing on his mind. But one always hopes that some of his wealth will be expended to relieve the cares of the poor, as we do in the church, also, when we can. I do a little, but my living is such a poor one that there is but little to spare."

"A poor living? That surprises me, Mr Parker, when your church is such a splendid building."

"Splendid building? Oh, I see, you are thinking of the new church in Ballard Square. No, I am parson of Old Drifford Church, my lord, which is a much less imposing affair, I assure you."

This statement, trivial as it may have seemed on the surface, hit Gus with all the force of a bolt of lightning. He shot upright, his cane clattering to the ground. "There is another church? Why did we not think of that? Good God, but perhaps...? Tell me, Mr Parker, does your church have a register for recording marriages?"

"It does, but—"

"Aha!" He jumped to his feet. "Please, may I see it?"

A wary look crossed the clergyman's face. "My lord, I—"

At that moment, Willerton-Forbes and Merton reappeared, half-running across the little square. "Marford! There is another church! There may be a register there."

"There is," Gus said. "Gentlemen, this is Mr Parker, the parson of Old Drifford Church. My friends Mr Willerton-Forbes and Mr Merton."

"Then pray, sir, take us there at once and allow us to examine the register," Willerton-Forbes said excitedly. "This may be the final piece of the puzzle."

Parker drew himself up to his full height, which brought him almost level with Gus's shoulder. "I regret, my lord, gentlemen, that I cannot do that."

Willerton-Forbes puffed out his chest and said with all the gravitas of the judge he would surely be one day, "Then, sir, you would be breaking the law, for the register is a public document and may not be withheld."

Parker deflated a little, but said, "I must ask your reason for seeking to examine the register."

Willerton-Forbes glowered and would have answered him robustly, but Gus waved him to silence. When he spoke, his voice was sympathetic. "I think, Mr Parker, that you have been keeping a secret these five years past, as you were undoubtedly asked to do. But there are those who have the right to know this secret, those who would not for the world do anything to harm the lady concerned. The matter cannot be kept hidden indefinitely."

Parker's eyes flicked from one to the other of them, weighing Gus's words. "I think you know the secret already," he said heavily.

"We seek only the proof," Willerton-Forbes said. "For myself, it is a legal matter, not to be made public except to the duke himself. Lord Augustus's interest in the question is… more personal."

"Ah." Mr Parker looked at Gus, and nodded. "That is a different matter. Come with me, gentlemen, and I will show you the register."

~~~~~

Gus hummed all the way back to the castle, to the amusement of Merton who sat beside him. He hummed through his bath, and he hummed while Willett was fussing over his cravat. Willett was in high good humour too, for the duke had summoned half the county to attend a grand dinner at which he would announce his betrothal, and that meant full evening dress. Willett approved of full evening dress, considering it the height of elegance in male attire. Gus cared nothing for elegance, especially not tonight, but he submitted meekly to Willett's ministrations and decided not to distress the valet by any mention of fleas.

He could hardly believe that he had finally got to the truth. At last, his way was clear and he need no longer agonise over the proper way forward. It would mean giving up his horses and living more quietly than he was used to, but the compensations would be immeasurable. If she would have him, of course. He must not presume. But at least he could court Amaryllis in good earnest now, and not be coy about it. Whether she would want him... he could not tell. She had not been very encouraging so far, but then he had not been able to demonstrate his intent previously. He would—

Shouting broke out somewhere nearby. Several male voices, loud and harsh, and a female voice, rising to a wail. "Lord Gus! *Lord Gus!* Lord Gus! Help!"

Lucy, he thought, a spasm of terror spearing through him. Amaryllis! She was in danger, in need. He was outside like a shot, and racing towards the voices. Three footmen were trying to hold Lucy back, her face chalk-white, eyes wide with terror.

"Lord Gus!" she cried when she saw him. "Quick, please, help us!"

"Your mistress? At the lodge?"

"Yes. Mrs Ballard... taking Ned away. *Please* help!"

Gus poked a finger at the nearest footman. "You, fetch as many men as you can and get to the north lodge. Find Captain Edgerton, if you can, and tell him to bring his pistols. Lucy, find my grooms, tell them to have Jupiter ready for me, just in case. Go, go, go!"

Grabbing his cane, he ran. Coatless, heedless of the startled servants leaping out of his way, he tore down the stairs, out in to the grounds and across the gardens. Please God that he would be in time! Please God let nothing happen to Ned! Please God, please God, please God!

23: *Pistols And Rapiers*

Gus flew across the castle grounds towards the lodge. The gravel path was straight and pale enough that he could just make it out in the darkness, but even so, twice he stumbled, regained his footing and sped on. Into the sheltering belt of trees, running blind in the pitch dark, hoping he was going aright. Then lights ahead, shouting, a child's high wail, and he burst out of the trees.

A carriage was drawn up on the drive, the coachman and a groom standing at the horses' heads. As he approached the house, a figure emerged from it, carrying the screaming Ned. Mrs Ballard, striding purposefully towards the carriage. Running behind her, crying and pulling at her sleeves, a figure so familiar, so dear to him that he was swamped with pain at her distress.

"Stand!" he yelled. "Release him at once!"

Unhurriedly, Mrs Ballard turned to face him as he panted up to them, hot, dishevelled and furiously angry.

"Release him *at once!*"

She looked him up and down, then with a supercilious sneer, she said, "Ah, Lord Augustus Marford. This does not concern you."

Before he could reply, Ned wriggled violently, then sank his teeth into the nearest flesh, which happened to be her neck. Mrs Ballard screamed and dropped him. Amaryllis snatched him up, clutching him to her bosom, as Mrs Ballard lurched towards her and managed to grab an arm. Maggie and John, who had followed Amaryllis out of the house, rushed in to help. In the tussle, Amaryllis fell, and twisted so that her body was arched protectively over the still screaming Ned, with Mrs Ballard pulling ineffectually at Ned's arm, while Maggie and John in their turn pulled at her arms.

"Move away!" Gus yelled. "Move away *now* or I run you through!" With a twist and a swift tug at the head of his cane, he withdrew a long rapier.

"Oh, so brave!" Mrs Ballard mocked, but she took a step back all the same.

"Go, now," Gus growled. "You have no business here, madam."

"I have every business!" she said, chin lifting. "I am come to reclaim what is mine, what was *stolen* from me."

"Ned is not yours."

"He is, he is!" and her voice was high, on the verge of hysteria. "He is *mine*, my son's only child, and he belongs with me."

"Ned is *not* yours. He is the son of Lord Edward Winfell and grandson of the Duke of Dunmorton."

For the first time, he saw hesitation in her. "Nonsense," she said, but without conviction. "What story is this?"

"It is the truth, as God is my witness, and if you do not leave here *immediately* I shall be forced to take the appropriate measures."

A couple of footmen appeared, puffing, from the trees, and then two more, followed by Captain Edgerton, brandishing a fearsome pair of pistols.

"Well, now, Marford, who would you like me to shoot first?" he said, as affably as if asking his preference between beef and mutton.

Eyes narrowed, Mrs Ballard spun round and stalked back to her carriage. The groom, his face struggling to stay impassive, held the door open as she entered, shut it behind her and climbed up behind as the equipage rumbled into the night, passing a cluster of grooms arriving with pitchforks and even a couple of axes, fully prepared for a pitched battle, instead of a tussle between two ladies for possession of one small child.

Gus threw aside his rapier and rushed across to Amaryllis. "Are you hurt? May I help you to rise?"

She scrambled into a sitting position, Ned cradled in her arms, both of them crying. Gus helped her to her feet, and, arm protectively around her back, ushered her towards the house. He saw Edgerton watching, and nodded his thanks.

Edgerton smiled. "I shall secure the defence while you dole out brandy to the casualties."

Gus shook his head in bemusement. He supposed Edgerton had seen some action in his years with the East India Company Army, and that gave him the ability to keep a cool head in battle, but Gus was too intimately connected to those involved to be so calm about it. Amaryllis had been so close to losing Ned! And if Mrs Ballard had succeeded in taking him, it would have been the very devil to get him back again.

He took Amaryllis into the parlour and settled her on the sofa there, Ned on her knee. They were both still crying, Ned a steady, grinding sort of cry, and Amaryllis in deep, convulsive sobs. He would have let go of her then, but she clutched at him so fearfully that he sat down beside her, his arm resting around her shoulders. It was dreadfully improper, and yet it felt like the right place for it, and after all that had happened, his own nerves needed the reassurance of her nearness just as much as she seemed to need him.

Outside, he heard Edgerton barking commands, very much the army captain in charge. Inside, murmured voices as John and Maggie came and went, lighting lamps, bringing brandy which no one wanted, and conferring in whispers in the passage outside the parlour with the returning Lucy. Gradually, quiet returned to the lodge, Ned's cries reduced to an occasional sob. After a while, Maggie came in and took him away to the kitchen for milk and cake and the quiet comfort of the servants.

Only Amaryllis wept on, her thin body wracked by sobs. With Ned gone, she leaned across Gus, resting her head on his chest and grabbing his shirt with one hand, clutching at it as if she could not bear to let go of him. He had no complaint to make over this arrangement. Somewhere in the scuffle, her cap had been lost, and her smooth hair now lay just an inch or so below his chin. If he bent forward ever so slightly, he could feel the silken touch of it on his skin, could smell the herbs she must use in her soap. He hardly dared to breathe, for fear that she would recognise the impropriety of their closeness and move away from him.

A knock on the door was followed by Edgerton's head. He leaned the cane, the rapier hidden inside it once more, against the wall. "The perimeter is secured, and the night guard is in place. Anything else I may do for you?"

Gus spoke low, trying not to disturb Amaryllis. "I should be obliged if you would send word to my grooms that I shall not be needing Jupiter tonight after all. I thought I might have to give chase, but it was not necessary in the end."

"Very well. If there is nothing else, I shall go back to the castle briefly to find out who the old man chose, but I shall be back directly."

Who the old man chose... Gus had forgotten that the duke was to select a duchess from the unlikely bevy of hopefuls hanging around him. He could not see the clock, but he was fairly sure that he had missed dinner and perhaps the announcement too. Not that he cared any more, but he felt a prick of conscience for the lady concerned. And the duke himself should know about Mrs Ballard, and all that had happened that day.

As the door clicked shut behind Edgerton, Amaryllis shifted so that her head rested on Gus's shoulder and her blue eyes gazed up at him. But still she clutched his shirt, and made no attempt to pull away.

"Thank you," she said, her voice as thin as paper. "Thank you for rescuing us. I did not know who else I might call upon."

"You may always call upon me," he said quietly. "I will always come to you if you have need of me."

Her eyes filled with tears again. "Thank you." After some effort, she composed herself. "How long have you known… about Edward?"

"I guessed a long time ago," he said. "But I do not understand why you keep it such a secret."

"I had to hide Ned away, to keep him safe from *that woman*. Everything I have done for the past four years has been to keep him hidden from her, so that she would not take him away from me. I have told so many lies… even to the duke. And to you! But it was imperative to keep him from her."

"She has no right to him, and the law would support you."

She smiled up at him. "Oh, Gus!" His heart tightened at the use of his name, and he could not resist returning her smile. "You are a man, and one with a powerful family at your back. The law would support *you*. But a woman alone, with no husband or brother to protect her, is weak and vulnerable. I was supposed to marry him, you know. Her son. James. He pursued me almost from the moment

Papa and I moved to Drifford. When I was sixteen, he became... persistent, and *she* encouraged it. We lived next door to them, in the very shadow of their house, and they owned it, so they imagined they owned *me* too. There was no escaping them."

"I saw the house," he said softly. "She was there, and she told me all about James."

"Oh, she would! She is obsessed with him! But I did not like him at all. There was a cruel edge to him that repelled me. He beat his horses and his servants, and I daresay he would have beaten his wife, in time."

"Good God!"

"I refused him, of course, but he would not leave me alone. I was not of age, and Papa would never have given his consent, but he would not give up. Gus, may I tell you all? You will be shocked, but I would have you know the worst of me."

"It would please me greatly to hear everything of your life, good or bad." He ran a finger down her cheek, smiling, and she gazed up at him, so trusting, so guileless. He could not believe that the worst of her was anything terrible. How could it be? She was an angel, and could no more do a wicked thing than stop breathing.

"Very well, but do not think too badly of me, I beg you. I did everything I could to avoid James, but he followed me everywhere, and I was afraid to be alone with him. Papa was very ill by then, and we all knew he could not live much longer. I spent long hours in his room, even at night, and I scarcely left the house except to go to church, but sometimes I needed to be outside, to feel the sun or wind or rain on my face, otherwise I should have gone mad. I used to wait until I saw James go out on his horse before I dared to leave the house, but one day... he tricked me. He must have realised my scheme, and lain in wait for me. He caught up with me in the woods above the town. I was quite alone, and he was bent on *forcing* me to marry him. You understand me, I am sure."

He nodded, not trusting himself to speak.

She went on, "I was terrified. For the first time, I was totally in his power. It was just a game to him, and I think he enjoyed my fear. If he had just… grabbed me…" She took a heaving breath, and Gus tightened his arm around her. She gave him a tremulous smile. "But he wanted to taunt me first, and so he let me run away. He chased, I ran. And quite by accident, I ran to the edge of an old quarry, the ground littered with broken rocks. So I picked one up, and threw it at him. And another, and another. He laughed, thinking it a fine game, for we both knew I could not escape him in the end. But… but one of my rocks hit him on the head. He stumbled backwards, fell and lay still."

"Oh…" Finally, Gus understood the reason why Amaryllis was so terrified of Mrs Ballard. "He was dead?"

She nodded. "I did not know that at first. He lay still, and I ran for help, down towards the road. And the first person I saw was Edward, riding with his batman. I told him my trouble, and showed him the place where James lay. He told me that James was dead. Gus, he was so kind. He understood everything, even though I was hysterical, and making no sense, I am sure. He found where James had tied his horse and let him loose near where he lay, so it would seem that he had been thrown while riding. And he got me back home without anyone seeing. Only Maggie knows what happened that day. And now you, of course. Are you very shocked?"

"Shocked that any man should seek to use you so ill, yes. Relieved he failed. Glad that Lord Edward was there to help. And… it is wrong of me, I dare say, but I cannot but be happy that James Ballard met the end he deserved."

"Oh. That is just how I felt... still feel. I should have pitied him, but I could not. God guided my steps that day, I am sure of it, in leading me to a place where I could defend myself, and in bringing Edward to my aid. You remind me of him, for you would have done just the same, would you not?"

"Of course I would! Any man of honour would have done as much."

"As you did tonight," she said.

"So that was how you met Lord Edward?"

"Yes. He came the next day to see how I did, although secretly, through the woods, so that the Ballards would not see him. And almost every day thereafter."

"And so you fell in love with him," Gus said, with only the slightest pang of jealousy.

"Oh no!" she said, eyes widening. "I liked him very much, and I felt safe with him, but... no, I was not in love with him. It was all on his side. But he did not press me, for he said his father would not like it one bit, since I was not titled. The duke wanted his sons to marry noblewomen, you see, so it would take time to bring him round. But he promised me... he promised Papa too... that he would take care of me, after Papa died, even if I chose not to marry him."

She paused, taking a deep breath before plunging on. "It was so difficult. *She* had come — Mrs Ballard — just after James's death. The day after the funeral, it was, and she berated me for not attending, but then she said that she forgave me for killing James — those were her exact words! — but now I would have to marry Richard, her next son. I refused, of course. How could I possibly marry into that family? It was out of the question. So she threw us out of the house, even though Papa was so ill, and we had to move very suddenly to the old town. We had friends there, for I had been going to church there for some time, to avoid James, and Edward helped us move. In some ways, it was better there, for we were no longer under her eye all the time, and Edward could visit more easily. But then… he was ordered to the Peninsular, and he had to go, it was his duty. And there was no time, and he wanted it so much and Papa wanted it too… to set his mind at rest. So I agreed but… Edward could not take me to Castle Morton, to the duke, because they had had the most violent quarrel. He had tried to tell his father of his plan to marry me, but the duke flew into a rage. He was quite irrational about his sons marrying commoners. Edward dared not leave me with him for there was no knowing what he might do without Edward to protect me. Besides, my father was so sick, and I did not want to move him. So we agreed that we would marry secretly, and I would stay in Drifford with my father, just as before, until his end came. Edward was such a kind man, and understood all my fears. So I married him."

But her voice had diminished to the merest thread, and Gus was helpless to relieve her distress except by holding her tight and listening. So he sat silent, rocking her just a little, letting his emotions wash over him as he heard her dreadful tale.

"Three days," she said, her voice laden with sorrow. "That was all the time we had, but Edward was happy and Papa was content, and it gave me Ned, so I could never regret it. But then Edward died… the lawyers came, for he had left me money in his will, but they called me Miss Cordwainer, so they knew nothing of my marriage. I felt safe, at least. And then Ned was born and Papa was so happy, you cannot imagine. But not long after that he died, and… and then…"

She stopped, and the tears flowed again. Gus rocked her, and murmured to her, although he had not the least idea what he said, and eventually she recovered a little.

"*She* came to see me again, after Papa died. She came to Holly Cottage and told me again that I must marry Richard, and if I did not she would make me go to the Girls' Academy, which sounds so worthy, does it not? But it is a dreadful place, where men go to… to…" She shuddered.

"I know the sort of place you mean," Gus said quickly. "Do not distress yourself by describing it."

"But then… oh Gus, Ned cried! And she heard, and naturally she assumed it was James's baby, for she knew nothing of Edward, nothing at all. No one knew of him, except, I suppose, a few of our neighbours, but they had no idea who he was or that I had married him. She would have taken Ned at once, but I fought her and Maggie came in with a knife and slashed at her, and cut her face. Then she said she would send a carriage for me the next day, to take us to Drifford House to live! So I ran away. Mr Parker helped, and Mr White, the physician who had attended Papa. I went to Newcastle for a while, since Edward had given me money to use, and a house to live in, far from Drifford." Another long pause. "He had considered every eventuality. If I had a son, he told me, he would perhaps be the heir to the dukedom, and therefore of great importance and I must not hide him away. He would need to know of his father's family and the inheritance that might one day be his. He must grow up at Castle Morton, but the duke's temper was too uncertain to tell him openly, and his brother has a poisonous wife, so he would not entrust me to him, either, not until he was duke and could protect me. So we devised a story. I was to say I had been his mistress, and he gave me a letter to give to the duke, asking him to take care of me. He was honour bound to do so, Edward said. So in time, when I felt it was safe, I came here, and told the duke the story we had agreed, and how I wanted to live a quiet life, very secluded. He was very suspicious, for he said Edward would never have taken a mistress, and flatly refused to believe Ned was his son.

Even so, he agreed to let me live in the lodge. We have been here, ever since, waiting... waiting until the duke should die and I could go openly to Edward's brother. But then Henry died and Ned became the heir, but I dared not say anything in case the duke threw us out. At least we were safe here, but now we are *not* safe, and I am so afraid. How did she know where to find me? And what will I do when she comes back, as she surely will? Gus, you must protect us, you must! Please help us!"

Gus hesitated, but it was a night of confessions and he could not withhold the truth from her. "One of those questions I can and must answer," he said. "I am so sorry, Amaryllis, but it is my fault that she found you tonight. She showed me your likeness in the church window, and she must have seen from my unguarded reaction that— Why are you smiling?"

"You called me Amaryllis," she said, the smile so wide it almost reached her ears.

"Oh. Oh... I beg your pardon."

"Oh no, do not apologise, not in the least. But you will protect us, will you not, Gus? You will keep us safe from her?"

"If I had the right, I would, but not without taking you both away from here, which, for Ned's sake, I cannot do. His place is here, with his father's family. But it is time, I think, to take you to the one man in the county who has both the right and the power to protect you and Ned from any threat, even Mrs Ballard."

"The duke?" she whispered fearfully. "He will not acknowledge me."

"He must and he will. You were legally married to Lord Edward, and there is proof."

"Not here! The entry in the parish register is with the clergyman in Drifford, and my marriage lines are with an attorney in

High Morton, and they will only give them up to the duke himself. What if he refuses to believe it?"

"We can convince him, but we must do it tonight, so that you and Ned may be protected within the castle. Nowhere else is safe."

"I... am not sure."

"Amaryllis, do you trust me?"

"With my life," she said without a second's hesitation.

"Then put your trust in me tonight, and I will make him acknowledge you, and Ned too, I swear it."

24: Humiliation And Grace

Amaryllis changed her torn and muddied gown for one of her seldom-worn evening gowns. It had never been very fashionable, even when new, and was less so now, so she had no doubt she would look like the provincial nobody she was — the unsophisticated daughter of a country parson. But she let Maggie dress her hair, and wrap her in the fine silk cloak that Edward had bought for her, which she had never worn, and fasten a garnet necklace around her throat. It had been her mother's once, part of her very small collection of jewellery.

Apart from her wedding ring, Edward had only had time to buy her a small locket containing a curl of his hair, and it was not fine enough for evening. "When I come home, my love, I will shower you with bracelets and rings and jewelled combs for your lovely hair, and you will look like the daughter-in-law of a duke that you are," he had said. But he had never come home, and now she hardly remembered him, and had never missed the shower of jewels. As she looked at herself in the glass, the garnets sparkling in the candlelight, she wondered when Gus would buy her jewels. He had already bought her a pianoforte, but jewels were only for a betrothed, or a wife. Or perhaps, knowing Gus, it would be a horse instead. The thought made her smile.

"Ah, that's better," Maggie said. "It's been so long since you smiled much, Amaryllis. There, now. You look beautiful."

Was she beautiful? Edward had said so, and Gus had looked at her with the same admiration in his eyes, but she could not see it in herself. Her skin was too pale, her face too thin, her eyes too large for beauty. Even her hair was no crowning glory, for it lay smooth and flat, and no amount of curling papers or irons could induce a curl that would not drop out within the hour. But there was nothing to be done about that.

Gus smiled when she emerged from her room, gloved and gowned for the evening, and Ned, too, wore his very best clothes to meet his grandfather.

"What about you?" she said, gesturing at Gus's disarrayed cravat and shirt, muddied where he had lifted her from the ground.

"My valet will meet me at the castle entrance and make me respectable," he said, smiling, and gazing at her in that way he had. "You look so beautiful in that gown." And he swept up her hand and bent over to kiss the back of her glove, making her cheeks flame.

They had an escort of a dozen men across the castle grounds — several burly footmen, two or three grooms and the rest she recognised as gardeners, led by Captain Edgerton in his flamboyant waistcoat, pistols ready in his hands. At the castle doors, they were met by Gus's valet, who tutted and fussed and pleaded to be allowed to replace the shirt and neckcloth.

"No time," Gus said firmly. "Do the best you can, Willett." But the poor man was almost in tears.

The butler hovered in the background, with several more footmen. So many footmen, to attend upon one elderly gentleman!

"Where is the duke, Bedford?" Gus said to the butler.

"In the Grand Gallery, my lord. The dancing has started but his grace has not yet announced his betrothal. I shall take you there myself, but..." His gaze swept up and down Amaryllis, and then to Ned, clutching her hand and sucking his thumb. "His grace will not permit the lady or the child to enter."

"Nevertheless, we are all going to see the duke, and if that is where he is to be found, that is where we must go. All of us."

"But my lord..."

"You may announce them as the Lady Edward Winfell and the Marquess of Darrowstone."

Bedford blanched, looked at Amaryllis again, then back to Gus. "You are quite sure of this, my lord? Because his grace has had his hopes raised before." Again he looked at Amaryllis.

"Bedford, it is the truth, as God is my witness."

Amaryllis bowed her head. If even the butler would not believe it, what hope had they of convincing the duke himself? He had already decided the matter in his own mind, and she was not sure what arguments Gus could bring to bear that the duke had not already considered. She could prove it, given time, but here and now? Tonight? All Gus had were words, and words would not be enough.

But the butler accepted Gus's statement. Her cloak was whisked away, and Bedford led them through dim passageways to the main stairs, lit by so many lamps that it was as bright as day. They ascended one flight of stairs and then another, Gus carrying Ned to the top. Then he set him down and Ned clasped her hand firmly again. Gus offered her his arm, and so they walked forward slowly behind the butler to a pair of carved oak doors, standing open to reveal an even brighter scene within. Music played, whirling couples danced, the ladies' gowns shimmered, their jewels dazzled and Amaryllis had almost to turn her head away at the brilliance she saw before her.

She would have hesitated, but the butler marched on with stately tread, and Gus directly behind him, and she was swept along too on the current of his determination. Yet all her fears, all her foreboding were before her now. Here was the aristocracy in all its glory, but that was Gus's world, not hers. She should not be here, this was all dreadfully wrong...

But Gus turned and smiled at her, and patted her hand with his, so that even through her glove and his, she could feel the warmth of his touch. "Be brave. This is for Ned, remember?"

For Ned. Yes, she could do that. Everything she had done thus far had been for Ned, to keep him safe. She could be brave for Ned, and also for Gus, for she did not want to let him down, not when he had done so much for her. And after this evening was over, after she had been humiliated in public, he would take her away and perhaps she could forget and be happy.

Then they were inside the doors, and the noise, the light, the brilliance were all around her. But Gus squeezed one hand and Ned clung to the other, and she lifted her chin defiantly. She would not crumble. She would not be a coward. She would face the next half hour with humility and a belief in God's grace, and she would get through it, somehow.

The butler took a staff from a footman, and banged it three times on the floor. Heads turned, the dancers slowed, even the musicians faltered and then stopped.

"The Marquess of Darrowstone, the Lady Edward Winfell, the Lord Augustus Marford, your grace."

Amaryllis wondered a little at the order of announcements, but supposed it was a matter of rank and beyond her comprehension. But there was no time to wonder about it, for the butler was standing aside, and then they were moving forward. Gus moved slowly, so that she and Ned could keep pace with him, but still it was inexorable, and she could not resist being drawn forwards too. All around them, she heard whispering, and fans were raised to hide the shocked expressions. The dancers parted like the Red Sea as their little party moved down the long room, and then she could see their destination, a dais at the far end, where sat several figures she did not recognise, and one she did. The duke. She knew that glowering expression of old. She lowered her gaze.

Gus came to a halt a few paces from the dais. The duke was on his feet, his legs spindly in his knee breeches and stockings. Evening dress was not kind to the elderly, and from her position below the dais, even with eyes lowered, she had an excellent view of his grace's bulbous knees.

Gus bowed, and she managed a curtsy of sorts. Not her best, but at least she did not wobble or fall over.

"Good evening, Duke," Gus began, in the sort of friendly tone he might use to an old acquaintance encountered unexpectedly. "A thousand apologies for interrupting your festivities, but we must discuss a matter which will brook no delay."

The duke made a low growling sound, like a dog. "You young people are so impetuous. It must all be done *now*, this very minute, or the world will no doubt end. But you are a meddlesome fool, Marford, and you bring great shame on the lady here by your actions. You had much sooner have waited, or better yet, done nothing at all."

"No, for events this evening have made it imperative that we resolve this issue."

"There is nothing to resolve, but if you insist, then you and I will withdraw and discuss the matter privily."

"No," Gus said, his voice a shade louder. "We will say what must be said here and now, for I will not leave the lady."

Amaryllis wished she could curl up into a ball like a hedgehog, and pretend none of this were happening, or if it were, that it had nothing at all to do with her. All that could come of this confrontation was that the duke would say publicly all that he had once said to her privately. But she trusted Gus, she had placed her confidence in him, and now, however much she trembled, she must see it through and not disgrace him. And there was Ned to consider, too, clinging tightly to her hand, silent and terrified, just as she was.

"As you wish," the duke said, drawing himself up to his full, imposing height. He raised his voice, so that he could be heard throughout the vast room. "Before you all, I declare that this woman is not my son's wife, and the child is no heir of mine, however much I may wish it to be so. I have examined all the facts and found no evidence to support the claim."

"But I have," Gus said, and his voice, although quiet, resonated throughout the room. "The Lord Edward Winfell married Miss Amaryllis Cordwainer by special licence at Holly Cottage in the town of Drifford. The officiating clergyman was Mr William Parker, and the marriage was witnessed by Mr Anthony White, a physician of that town, and Mr Joseph Cordwainer, a retired clergyman, and father of the bride, who gave his consent freely. The marriage was recorded in the register of the Old Drifford Church. Three months later, Lord Edward Winfell was killed in action in the Peninsula. Six months after that, his son was born, and the baptism of Edward John Henry Winfell was recorded in the same church register."

The silence in the room was absolute.

"You know all this?" the duke whispered.

"I do."

"But can you *prove* it?"

246

"I can. The special licence, the letter of consent and the church register are all presently within the walls of this castle, in the care of Mr William Parker and Mr Willerton-Forbes, awaiting the inspection of your grace's lawyers. Lady Edward's marriage lines are in the safe keeping of an attorney in High Morton."

The duke sat down heavily in his chair. Then he lifted his head and emitted an unearthly keening sound, the primal cry of the warrior after a successful battle when the enemy is finally slain, a cry that owed nothing at all to civilisation.

"God be praised!" he cried, his voice shaking with emotion. "I have a grandson at last."

~~~~~

Within an hour, a many-roomed apartment in the keep had been allocated to the duke's newly-found daughter-in-law and grandson, and an army of servants sent in to sweep and brush and polish, and whisk away holland covers and lay fires and smooth crisp, white linens and fluffy blankets on the beds.

From some obscure attic, footmen had wheeled in a scale model of the castle, the sides hinged to open up the interior, and boxes upon boxes of tiny furnishings and horses and carriages and even a battalion of miniature footmen to stand about in silent servitude, just like their larger counterparts. Ned was busily engaged in placing the horses in the Great Gallery, so that they might have room to gallop about, and beds in the stables, so that the grooms might not have to sleep upon the rigid blocks of wooden hay, while his grandfather sat on a stool nearby, unashamedly wiping away tears of joy.

"He will never sleep tonight," Amaryllis said to Gus, watching her son fondly. "What hour is it? Surely it is past midnight?"

"It must be," Gus said. "It hardly matters, for this one night. He will sleep when he is ready."

"But then it is already the Sabbath," she said, shocked. "He should not be playing today."

Gus picked up her hand, now relieved of its glove, and tucked it comfortably around his arm, so that he could stroke it, making her blush. "For this one night, let us not worry too much. It would be very hard to take him away from his grandpapa just yet. He will remember he is tired soon enough."

On a chair nearby, the Lady Rachel Medhurst sat in languid composure, fanning herself lazily. As the duke's newly chosen intended, she was entitled to feel disgruntled that her hour of glory had been upstaged by a slip of a girl and a four-year-old boy, but she gave no sign of anything but boredom.

The butler came into the room with another train of servants behind him, all laden with bags and boxes. "I beg pardon for the intrusion, milady, but where should we place these items from his lordship the marquess's bedroom at the lodge?"

She rubbed her eyes tiredly. "Is there an empty room where they may be left for now?"

"Of course, milady."

With many bows, he withdrew, his train of followers in a long line behind him, for all the world like a mother duck with her ducklings.

"It is going to take me a while to get used to these new names," Amaryllis said.

The duke looked up at her and cackled gleefully. "No need to get used to *yours*, I daresay, little lady. Marford here has plans for you to change it soon enough."

That made her blush all over again, but Gus just laughed. "Ah, there is no hiding anything from you, Duke." Which made the duke cackle even more.

Lady Rachel rose languidly to her feet. "Well, I am no longer wanted here, that is clear to see, so I shall go to my bed."

"Very well," the duke said. "On Monday I shall write to the Gazette, to have a notice posted of our betrothal."

"Do not bother," she said. "As if I would marry an old man like you."

"Then why did you pretend that you would, you silly woman?" the duke said.

"Why, to make you look ridiculous, of course. I had planned to wait until you formally offered for me the end of the evening before rejecting you, for the greatest possible humiliation, but the scheming hussy with the big, innocent eyes has rather sunk that idea. So I will just leave first thing tomorrow. Today, I suppose."

"But you cannot travel on a Sunday!" Amaryllis said, shocked.

Lady Rachel looked her up and down. "I am the daughter of a duke. I may do whatever I please."

"Then you would be very wrong," Amaryllis said stoutly.

With a titter that might have been embarrassment or annoyance, Lady Rachel swirled her skirts and strode out of the room without another word.

But the duke cackled again. "You put *her* in her place, little lady. Ha! Very wrong, indeed! These Medhursts are all the same, but what can one expect with these new dukedoms? Not much more than two hundred years old, Wedhampton's line. Upstarts, the lot of them."

"I find it is viscounts who are the most encroaching," Gus said. "No manners at all. But I think you have had a narrow escape there, Duke. She would have made your life miserable."

"You are probably right, but *she* is right too. What is more ridiculous than an old man bent on taking a new wife? I should have had more sense." He struggled to his feet, wincing. "Damnation, but this gout is a great trial to me. Where is Emma, that is what I should like to know? She had a way of getting me straight that none of these fool medical men can manage. Pleasant little thing, too. Not one for putting herself forward, like her dreadful sisters, or that Medhurst woman. Why was she not here tonight?"

"She left because you humiliated her with this contest of yours, Duke," Gus said. "She would have married you in a moment and made you very happy had you ever looked her way, but you never did. She would not perform for you like a circus animal, she said, so she left."

"She would have married me?"

"Certainly, and been thrilled about it. She told me some tale about watching you dance when she was just a girl, and how you were the handsomest man in the room. She has harboured a secret passion for you ever since."

"Emma?" the duke said, sitting heavily back down on his stool. "Emma Frensham? And you think she would not mind — me being such a grouchy old fool?"

Gus laughed. "She told me you were not really grouchy at all, that it was just the gout that made you cross."

"Good God! Oh, I beg your pardon, Amaryllis. I must learn to watch my language, eh? But where is she, Marford? Where is Emma? I must write to her. I must write this minute... no, not on the Sabbath, eh? Not on the Sabbath. I shall write first thing on Monday. But today, I shall attend chapel for once, and we shall have some fine uplifting hymns, and thank God with the greatest sincerity for His infinite grace."

And Amaryllis could agree with that with all her heart.

25: Well-Wishers

For three days, Amaryllis walked about in a dream. Servants bowed and curtsied deeply to her, those of importance from High Morton and the country around all came to pay their respects to her and admire the newly-discovered heir, a steady stream of gifts arrived, the duke was affable and smiled whenever he saw her, teams of seamstresses came to fit her out for her new position in society, and she was suddenly surrounded by kindness and gentleness and *people*. From her quiet solitude with Ned and three servants, she had been dropped into a maelstrom of callers and servants and no peace at all.

Her world had expanded greatly. The whole of the north lodge could have fitted into her new bedchamber, and she seemed to spend hours each day traipsing along endless corridors or up or down stairs to get from one place to another. And that was just the keep, for she had not yet been permitted to venture into the greater part of the castle for fear of Mrs Ballard leaping out from behind a pillar. Everywhere she went, three or four footmen trailed behind her to protect her.

But there was one great benefit to this restriction, in that all her visitors must be allowed into the keep itself, and the duke's long-held stricture that only those of blue blood be permitted therein was blown to smithereens. All the callers were shown into the nursery, where Ned could not be separated from the model castle, now populated with a great array of tiny residents in hooped skirts and enormous wigs, and his grandfather could not be separated from Ned. The duke spent most of his time sprawled full length on the floor, arranging the furnishings and wooden people according to the whims of his heir. So it was Amaryllis who dispensed tea and received the congratulations of the populace and tried to remember even one tenth of their names.

Fortunately, Gus was usually there too, and somehow the formal visits of strangers were less of an ordeal when he was there, talking on the easiest terms with everyone, gently chaffing the duke's occasional outbursts of ill-humour and unceremoniously carrying Ned away when he became fretful. Dear Gus! His calm good sense was so soothing to her.

The former heir and his wife, Mr and Mrs Richard Winfell, were amongst the visitors, greeting Amaryllis with wide smiles.

"*Such* a relief, you cannot guess!" Mrs Winfell said, sitting beside Amaryllis and patting her arm in a friendly way. "We was so happy to hear the news, for now we may go home to Cheshire and not trouble ourselves about being duke and duchess and living in a great stone monstrosity like this. Begging your pardon, my lady, I'm sure, for it's your home now, but I should find it an uncomfortable sort of a place. And we was never suited to being so high, you know, and certainly never wanted it. Why, my father is nought but an apothecary, and although he's perfectly respectable, it's not like being a duke, is it? Goodness, what a fine little man you have there! Such a sturdy little chap. Now my Peter is five now, but I declare he is not so tall as your boy. William, on the other hand…"

Amaryllis found it very restful to listen to Mrs Winfell rattling away about nothing in particular.

"Mama! Mama!" Ned yelled, brandishing a brown-paper-wrapped package. "Another present! May I open it?"

"Bring it over here, and you may open it in front of me, for if it is more pistols—"

"It is sweeties! Look! May I have some now?"

"Just one, no more. If you eat up all your dinner, you may have some more afterwards."

Ned took a bite of one of the sugar-coated sweets, pulled a face and wandered away again. Amaryllis laughed. "He is getting so spoilt! A few days ago such a gift would have been a rare treat, and I would have been hard pressed to prevent him eating the whole box in one sitting."

"Mine are like that too, and they are accustomed to such treats," Mrs Winfell said, looking after Ned with a frown. "May I see the box? Oh, this is from a very good shop in the town, but they are strangely misshapen, are they not? What does the note say?"

"Just *'From a well-wisher'*," Amaryllis said. "But—"

Mrs Winfell picked up the half-eaten sweet and sniffed at it. "Tell me, would anyone wish to harm Ned?"

Amaryllis turned cold. "*Yes!*" she cried. "There is one who might— Oh God! Ned!" As she watched, Ned's feet faltered. He turned glassy eyes to her, and took one wobbly step before collapsing.

"Quick, a basin, a bowl, anything!" cried Mrs Winfell. "No, stand aside from him, all of you. I am an apothecary's daughter, I know what to do."

And she did, too. Without hesitation, she picked Ned up, rolled him onto his side and pushed her fingers down his throat. His whole body heaved, and he vomited copiously over Mrs Winfell's and Amaryllis's skirts, and the duke's shoes. Then he vomited again.

"Well done, little man," said Mrs Winfell in pleased tones. "An excellent response."

"Will he... be all right?" Amaryllis whispered, gazing at the pale, unmoving form of her son.

"I will not lie," Mrs Winfell said. "Without knowing the precise form of poison used, it is impossible to be sure. Some poisons are so virulent that the patient cannot be saved. But see, there on my gown, the half sweet that he ate, quite intact. He did not even chew it. That gives me some hope that he has only absorbed a small amount, and may well make a full recovery."

And within a very few minutes, even Amaryllis's anxious eyes could detect a greater colour in Ned's cheeks, and not long after that his eyes fluttered open. Within an hour, he was declaring himself famished, and could he please have something to eat now?

Amaryllis and the duke wept quietly together in relief.

~~~~~

Gus waited only to be sure that Ned would live before riding out. The duke was organising constables and deploying troops, but Gus could not delay. He took with him Edgerton and Merton, and as many grooms as could ride fast. Since not all could jump, they took the road to Drifford, terrorising the sedate matrons' carriages and forcing aside farmers' carts, for no one was to stand in Gus's way when Ned's life had been threatened. His anger burned inside him like a simmering volcano, and his only thought was to find Mrs Ballard and reduce her to gibbering terror, for putting Amaryllis — all of them — through such an ordeal.

What kind of woman avenges herself by the killing of a child, an innocent? What insanity must inhabit her mind to make anyone want to do such a thing? He knew not, but of one thing alone he was coldly and irrevocably sure — that Mrs Ballard was responsible for this devilry. She was a wicked, wicked woman, and she would hang for what she had done, on that he was determined.

They tore into Drifford Square and turned towards Drifford House. The gates were closed, but they were arched in the middle and low at either end, and Jupiter jumped them without breaking stride. Gus pelted up the drive, slithered to a halt, sending gravel pinging against the walls, and tossed Jupiter's reins over a bush. Then he took the steps two at a time, and banged on the door with fists and riding crop, then the knocker, and then his fists again.

"Open up!" he yelled. "Open this door at once!"

Edgerton and Merton came up behind him, and Merton rang the bell, explaining mildly, "They may not hear knocking from the basement."

Eventually a footman answered, but before he could speak, Gus had barged past him and into the hall. "Where is she? Where is Mrs Ballard?"

"I regret, sir—"

"No, tell me no lies. I *will* see her, and I will search this house from top to bottom to find her and so you may tell her."

"What is happening?" said a gentle voice from the stairs. "What is all this noise, Terence?" A young man appeared, very finely dressed, and with a cultured accent. Gus guessed him to be about thirty.

"Sir, these gentlemen—"

Gus pushed past him. "I am Lord Augustus Marford. I have no idea who *you* are, sir, but I am looking for Mrs Ballard on a matter of great urgency. Is she within?"

"My wife is within, but—"

"Your *wife?* Oh but—"

"—she has just this past hour presented me with a fine son, our first."

Gus was momentarily taken aback. It was Merton who stepped forward. "You are Mr *Richard* Ballard, I surmise? Then it is your mother whom we seek, Mrs Charles Ballard."

Ballard seemed himself to understand the situation, for he ushered them into a strongly masculine room, bade them sit and offered them refreshments.

"We have no time for this!" Gus burst out, but Merton placed a hand on his arm.

"Let us be patient, my lord. Mr Ballard will, I believe, explain all to us. For I suspect that the Mrs Ballard *we* want is no longer here."

"You are correct, sir," Ballard said. "My father returned unexpectedly two days ago, and took my mother away. He was very angry, for she had tried to take a child from its mother, something of which he strongly disapproved. They quarrelled but my father had the better of it, as he always does. He said they must leave at once, and never come back, and I am not even to know of their whereabouts. And so I am Master of Drifford now, a little earlier than expected, and this house is mine. We have not properly moved in yet, but my wife wanted the baby to be born here. I am sorry, was your business with my mother a matter of great import?"

"It was a matter of justice," Gus said. "A child almost died today because of your mother, sir."

"I do not see how that could be," he said calmly, "when she left here two days ago."

Gus was so flummoxed by this that he could not even form a reply, and jumped up at once to leave. Ballard accompanied them to the front door.

"I daresay we will see more of each other in future, Lord Augustus," Ballard said. "Mrs Ballard is keen to move in a wider society once she is able to go out again, and so we will be spending some time in High Morton, and perhaps even London, who knows?"

Gus bowed stiffly, but could not find it in him to express pleasure in such a prospect. Instead he said, "So you have ownership of Drifford now, sir?"

"I do." There was no mistaking the avaricious grin on his face at the change in circumstance.

"It would please me to know that a man who controls the lives of so many would have a greater care for them than his predecessor. There is much poverty in this town, Ballard, and great need of a benevolent master."

The smile widened. "There is also much idleness here, Marford, and great need of discipline. If a man gives food to those who will not work for it, he only encourages sloth. My mother brought this town from nothing to be a shining beacon of profit in this wilderness of ignorance. I intend to follow her precepts to the letter. Good day to you."

And he shut the door in their faces.

"That was rude," Edgerton said, as they remounted and rode at a more sedate pace down the drive. "He called you Marford, too. Ignorant little runt."

"He is very full of himself and his new dignity," Merton said. "I wish I could stay to see society reject him and his wife."

"Society will receive them," Gus said with certainty. "He is a gentleman, his wife is a lady and they are rich. But can we be mistaken in Mrs Ballard? If she left two days ago—"

"Did you not see the triumphant gleam in his eye when he spoke of it?" Merton said. "And he was neither surprised nor shocked to hear of it. No, he knows all about the business. And no one supposed that Mrs Ballard herself delivered the present to the castle. It must have been arranged before she left, and perhaps Mr Richard Ballard himself arranged the delivery. The duke will find it all out, and you may be sure that Mrs Ballard was behind it."

"But is Ned safe now?"

It was a question none of them could answer.

Merton dismounted to open the gates, since no gatekeeper had materialised. As he was fumbling with the latch, a great commotion could be heard at the far side of the square, momentarily hidden from them by the plinth and voluminous skirts of Mrs Ballard's statue. From behind it appeared a cavalcade of many horses bearing banners and trumpeters and a whole host of attendants surrounding a large man on a horse massive enough to have carried a medieval knight in full armour.

"Good God! The duke!" Edgerton said. "What a splendid old fellow he is."

One of the trumpeters blew a violent blast, a sound to which Jupiter took extreme exception, and Gus was fully occupied in controlling his mount for some minutes, aware of some announcement being made but unable to listen.

"What did he say? What is happening?" he hissed to Edgerton, as soon as Jupiter had calmed down.

Edgerton laughed. "Inspection of all warehouses, weaving halls and manufactories, in his role as local magistrate. Also investigation of the Ballards' claim to ownership. Oh, and look, he has invited all his friends to the party."

From the other end of the square, neat lines of soldiers marched in perfect synchrony and began to parade around the perimeter, before forming up in orderly fashion. The local population, drawn onto the streets by the commotion, began to cheer and wave handkerchiefs.

"Too much of a rabble for me," Gus muttered, struggling to control Jupiter as the crowds became rowdier. "I shall expect a full report later, Edgerton."

And with that, he released Jupiter and, scattering riders and townsfolk in all directions, let the horse race for home.

Gus settled Jupiter in the stables and went to check on Ned, who was sleeping peacefully. Fortunately, Amaryllis was not sleeping and was very happy to see him, and ply him with tea and cake, and hear all about the afternoon's adventures. Somehow, by the time he got back to his own rooms, the others were back.

"You should have stayed, Marford," Edgerton said. "Young Ballard came marching out of his fine house to see off the miserable interloper who was making the town square look untidy, and ran up against a peer of the realm in all his splendour. I do like the old boy, you know, but I am very glad he is on our side. He is magnificent at one and sixty, so I cannot even conceive how glorious a sight he must have been in his prime. He dispatched Ballard in two minutes, and by the end the poor boy was very grateful to be allowed to stay on until after his wife's lying in. In a few weeks, the place will be free of Ballards and that hideous statue will be pulled down. There will be champagne for you in the keep tonight, I wager."

"Shall I order some for you?" Gus said, amused. "You may celebrate too, if you wish."

"We are going to celebrate by relieving Mr Parker of his vicar's stipend," Edgerton said cheerfully.

For the first time Gus noticed that the cards and Madeira were out, and the clergyman was shuffling expertly, and dealing to Edgerton, Merton and Willerton-Forbes.

"Are you a keen card player, Mr Parker?" Gus said.

"I am accounted a tolerable player, my lord, and I must do something to pass the time, since I cannot return home until his grace's lawyers arrive from London. Shall I be dreadfully out of my depth, do you suppose?"

"You will need to watch Merton and Edgerton very carefully," Gus said. "Merton because he is almost as good a player as my brother Humphrey, and Edgerton because he will bamboozle you into a mistake. As for Willerton-Forbes, he is a lawyer, so all in all, I should say you are sunk, Mr Parker."

"Oh dear, oh dear. Well, I shall just have to do the best I can," Parker said cheerfully.

"There are letters for you," Merton said. "On the mantel. One is from Lady Carrbridge."

"So it is, but this one I do not recognise." He broke the seal, and unfolded the sheet. "Good God! It is from Charles Ballard. Listen to this. *'My lord, Forgive my presumption in writing to one who is quite unknown to me, nor likely to be, as being quite above my humble station in life. However, if I may beg your indulgence to read these few words, I hope I may ease your mind about a recent dreadful event occurring to one close to you. My wife has confessed to me that she has done a dreadful thing, in attempting to remove a child from the arms of its mother. I need not tell you how horrified I was that such a thing should happen, and my own wife be the cause. She, of all people, should understand the distress of a mother upon the loss of a child. She has been, perhaps, too much indulged and allowed to dwell upon a tragedy in our own family, the details of which you already know, I understand. My wife's despair has long been a concern to me, and can no longer be ignored, nor may she be left unattended to cause what misery and evil she will. I have therefore taken steps to have her admitted to an asylum where her particular needs may be addressed without risk to any innocent person. To avoid the shame necessarily attendant upon such a measure, I have chosen to give her a false name for this purpose. I trust that in revealing these details, I may alleviate your mind from any further concerns on her account. She will cause no further injury to anyone close to you. I have the honour to be your lordship's most obedient servant, Charles Ballard.'* Well, Merton, what do you make of that?"

"Do you wish my honest opinion? Then it seems to me that he wishes the constables to stop looking for his wife in order to bring her to justice. Admitted to an asylum? Under a false name? How convenient!"

"Oh, that does make sense." Gus was immediately deflated. "But the more important point is this — can we assume that Ned is no longer in danger from this woman? *'She will cause no further injury to anyone close to you.'* That sounds almost like a reference to the poison."

"Possibly. One fact I think is now established beyond doubt — that all the Ballards will shortly be removed from the neighbourhood. That must be a great relief to all who care for the boy's welfare. It seems to me that the poison was a last vicious attempt at revenge."

"That is my feeling, too," Gus said. He turned to Connie's letter, which was bound to be full of trivial news and therefore a perfect distraction.

'My dear Gus, Once more we are all in uproar here, and I can scarce believe the words I must write, but nevertheless it is true — Mr Sharp has been here! He arrived quite unannounced, as he always does, but his poor wife had become so terrified of him with all these revelations about mistresses and falseness and the misappropriation of money that she ran screaming into the stable

court that he was come home and may the Lord help her. The Lord was not on hand, but Lady Humphrey was, having just ridden in, and she went straight into Mr Sharp's cottage and laid about him with her riding crop, whereupon the villain ran out and mounted a horse already saddled and waiting and rode off. And Lady H then mounted up and rode after him! And half the grooms went after, and then Humphrey and Francis in great anger, all chasing after Mr S. But luckily for him, Lady H's horse was already tired or else she would surely have caught up with him and killed him and then where would we all be and Humphrey would have been very upset if his wife had been hanged, and all for murdering a wicked man like Mr S. So he got clean away. But inside his cottage was found a hidden safe under the floorboards, already opened and containing no end of money which no doubt he had hoped to get away to fund his continued wickedness. Francis had never seen so much, and all his, of course. Pray tell Mr Merton that it has all been locked away in the safe in the library, awaiting his return to count it, for Francis becomes dizzy at anything more than a hundred pounds. And as if that were not enough upset for one day, word came from Gil's colonel that he has been injured, although in a duel not a battle for he has not yet left Dover and there are not many Frenchmen in Dover. And Francis is beside himself and swears that he never sent Gil into the army to be killed although what he expected with Gil I do not know, for everyone else thought it very likely that he would be killed at once, for he is so wild it is inevitable but if he could kill a few Frenchmen first, then he would not have died in vain. Although I am very glad that he has not been killed, naturally. But we do not quite know what is to happen to him, and Humphrey talked very gloomily of cashiering which sounds very dreadful and I hope it will not come to that. But you must not worry about us for we are all well and little William has not one but two new teeth, and Lady H is increasing and Humphrey is so proud it is very sweet. Please write soon, Gus, for I *have not heard anything for days and I want to know <u>everything</u> about your widow. Your affectionate sister-in-law, Connie.'*

Gus retailed the bulk of this to Merton.

"Ah! Then I must hasten my departure," Merton said. "Indeed, there is little purpose to staying longer."

"You do not think Sharp — or Harcourt — will come here now? He will not take your bait?"

"I do not believe so, for he must have received my letter long since. He knows me too well to be convinced by any hint of corruption, I suspect, and is too astute to allow himself to be taken in. No, I imagine if we were to return to the White Cottage now, we should find it all closed up. Sharp or Harcourt is long since away in that fancy carriage of his."

"Oh…" Something fell into place in Gus's mind. "The carriage… the one from the White Cottage. I have seen it recently."

"Really? Where?"

"Here, at the castle. It was the one that brought Mrs Ballard here when she tried to take Ned away. But… how is that possible?"

Merton groaned, and threw down his cards. "I have been a fool. Why did I not think of that possibility?"

"What possibility?"

"That Sharp — and Harcourt — are also *Ballard*. Charles Ballard is Ambrose Sharp. He must have left here and gone straight to Drummoor. And I do not imagine his way took him past an asylum."

Into the shocked silence, Mr Parker coughed politely. "My trick again, I think, gentlemen?"

26: Proposals

There were many delightful aspects to having Amaryllis living within the castle, Gus decided, but not the least of them was the inestimable joy of dining with her every night. He now raced impatiently through the dreary duty of bathing and dressing in order to rush across the bridge to the duke's drawing room. She was always there before him, so elegant in her simple gowns and her hair adorned with no more than a ribbon or two and a few silk flowers.

"How lovely you look," he murmured, bending over her hand, and smiling at her blushing confusion. She had never learnt the sophisticated art of accepting a compliment as if it were her right, and he loved her all the more for it. "How is Ned?" It was two days since he had fully recovered from the poison, and Gus had seen him not three hours ago, but nevertheless the question had become a habit.

"He is well. The duke is very out of sorts, however."

Gus could hear the grumbling from across the room. He still had a small coterie of ladies about him, for although most of the candidates for his hand had long since left, a few persistent souls lingered, amongst them Emma's sister Maria.

"Marford!" the duke called out. "Stop making love to my daughter-in-law and get rid of these pestilent women for me. I cannot imagine why they are here, for I am sure I do not want them. Make them go away, Marford, for they give me no peace."

Maria tittered. "Such a wit you are, Duke, to be sure. As if we do not desire your comfort above all things. Do let me straighten your cushions for you."

"Get away from me, woman!" He flapped at her ineffectually, as she pulled out one cushion after another from behind his back. "Leave me alone! If I want your— Emma! At last!"

The door burst open, and Emma marched in, still wearing her travelling clothes as if she had just that moment stepped from the carriage. She strode across to the duke's chair, scattering his little entourage, and dropped to her knees in front of him, so that her eyes were level with his.

"I am here."

"Emma, why did you go away? I did not tell you to go. You must never go away again, do you hear?"

"Well, I shall not, then, if you dislike the idea so, but Harry, you must not tease me any more with this nonsense about competitions and enticements. It was unkind in you."

"It was just my foolishness, my dear," he said. "Bedford? *Bedford!* Get this rug away from me, and help me up."

Emma jumped up. "No, Harry, your feet—"

"Got to do this properly," he said, wobbling on Bedford's arm. Then, using the chair arm for support, he slowly lowered himself to one knee. "Emma Winifred Charlotte Frensham, would you make an old man very happy and do me the very great honour of becoming my wife?"

"Oh, Harry, how romantic!" Emma cried, clapping her hands together. "And you even looked up all my names in Debrett's. Yes *please*. I should like to be your wife of all things. Oh, but do get up, for I see how much your gout pains you. Here, let me help you. There now." She sat him back down in his chair, and again knelt at his feet. "That was quite the loveliest proposal I have ever had, Harry, although it must be said that there have not been a *great* many others. Still, it was delightfully done. But we must be married very soon, you know, for I want to get busy with babies and so forth as quick as may be, and I am sure *you* do too."

The duke chuckled. "I find I do not care very much if there are any babies or not, but we shall have fun finding out, eh, my dear?"

And Emma, quite unembarrassed, laid her head on his lap and sighed contentedly.

Beside Gus, Amaryllis sighed too. "That was charmingly done."

"Although as offers go, it was deficient, I felt," Gus said gravely. "He said nothing about his income or position in society or how well suited they were, nor did he mention love."

Amaryllis laughed at the idea that a duke needed to say any of those things. "As for love, he said she would make him happy, and who could doubt it? Everyone must be thrilled for them."

"Except her sister," Gus whispered. "She has a face that would freeze the fires of Hell just now. Poor Maria! To be outranked by Emma at last. How will she bear it?"

~~~~~

The lawyers from London arrived in great state, accompanied by several learned gentlemen from the House of Lords, to examine the documents relating to Amaryllis's marriage.

"You will need to be interviewed by them, little lady," the duke told her, as they sat at dinner one day.

"Oh, must I? For it is all set down in the papers, is it not?"

"They will not ask anything terribly difficult, I am sure," Emma said. "I daresay they just want to know your father's name and so forth, so that everything may be set down correctly in the Rolls."

"I shall be there, too," the duke said, then gazed at her from beneath bushy eyebrows. "Hmm, you are a timid little puss, are you not? Should you like it if Marford were to be there too?"

"I should like that very much," she said, with a little warm feeling inside. Everything was so much easier if Gus were with her.

"Lady Edward is not so timid when her child is threatened," Gus said. "She becomes a tiger then."

Amaryllis blushed, but she glowed a little too. Such a fine compliment! And he never made it sound outrageous, as some men did when they complimented one. He said such things as if they were mere statements of fact.

"True, she did well against that Ballard woman, holding out until the cavalry arrived. Well done, indeed, little lady. And now I have charge of the boy's safety, and I shall not rest until every last one of that rats' nest of Ballards is gone from here. Ned will have food tasters and bodyguards and whatever is necessary to keep him from harm."

"And he also needs fresh air and to run about and be a child," Amaryllis said firmly. "I will not allow you to keep him imprisoned, even for his own safety."

The duke glowered at her for a moment. "Hmpf. He is my heir, you know, my only bulwark against the attorney from Cheshire."

"Then you had better get busy with Lady Emma and produce some more bulwarks," she said sweetly.

And the duke gave a bark of laughter, and patted her arm and called her a cheeky little monkey.

Emma was quite right about the lawyers. They questioned Amaryllis in the gentlest manner possible about her family, trying, it seemed, to connect her to some noble line, although without success. But they were quite satisfied in the legality of the marriage, and congratulated her heartily, and the duke too, for his acquisition of an heir.

The retrieval of Amaryllis's marriage lines from the attorney in High Morton had also produced another will, written with Lord Edward's marriage in mind. It was very similar to the previous will, except that there was a settlement for Amaryllis, and the residue of the estate was left explicitly to any issue of the marriage, or, if there was none, to Amaryllis herself.

"Like a sensible man he made provision for the change in circumstances," the lawyer said, beaming. "It all goes to the young Marquess of Darrowstone, to be held in trust until he attains the age of one and twenty, with you as the sole trustee, Lady Edward. And the first decision you will have to make in that role is to decide the future of the stud. Have you thought at all about whether you wish to sell the horses? For Tattersall's has been waiting for some time for a decision."

"And they may wait even longer," Gus said quietly. "Lady Edward may take as much time as she needs to make such a decision."

"Oh, no, I do not need time to decide," she said at once. "I do not wish to sell the horses. My husband bought them for his brother, because he believed in his ideas. It was something he talked about to me on occasion. I should like to see the stud thrive."

"Well, that is very decided," the lawyer said. "Very decided indeed. Very well. As for the rest of Lord Edward's estate, it is all invested here and there, and the income is entirely yours until such time as your son comes of age, and one third thereafter, for your lifetime. And should you remarry…"

His eyes twinkled at her, making her blush. She dared not look at Gus, but she knew exactly what was meant. And she held her breath… would she lose everything if she married Gus? Would it make a difference? Not to her, but to him and to his family, perhaps it might.

"There are no conditions," the lawyer said. "None whatsoever. Lord Edward was a generous man, Lady Edward, and trusted you implicitly. And I do not believe his confidence was misplaced, do you?" He threw a quick glance at Gus, and chuckled.

~~~~~

Gus was up early the next morning to see Edgerton, Merton and Willerton-Forbes on the road south. Edgerton was uncharacteristically glum.

"Did you not enjoy your stay in the far north, Michael?" Gus said, amused.

"I should have enjoyed it more if the ladies hereabouts had been a little friendlier," he confessed. "All promise, they are, and none of them willing to make good on it. I have never expended so much effort for so little reward. If you see Mrs Masterson wearing a very pretty pearl necklace, you may wish her joy of it from me. I do not like being bested by a woman like that. And as for gentle little clergymen, who innocently claim they hardly ever play cards… do not believe a word of it. I shall be hard put to it to pay my way home."

"I think I lost more to him," Merton said.

"Aye, I believe you did," Edgerton said.

"You mean Mr Parker?"

"The very one. Willerton-Forbes gave it up after an hour or so, and we should have done the same. If ever Lord Humphrey comes up here to visit, you may set him the task of recovering my blunt from Parker. I take it you are staying?"

Gus nodded. "I have already sent my resignation to Tattersall's, for I cannot leave Lady Edward just now."

"Well, I shall take the liberty of wishing you joy, even if it is a little premature," Edgerton said. "Heaven knows when we may meet again."

Later that morning, Gus took Ned to see the stud horses that were now his, accompanied by Amaryllis, six solid footmen and a couple of maids.

"Good morning, Lord Gus!"

Gus was getting used to his new epithet. "Waterbury. How are you?"

"Very well indeed, as you may imagine. Oh, I can see that you do not know! Do you remember Light As Air, the pretty little filly you suggested we race? Well, we took you at your word, and sent her to Newcastle and she won! Can you believe it? It is the most famous thing, and..." He lowered his voice conspiratorially. "I hear that Lady Edward is not inclined to sell. That is excellent news, for with a victory under our belts, all these horses are immediately more valuable. Is it not wonderful? The marquess's theories on breeding are quite vindicated."

Ned was enchanted with the idea that he owned all the horses, and wanted to know the name of every one, and pat each one on the nose and offer a lump of sugar. His tour of the stables took a very long time.

"He is exhausted," Amaryllis said. "Look at the way he pulls his hair. Lucy, will you take him back to the castle for a nap?"

"Shall we go back too?" Gus said.

"Will you walk with me?" she said, and he nodded his acquiescence.

Somehow it did not surprise him when their walk led to the little arbour with its seat. They still had three footmen and a maid dogging their footsteps, but when they stopped, Gus said to them, "Stand further off, will you? You may protect us just as well from twenty yards as two."

"Thank you," Amaryllis said, smiling up at him in that heart-stopping way of hers. "So much attention is rather overwhelming. Gus… will you take your gloves off? I should like to hold your hand."

He was delighted to oblige. Her hand was so soft and warm in his, yet so tiny, like a little bird settled in his palm, fluttering there, afraid but trusting.

She sighed. "That feels so lovely. I had never realised how much I needed this — touching. Being held, as you held me that night we nearly lost Ned to *her*. I have always been so… alone. Papa was like a friend to me, but it is not the same, is it? There were things I could not share with him. But when I married Edward… he made me feel very safe. Protected. For a brief time, I did not have to be strong and think of everything and make all the decisions."

"You are safe now," Gus said. "The duke will protect you."

"That is not the *same*," she cried with unexpected passion. "Papa protected me too, but it is not the same. Will you protect me?"

He hesitated. "Amaryllis, I am yours to command, always, you must know that. But I am a simple man, and do not understand subtleties. Tell me in plain terms what you want from me, and you shall have it."

She looked at him with her guileless blue eyes, as if debating whether he truly meant it. Then she said, "I want to know... why you have not yet asked me to marry you."

The honesty of it took his breath away. He could only be equally honest in return. "Because... I did not know who you were, for a long time. Now, because your life is in turmoil and I would not add to it. Because it is not clear to me how to fit into your new life. Because I did not know when it was the right time. And more than any of those things, because you are a very wealthy woman and I have *nothing*, not a penny to my name, except for my brother's charity. I am not worthy of you, and I do not yet know how to overcome that obstacle."

"That is *not* an obstacle," she said fiercely. "My husband trusted me enough to make me independently wealthy, quite apart from Ned's inheritance. He settled twenty thousand pounds on me, and a house too, all in my own name, and those are mine no matter what happens. Edward trusted me to choose my *next* husband well, to choose a man worthy to succeed him, and I have done that. Gus, you have asked me what I want from you and I cannot speak plainer. I want you in my life, in my arms, as you are in my heart. And if you truly need me to tell you... this is the right time to propose."

He closed his eyes momentarily, swept by joy, by relief... by love. Then he took both her hands in his.

"Amaryllis..." He stopped, mesmerised by those blue eyes that had haunted his dreams. "I... do not know the right words. All I know is that I love you more than anything in the world – more than my horses, which I never thought was possible, and I would cherish you more, far more, than I ever cherished them. I would love you and protect you and stand beside you for ever, if you will have me. Will you? Please?"

"I will," she said, smiling up at him and making his heart turn over, then added in severe tones, "Although… you said nothing of income or your position in society, you know, which an offer should always include, if at all possible."

He laughed at that, remembering his own words after the duke's proposal. "But at least I mentioned love."

"So you did, and that is all that matters. Dear Gus… the love of my life.

He scooped her into his arms, and pressed her close. "My darling, my sweet angel…"

Her lovely face was so close to his, close enough that he could feel the warmth of her breath. He ran one finger wonderingly down her soft cheek, trembling with joy at her nearness. Finally, after all the doubts and long anxious days of wondering who she was and how he could ever win her — she was his own love, his Amaryllis. She would never leave him. Almost imperceptibly, he moved closer to her, and then his lips were on hers — oh, such sweetness! — and, wondrously, she was kissing him back with such fiery passion that he was almost overcome. For a long, long time they clung together, until his lips were bruised and he was sure he would explode with happiness.

"When?" he whispered, as soon as he could formulate the thought. "When may I make you mine?"

"Whenever the banns can be read," she said. "I have waited such a long time for you, my beloved Gus, for a man who truly owns my heart. I do not want to wait a moment longer than I have to."

"I have no objection to such a plan," he said. "But I must go home for a while…"

She pulled away from him, her face fearful. "Why? Why must you go? Do not leave me!"

"Well, perhaps it may be done by letter. But I must make arrangements."

"There must be people who can pack up your clothes for you," she cried.

"It is not my clothes that concern me. I need to dispose of my horses, and—"

"Your horses! But why?"

"Because I have more horses than any sensible man needs. I decided some time ago that I would get rid of them. It was when I thought, you see, that you were Lord Edward's mistress and that I should be cast out of all good society when I wed you. I would only have my brother's allowance to live on, and so—"

"You would have married me, even thinking I had no reputation at all?"

"Of course. Why should I care about that? It might be significant to society, but you are the same person, the same sweet, good-natured, delightful person, and you matter to me more than anything in the world."

"Oh Gus!" She laid her head on his shoulder. "As to your horses — that is up to you. If — *when* we marry, there will be money enough for as many horses as you want, but you must decide that for yourself. The question of how you will fit into my new life is difficult, because I do not yet know how *I* will fit into it. But I feel that Ned must stay here, and therefore I must stay here, and that means that you must stay here, too."

"I understand," he said. "But I shall feel very useless."

"No, you will not, for you will have work to do, if you want it. I very much hope that you will manage the stud for Ned."

"Oh..." Joy bubbled up inside him. "That is... perfect!" he said. "I should like that very much. And if I write to Humphrey, he can arrange to sell my own horses for me. He will see that they go to good homes, where they will be well looked after, and cherished just as I have cherished them. It would tear at my heart to send them to be auctioned to strangers at Tattersall's. There is an irony, is it not? I came here to sell the stud horses, and in the end it is my horses which are to be sold."

"But not Jupiter," she said firmly.

"No?"

"No. For that is how we met, remember? First he nearly ran me down, and then Ned. Without Jupiter we should never have known each other, so you must never sell him, never."

"It shall be just as you wish, my love," Gus said, and bent his head to kiss her again.

Thanks for reading!

If you have enjoyed reading this book, please consider writing a short review on Amazon. You can find out the latest news and sign up for the mailing list at my website: http://marykingswood.co.uk/

A note on historical accuracy: I have endeavoured to stay true to the spirit of Regency times, and have avoided taking too many liberties or imposing modern sensibilities on my characters. The book is not one of historical record, but I've tried to make it reasonably accurate. However, I'm not perfect! If you spot a historical error, I'd very much appreciate knowing about it so that I can correct it and learn from it. Thank you!

About Sons of the Marquess: *the Ninth Marquess of Carrbridge is happily married to the former Miss Constance Allamont, he has an heir and a spare in the nursery, and all seems set fair for a life of perfect bliss. His five younger brothers are a bit of a handful, but young men like to spread their wings a bit. If only they weren't so expensive! And whatever happened to that huge income his father used to boast about? It seems to have vanished in a generation. And now there's the unknown son of his father's who claims to be the legitimate heir to the Marquessate. It's a bit much for a Marquess to deal with. Fortunately, his wife has some ideas about recovering their position...*

Book 0: The Earl of Deveron (a novella, free to mailing list subscribers)
Book 1: Lord Reginald
Book 2: Lord Humphrey
Book 3: Lord Augustus

Book 4: Lord Montague
Book 5: Lord Gilbert

About the author

I write traditional Regency romances under the pen name Mary Kingswood, and epic fantasy as Pauline M Ross. I live in the beautiful Highlands of Scotland with my husband. I like chocolate, whisky, my Kindle, massed pipe bands, long leisurely lunches, chocolate, going places in my campervan, eating pizza in Italy, summer nights that never get dark, wood fires in winter, chocolate, the view from the study window looking out over the Moray Firth and the Black Isle to the mountains beyond. And chocolate. I dislike driving on motorways, cooking, shopping, hospitals.

Acknowledgements

Thanks go to:

My mother, who first introduced me to the wonderful world of Jane Austen.

Shayne Rutherford of Darkmoon Graphics for the cover design.

My beta reader: Mary Burnett.

Last, but definitely not least, my first reader: Amy Ross.

Sneak Preview of Lord Montague: Chapter 1: A Debt Of Honour

"Melissa, I hope you have a pretty gown for evening tucked away somewhere," the new earl said. She still thought of him as the new earl, although his father had died more than two years ago.

"My lord?"

"You will be dining with the family tonight, so be sure to look your best."

"With the family? Me?"

"Ah, I see your pleasure," he said smugly. "A rare treat for you. But why not, just this once, eh?"

So rare a treat was it, that Melissa could never remember it happening before, and was mistrustful. Lord Bentley was not a man who dispensed largesse, or even kindness, as a rule, and she was quite certain this outburst of generosity had some dark motive.

But still, a dinner in company was a welcome event. She curtsied and thanked him with sincerity, and went to see which of her two evening gowns might manage to rise to the occasion. Neither were worn very often, and both had been cast-offs from the present earl's stepmother, taking pity on Melissa before the annual servants' ball. The pink, she supposed, being the newer and least faded of the two. The previous Lady Bentley had had a pale prettiness that was well-suited to delicate colours, and the gown had looked charming on her. With Melissa's dark complexion, it looked less well. How she wished the present Lady Bentley would offer her a gown, for the striking colours she liked would suit Melissa admirably.

When the dressing gong sounded, Melissa was already in her little room, half undressed and trying to decide whether the addition of ribbons in her hair made her look even more ridiculous or not, when a tap at the door revealed Miss Thompson, Lady Bentley's maid.

"Milady sent me to help you dress, miss," she said, with an audible sniff of disapproval.

"Oh. How very kind of her ladyship." And how very unexpected. Now Melissa was deeply suspicious. She had a sinking feeling that she was being wrapped up like a gift, to be shown off to someone. Perhaps the countess had found her another position, now that she was no longer wanted at Bentley Hall? Although prospective governesses were not usually paraded at dinner. Well, she would find out soon enough.

Miss Thompson primped and curled and fussed until Melissa hardly recognised herself in the glass.

"There, miss, you look very pretty," Miss Thompson said, and her thin lips almost twitched into a smile.

Was she pretty? She would love to be pretty, or perhaps handsome. Everyone said that the present Lady Bentley was handsome, and it seemed to be a compliment, but Melissa was not quite sure what they meant by it. Lady Bentley was elegant, to be sure, in her exquisite colourful gowns, and her manner of piling her blonde curls on top of her head gave her an imposing height, but her countenance was not pleasing. But perhaps that was because she was always scowling when Melissa saw her.

She was not scowling when Melissa entered the drawing room. When she smiled, however insincerely, she did indeed look quite handsome.

"Ah, here she is at last! How impatiently we have awaited you, Melissa dear, but we do not mind in the least, for see how we are rewarded. I never saw you look better, my dear."

"I did not mean to be late. I beg your pardon."

She tittered. "My dear, I intended no rebuke."

Melissa was silent. Since when had Lady Bentley not had a rebuke on her lips? Her first lesson as soon as the new earl had married was to learn to keep out of his wife's way.

The countess rose smoothly from her chair and crossed the room to where her husband and brother-in-law stood with a third man, unknown to Melissa. The earl was shorter than average, with an undistinguished air. His brother tended to foppery, with an excessively complicated cravat, a bright red coat and such an array of rings and pins and fobs as to quite dazzle the eye. The stranger was excessively fat, his coat buttons straining across his vast stomach, and a balding head already shining from the heat.

"Here she is, gentlemen. Mr Pontefract, may I present to you Lord Bentley's ward, Miss Frost?"

"Enchanted, my dear," he murmured, creaking as he inclined very slightly from the vertical in what Melissa supposed was a bow. As she rose from her curtsy, he was licking his lips as if she were a particularly tasty dish presented at the dinner table. "Delightful, quite delightful." His eyes ran slowly down to her shoes and back up again, before settling on her chest. "Charming!" He rubbed his hands together, and leered at her.

Melissa shivered.

Dinner was an awkward affair. The Miss Wilkeses, Lady Bentley's daughters from her first marriage, were late, which put the earl out of countenance. Then they giggled and whispered throughout the meal, which put the earl's brother out of countenance. Melissa was seated beside Mr Pontefract, which would have put her out of countenance if she had only dared. She was beginning to have some inkling of the reason for her invitation, and it turned the food to ash in her mouth. She ate but little, and took no more than two sips of her wine, and tried to make pleasant conversation with Mr Pontefract. It was hard work, for he ate prodigiously, leaving him little opportunity to speak, and when he looked at her, his eyes somehow never rose to her face and his breathing grew heavy. In addition, Melissa soon discovered that he had very few thoughts in his head beyond his plate and wineglass. A casual mention of his dogs led her to enquire further, and he then talked with great animation of his kennels and his numerous dogs, and which of them he had bred from and which others he intended to breed from, and so the meal was got through somehow.

When the ladies withdrew, and the Miss Wilkeses had disappeared in a giggling cloud of sarsenet and spangles, still whispering, Melissa would have retreated to her room, duty done, but Lady Bentley summoned her with a crook of one finger into the drawing room.

"You see how generous Lord Bentley is, my dear? For you could not have expected so handsome a gesture, I am sure. But so it is with my dear husband — no effort spared, even for someone like you. What a fortunate young woman you are, to be sure. You may be quite comfortable now, for your future is assured. If you and Mr Pontefract see Parson Albright tomorrow to arrange the banns, you may be married within the month."

"Oh, marriage," Melissa said, relieved that nothing worse was expected of her, as had happened at midsummer with the pretty under housemaid, who had left in tears the next day. Mr Cornelius Brockenhurst, the earl's brother, had a roving eye and, it was said, roving hands as well, and all the female servants had learnt to keep away from him and his lascivious friends. It had always surprised Melissa that she had never attracted his attention, but she supposed she was not pretty enough.

"Yes, marriage, of course. Mr Pontefract is an admirable man, I am sure, and a better catch than you could have hoped for. I trust you will express your gratitude to Lord Bentley."

"Indeed, I am very grateful to his lordship for all his trouble, but I do not in the least wish to marry Mr Pontefract."

"What you wish is not of the slightest consequence. Lord Bentley is your guardian and—"

"I beg your pardon, but I shall soon be of age, my lady. I shall be one and twenty in three months."

"Oh, very hoity-toity! And what other options do you have? Do you have a better husband in mind?"

"No, but I acted as governess to the late earl's daughters for several years, so—"

"And they are gone, and my own daughters do not need any tuition from a rustic like you. So you see, my dear, you have no place here."

"I am sure I could obtain a position as governess elsewhere, my lady. All I should need is a reference—"

A triumphant expression settled on Lady Bentley's face. "Not from me, and not from my husband's stepmother, either, not while he has control of her jointure."

"I see." Melissa's stomach churned with fear, but she tried not to show it. She found some stitchery to occupy her trembling hands, and when the gentlemen returned and sat down to cards with Lady Bentley, Melissa watched her future husband and tried to imagine herself married to such a man.

Mr Pontefract left in a flurry of creaking bows and smiles, kissing her hand with a smirk Melissa could not misunderstand. Lord Bentley went to the door to show him out, and the two men could be heard laughing together in the most amiable way.

"I congratulate you, Melissa," Lord Bentley said when he returned to the room. "Pontefract is quite charmed by you, and will return in the morning to make his offer in form."

"I am very honoured, my lord, but I shall not accept him."

Lord Bentley exchanged a glance with his wife. "You were always wilful, even as a child, so these flashes of disobliging behaviour are no more than to be expected. However, you will marry Pontefract. I am your guardian and you must do as I say."

Melissa jumped to her feet. "I may not marry against your wishes, but you cannot force me to marry a man I cannot like."

"No?" He crossed the room in two strides, and caught her wrist in a grip so tight that she cried out in pain. "Remember that your bedchamber has no lock to it. All it would take is for me to invite Pontefract to stay for the night, and show him the way. By morning, you would be happy enough to marry him, I swear. And if even that is not enough for you, I know the very place in Portsmouth for you, and once there, no man will ever want to marry you. Think carefully on it, Melissa, before you spew your defiance at me."

When she returned to her room, she found the housekeeper awaiting her, to help her undress, just as she had when Melissa was a little girl.

"Oh, Mrs Clark, what am I to do? He is quite dreadful! Yet I daresay he is respectable enough."

"Perhaps," the housekeeper said. "I've heard rumours... I don't like to think of you in the hands of a man like that."

"I suppose... they mean it kindly?" Melissa said. "Surely they do. It is nothing to their advantage, so they must feel it is to mine. Do you not think?"

Mrs Clark sighed. "I've heard that Mr Cornelius got into some difficulty with gaming debts, and rather than ask the earl for help again, he borrowed money from Mr Pontefract. I suppose this is his way of repaying the debt. Gentlemen regard such debts as a matter of honour."

"Mr Pontefract does not know his danger," Melissa said defiantly, not sure whether to laugh or cry. "If ever I were to marry him, I am sure I should make his life a misery and he should be very sorry he ever thought of me. Luckily for him, he is safe from me, for I have no intention of marrying him."

"But what will you do, Melissa? You have no family, no friends to take you in, no money and no possibility of respectable employment without a reference."

"I shall think of something," Melissa said stoutly.

And she knew precisely what she would do. She still had her letter, and there was another debt of honour to be repaid, but this debt was owed to her. Yes, she would go to Drummoor. As soon as Mrs Clark had gone, she pulled out her purse and began to count her coins.

~~~~~

Lord Montague Marford was bored. After the excitement of his brother agreeing — finally! — that he might become a clergyman, and then the joy of his ordination, and several months spent as assistant to Mr Callimont at York, now he was right back where he had started, at Drummoor. His brother, the Marquess of Carrbridge, had several livings in his gift, but none of them were vacant, nor likely to be soon. He could amuse himself as chaplain at the Drummoor chapel, but that was only one day a week. For the other six, he must sit and wait and wait some more. It was dispiriting. Even the weather was in dreary sympathy with his mood.

He laid down his book of sermons, and looked across the winter morning room at the only other occupants. His sister-in-law, Connie, was bent over the worktable, making a list. Guests to invite, possibly, or chores for the housemaids, or chutneys and preserves for the kitchen to make, or perhaps just one of her endless lists of Things That Must Be Done. Meanwhile she was chattering non-stop to her sister, Mrs Allamont, who was presently visiting. Mrs Allamont was more productively employed in trimming a bonnet, although she seemed to take her full share in the conversation, even though her fingers never stopped moving. Aunt Jane March said nothing, but she nodded and smiled at intervals, while steadily tatting.

Monty could hear Carrbridge and Mr Allamont out in the hall, laughing about something. No doubt Mr Allamont had come up with another of his outlandish schemes of improvement to his land, for he was full of ideas, while Carrbridge was much more conservative in his methods, and teased him unmercifully. It was all rather remote to Monty, the productivity of milking cows being very far from his concerns as a clergyman. His interest would be in the spiritual welfare of his parishioners, and if he kept a few chickens at his parsonage, that would be as near as he would come to agricultural matters.

If ever he had his own parsonage, of course. Eventually, Mishcombe would be his, which was a fine living within half a mile of Drummoor, but the present incumbent, Mr Hay, although elderly, was perfectly hale and likely to live for another twenty years at least. In the meantime, he had to wait with as much patience as he could muster for one of several clergymen to drop down dead so that he might have their place, and it was an uncomfortable feeling. He did not wish any of them dead, but nor did he much like sitting about at home, being bored. Perhaps the Archbishop would have some sudden need for one of the gentlemen, and summon him to York, leaving the way clear for Monty. That was a happier thought, a promotion rather than death.

Connie rang for tea, and that brought everyone into the winter parlour, including the usual array of aunts and uncles who had been invited to visit in the summer and had stayed on for months. For once there were few house guests other than family. Connie loved to have the place full of visitors, but with her confinement fast approaching, even her enthusiasm for entertaining had waned somewhat.

Daniel Merton came in with a note for Carrbridge, and the two whispered together for some time. They were an interesting contrast, Carrbridge every inch the aristocrat, his coat, his trousers, even his hair all of the first style, and his manner patrician. Merton, his secretary, was a gentleman and so there was nothing obsequious in his manner, but he never put himself forward, either, and his plain black coat was just as unobtrusive as the man himself.

Now the two of them came towards Monty. "There is news, my lord," Merton said.

"Good news or bad news?" Monty said. "I do not like to hear bad news, you know."

"It is both, I believe," Merton said, as Carrbridge chuckled. "Mr Whittaker, from Kirby Grosswick, has died."

"Oh."

"The living is vacant now, you see," Carrbridge said, beaming happily at him. "Congratulations, Monty. You will be installed there in time for Christmas."

"Oh." Happiness bubbled up inside him. "That... is good news! Not for Mr Whittaker, of course, but..."

And then they were all crowding round him, congratulating him, the gentlemen shaking his hand briskly, the ladies exclaiming in delight, and Connie shedding a tear.

From the door, the butler coughed. "Beg pardon, my lord, my lady, but there is... a person in the hall. A Miss Frost. She is asking to see the Earl of Deveron."

The room fell silent. "The Earl of Deveron?" Connie said, her tone shrill.

"That is what she says, my lady."

Merton cleared his throat. "Is Miss Frost a lady, Crabbe?"

"Hard to say, sir," the butler said in haughty tones. "Not a servant, I should say. She is carrying a portmanteau."

"Shall I investigate?" Merton said. But in the end Connie and Carrbridge and several others went out to the hall too, and Monty drifted along behind them, feeling rather sorry for this Miss Frost who was neither lady nor servant.

She was very young, perhaps twenty, and tall but exceedingly thin, as if she had not eaten properly for a long time. Her boots, travelling gown and pelisse were of reasonable quality, if rather worn, and her bonnet had once been quite stylish. Now it was so sodden that the remains of two feathers trailed listlessly onto her shoulders and dripped steadily.

"Miss Frost?" Carrbridge said. "I am the Marquess of Carrbridge and this is Lady Carrbridge. What is this about the Earl of Deveron?"

The girl lifted her chin defiantly. "I want to talk to him."

"Might one enquire as to the nature of your business with him?"

"I am betrothed to him." She looked Carrbridge right in the eye, as if daring him to disagree with her.

"Betrothed to him?" Connie burst out. "Impossible!"

"It is perfectly true," the girl said defiantly. "The engagement is of long standing, and now that I am old enough, I intend to hold Lord Deveron to his commitment."

It was so ridiculous that it had to be a joke, but Monty felt not the least desire to laugh. The girl — Miss Frost — was so sincere, so determined that it almost seemed a shame to unravel her plan, but it had to be done.

"Perhaps," he said carefully, "Miss Frost might care to meet the Earl of Deveron?"

"Oh, yes please," she said at once. "I should very much like to meet him, so that we may... begin making arrangements and so forth."

"This way," Connie said, leading the way towards the stairs. "Crabbe, tell Mrs Compton to prepare the rose room. Miss Frost will want a hot bath as soon as may be. My dear, you are quite soaked. Did you walk up from the village in all this rain?"

"From the village with the big cross in the middle. That was as near as the farmer could bring me."

"Mishmere Cross? Good gracious! That must be... a very long way."

"Close to ten miles," Merton said from behind her.

"Good gracious," Connie said again, faintly. "Here we are."

She threw open a door, and immediately the air was filled with squeals, as several children chased each other round and round the room on hobby horses. In a corner, three nursemaids sat in a gossipy huddle, leaping to their feet and hastily curtsying as soon as they realised they were observed.

Connie made no reprimand. Instead she waded into the melée and scooped up a sturdy boy of four, who immediately grinned and tried to grab the ribbons of her cap. Connie carried him back to the door.

"Miss Frost, may I present to you the Earl of Deveron. Dev, say hello to Miss Frost."

The girl's face grew ashen, and at first Monty thought she might faint from shock. Then she turned and stomped back out onto the landing. The others followed her out.

"I am so very sorry," Connie began.

"No, you are not," the girl said, her eyes flashing. "You think it a great joke, I daresay. Some poor deluded woman turns up to marry a child of... how old is he?"

"He will be five next birthday," Connie said, "and I do not think it a joke at all, for you have come all this way... where have you come from?"

Was that a hesitation? She licked her lips. "Cornwall."

"Well, that is a great way indeed. But you may see for yourself that you have been misled. Whatever understanding you have cannot be with Dev. You may stay here until the weather improves and then we will see you on your way back to Cornwall."

"Oh, that is very fine, and no mistake," Miss Frost cried. "So that is the end of it, is it? I was promised a husband, look, it says so here." She pulled a letter from some inner recess of her pelisse, and waved it at them. "The Marquess of Carrbridge — you, sir —

promised me to your son, and now you think you can just shrug and walk away, do you? Typical of you people. You have no sense of honour."

Carrbridge was reading the letter. "It does seem... Merton, read it, will you. The date is more than ten years ago, so it would have been my father promising you to me, Miss Frost. I was the Earl of Deveron then, you see. But I do not quite see what can be done about it now."

Merton looked up. "Miss Frost, it looks to me as if your father gambled you away to the eighth marquess in some wager that went badly for him. The eighth marquess tells him to keep you for the present, and he will marry you to the Earl of Deveron when you are of age."

"I know what it says!" she spat.

"But you must see that such an offer has no legal force. There is no obligation—"

"Yes, there is!" she said, stamping her foot. "I have been in expectation of the marriage for years. If the Earl of Deveron is not available, then you must find me another husband, that is only fair."

"I do not think—" Carrbridge began, frowning.

Monty raised a hand. "Carrbridge, this a matter of honour, a debt that we must repay."

"No, Monty, no!" Connie cried, realising what he was about.

"A matter of honour," he repeated firmly. "Therefore I will marry Miss Frost, if she will have me."

"And who are you?" she said, staring at him unsmiling.

"I am Lord Montague Marford, Lord Carrbridge's brother."

"Then you will do. I accept."

END OF SAMPLE CHAPTER OF *Lord Montague*

Made in the USA
Coppell, TX
03 August 2022

80874175R00173